KU-222-230

The Subterraneans and Pic

Jack Kerouac was born in Lowell, Massachusetts, where, he said, he 'roamed fields and riverbanks by day and night, wrote little novels in my room, first novel written at age eleven, also kept extensive diaries and "newspapers" covering my own-invented horse-racing and baseball and football worlds (as recorded in novel *Doctor Sax*).' He was educated by Jesuit brothers in Lowell. He said that he 'decided to become a writer at age seventeen under influence of Sebastian Sampas, local young poet, who later died on Anzio beach head; read the life of Jack London at eighteen and decided to also be a lonesome traveler; early literary influences Saroyan and Hemingway; later Wolfe (after I had broken leg in Freshman football at Columbia read Tom Wolfe and roamed his New York on crutches).'

Kerouac wished, however, to develop his own new prose style, which he called 'spontaneous prose.' He used this technique to record the life of the American 'traveler' and the experiences of the Beat generation of the 1950s. This may clearly be seen in his most famous novel, *On the Road*, and also in *The Subterraneans* and *The Dharma Bums*. Other works include *Big Sur*, *Desolation Angels*, *Lonesome Traveler*, *Visions of Gerard*, *Tristessa* and a book of poetry called *Mexico City Blues*. His first more orthodox published novel was *The Town and the City*. Jack Kerouac, who described himself as a 'strange solitary crazy Catholic mystic', was working on his longest novel, a surrealistic study of the last ten years of his life, when he died in 1969, aged forty-seven.

Ann Douglas is Parr Professor of Comparative Literature at Columbia University, New York. She taught at Princeton from 1970 to 1974, where she received a Bicentennial Preceptorship from Princeton for distinguished teaching in 1974. She received a NEII and Guggenheim fellowship for 1993–4. Her study *Terrible Honesty: Mongrel Manhattan in the 1920s* (1995) received, among other honours, the Alfred Beveridge Award from the American Historical Association and the Lionel Trilling Award from Columbia University. She has published numerous essays, articles and b......................culture in papers and periodicals su......................................, and introductions for .... and *Minor*

 700041333628

Characters, and *World Virus*, a William Burroughs anthology (1998). She is working on a book on Hollywood 1930–60 and a long-term project, *If You Live, You Burn: Cold War Culture in the United States 1939–1965*.

Jack Kerouac

THE SUBTERRANEANS
and PIC

With a new Introduction by Ann Douglas

PENGUIN BOOKS

PENGUIN CLASSICS

Published by the Penguin Group
Penguin Books Ltd, 80 Strand, London WC2R 0RL, England
Penguin Group (USA) Inc., 375 Hudson Street, New York, New York 10014, USA
Penguin Group (Canada), 90 Eglinton Avenue East, Suite 700, Toronto, Ontario, Canada M4P 2Y3
(a division of Pearson Penguin Canada Inc.)
Penguin Ireland, 25 St Stephen's Green, Dublin 2, Ireland (a division of Penguin Books Ltd)
Penguin Group (Australia), 250 Camberwell Road, Camberwell,
Victoria 3124, Australia (a division of Pearson Australia Group Pty Ltd)
Penguin Books India Pvt Ltd, 11 Community Centre,
Panchsheel Park, New Delhi – 110 017, India
Penguin Group (NZ), 67 Apollo Drive, Rosedale, North Shore 0632, New Zealand
(a division of Pearson New Zealand Ltd)
Penguin Books (South Africa) (Pty) Ltd, 24 Sturdee Avenue, Rosebank, Johannesburg 2196, South Africa

Penguin Books Ltd, Registered Offices: 80 Strand, London WC2R 0RL, England

www.penguin.com

First published 1958
First published in Great Britain by André Deutsch Ltd 1960
Published with a new Introduction in Penguin Classics 2001

017

Copyright © Estate of Jack Kerouac, 1958
Introduction copyright © Ann Douglas, 2001
All rights reserved

The moral right of the author of the Introduction has been asserted

Printed in England by Clays Ltd, St Ives plc

Except in the United States of America, this book is sold subject
to the condition that it shall not, by way of trade or otherwise, be lent,
re-sold, hired out, or otherwise circulated without the publisher's
prior consent in any form of binding or cover other than that in
which it is published and without a similar condition including this
condition being imposed on the subsequent purchaser

978-0-141-18489-0

www.greenpenguin.co.uk

MIX
Paper from
responsible sources
FSC
www.fsc.org   FSC™ C018179

Penguin Books is committed to a sustainable
future for our business, our readers and our planet.
This book is made from Forest Stewardship
Council™ certified paper.

ALWAYS LEARNING   PEARSON

Dedicated to Dr Danny DeSole

Contents

Introduction to the Penguin Edition

Jack Kerouac wrote his novel *The Subterraneans*, an account of his interracial love affair with Alene Lee ('Mardou Fox'), in a three day-and-night-long burst of creative energy in the fall of 1953. At thirty-one, Kerouac was a prolific if largely unpublished author, and the artistic leader of the 'Beat Generation', an informal literary movement dating from the mid-1940s that he had named. *The Subterraneans* represented Kerouac's first finished work written entirely in the 'spontaneous prose' style he had discovered in the spring of 1951. When his two closest Beat collaborators, Allen Ginsberg and William Burroughs, read *The Subterraneans* in manuscript, they asked him to write a brief how-to manual of his method for their use, a piece Kerouac eventually published as 'The Essentials of Spontaneous Prose'. Ginsberg and Burroughs wrote their own breakthrough works, *Howl* (1956) and *Naked Lunch* (1959), consciously adapting Kerouac's suggestions to their own needs.

The Subterraneans would not be published until 1958, but it announced the advent of a new charismatic ethos of virtuosic improvisation, anarchic individualism and confessional autobiography, a 'fury of subjective revolution', as one Beat writer called it, echoed and anticipated in the other major new developments in the American arts of the time, Bebop, Abstract Expressionism and the 'Method'-based Actors Studio. Kerouac's 'spontaneous prose' was quite possibly the most important and sustained experiment in American prose since Hemingway had unveiled his stark, elegantly laconic style almost thirty years earlier with the publication of *In Our Time* (1925).

A self-styled American 'Proust ... on the run' whose chosen subject was the haunted pathos, comic absurdity and sheer terror of the past, Kerouac confides at once to the reader of *The Subterraneans* that he is already past his prime. In 1948, at twenty-six, he was 'mad, cracked, confident, young, talented as never since'; today, he fears, not without cause, that he is an alcoholic, on the edge of nervous collapse, unable to fulfill even the responsibilities, to his art, his mother, and his friends and lovers (more or less in that order), that he has willingly undertaken. When Norman Mailer met Kerouac in New York a few years later, in the midst of the *succés de scandale* that attended the publication of *On the Road*, he recognized him as 'a pioneer', 'the first figure for a new generation'. Mailer liked Kerouac himself, 'more than I would have thought, and felt he was tired, as indeed why should he not be, for he has travelled in a world where the adrenaline devours the blood.' Mailer never forgot (nor did Thomas Pynchon) that, in contrast to himself, Kerouac had lived all his books as well as written them.

Born in 1922 in Lowell, Massachusetts, to working-class immigrant parents of largely French-Canadian and some Iroquois stock, Kerouac grew up speaking an unwritten French-Canadian dialect called joual. He did not learn English until he was forced to use it in school; by his own admission, he wasn't comfortable with it until his late teens. As *The Subterraneans*, in which Gabrielle Kerouac is a powerful off-stage presence, attests, he spoke joual with his mother for the rest of his life. Kerouac was a 'Canuck', one of a group sometimes called *blancs nègres* in his hometown, and on occasion he described himself as a member of the 'minority races', beset by 'that horrible homelessness all French-Canadians in America have'. He handled English easily and freely precisely because, he explained in a letter of 1950, 'it is not my own language. I refashion it to fit French images.' He early took what he described as 'mongrel America' and its many tongues as his subject. His books, like his life, were entangled in the Third World margins and urban back lots of capitalist civilization: in Lowell, a dying industrial town full of immigrants; New York and San Francisco, then the US capitals of miscegenation; and Mexico City, the home of the people Kerouac romanticized as the 'fellaheen', the ancient, dark-skinned races displaced by modern civilization who will witness and survive its collapse. Affluence had virtually no interest for Kerouac; again and again in his fiction he excavates Depression America from its postwar carapace of ill-gotten prosperity.

By his senior year in high school, Kerouac looked to be the hero of a fabulous American success story. Stunningly good-looking – Salvador Dali later pronounced him 'more beautiful than Marlon Brando' – and extremely smart, he was also an outstanding athlete, a star in track, baseball and football. He came to New York in 1939 on a football scholarship, first to the Horace Mann School, then to Columbia University, but he dropped out of college for good in 1944.

He had already met Ginsberg ('Adam Moorad' in *The Subterraneans*) and Lucien Carr ('Sam Vedder'), then students at Columbia, as well as Burroughs ('Frank Carmody') and Herbert Huncke, the drug addict con-man of Times Square who introduced the word 'beat' to Kerouac's circle. Neal Cassady ('Leroy'), the charismatic, fast-talking 'jail kid' from Colorado, who became the legendary inspiration for Dean Moriarty in *On the Road*, arrived in New York in 1946, shortly after the death of Kerouac's father Leo. With the additions of Gregory Corso ('Yuri Gligoric'), John Clellon Holmes ('Balliol MacJones'), Lawrence Ferlinghetti ('Larry O'Hara), and Gary Snyder ('Japhy Ryder' in *Dharma Bums* (1958)), over the next few years, Kerouac's Beat circle was virtually complete.

After serving sporadically in the Navy and Merchant Marines in the Second World War, Kerouac began to criss-cross the country with Neal Cassady, drinking, taking drugs (largely benzedrine uppers, then legal), talking to hundreds of significant strangers, and having affairs with a series of women, including a Mexican migrant worker he portrayed as 'Terry' in *On the Road* and the part African-American, part Native American Alene Lee ('Mardou Fox'). Kerouac married three times, producing a daughter by his second marriage, the lately deceased writer Jan Kerouac. Jan, however, didn't talk to her father until she was a teenager, and Kerouac never formally acknowledged that she was his child. The Beat revolt, as Barbara Ehrenreich has noted in *The Hearts of Men* (1983), was a masculine one, a protest against conventional 1950s suburbia and the conscription of men into the role of Organization Man and family provider on which it depended.

Kerouac's first novel, *The Town and the City*, a fairly conventional *Bildungsroman* written in ecstatic Wolfean prose, was published in 1950 to respectable reviews and no sales. Although he wrote six novels and two books of poetry in the next seven years, he found no publisher for his work until the critic Malcolm Cowley persuaded Viking to publish *On the Road* in 1957. Inspired by the stream-of-consciousness methods of Joyce, the anarchic extremes of Melville's most experimental prose, and the great Bop pioneer Charlie Parker (who makes a crucial guest appearance in *The Subterraneans*), Kerouac practised 'spontaneous prose' as a barely punctuated flood of images and words designed to capture on the printed page the actual body tones and talk of real people.

Deliberately smashing the taboos that separate author from reader,

Kerouac aimed to justify the greed on which reading depends, to satisfy the immemorial human wish that fiction be *true*. All his books were avowedly and entirely autobiographical, accounts of his own adventures and thoughts, full, in his words, of 'riotous angelic particulars', 'FREE OF HYPOCRISY', and told with '100% personal honesty'. 'What a man most wishes to hide, revise, and unsay', he wrote Malcolm Cowley in 1955, 'is precisely what literature is waiting and bleeding for.' This was the 'veritable fire ordeal when you can't go back ... all of it innocent go-ahead confession ... making the mind the slave of the tongue with no chance to lie or re-elaborate,' a style capable of delivering 'telepathic shock and meaning excitement'.

'Spontaneous prose' was a highly conscious, difficult technique requiring of the writer, in Kerouac's phrase, the 'heartbreaking discipline' of exhaustive, interminable rehearsal – in journal-writing and on-the-spot 'sketching' in words – to ready himself for the climactic act of writing a final draft; with the recent publication of his letters and some of his journals, we can see just how exhaustive Kerouac's preparation was. Although he famously claimed to have written *On the Road* in three weeks, he said nothing about the two earlier versions of the novel he had written and discarded. He later reminded an unsympathetic editor that it had taken fifteen years to tap and perfect the 'voice' in which *On the Road* and his subsequent works were written; 'I know what I'm talking about ... I'm an artist, old fashioned, devoted.' Kerouac laboured to craft a sound, a style, rather than a particular work; once unleashed, the style produced its own appropriate narrative forms. He felt no more free to revise his draft than a football player was to replay a game or a musician to repeat a gig, except in future practice and performance.

Because he had no money and a huge backlog of unpublished work, Kerouac used the visibility *On the Road* brought him to rush all his earlier novels into print, glutting his market and strengthening the critical misapprehension that he tossed off a book every few days. He was, indignant reviewers said, 'a know-nothing Bohemian', the 'latrine laureate of Hobohemia', 'a slob running a temperature', a 'high school athlete who went from Lowell, Mass. to Skid Row, losing his eraser en route', and 'a garrulous drunk drooling in your ear'. His books were mere 'self-indulgence', the 'self-abuse' of a 'Simple Simon', 'proof of illness', even 'psychoathic', and certainly 'unreadable'. On 5 October 1959, Kerouac sat horrified before his television, as he wrote Ginsberg the next day, watching a parody of himself as 'Jack Crackerbox' 'leap up (hair pasted on brow) and start screaming ... kill for the sake of killing!'

A shy, gentle, intensely unworldly and self-conscious man, devoid of media savoir-faire, Kerouac tried to explain that he was a 'prose theorist' and a 'strange solitary crazy Catholic mystic', waiting for 'God to show his face'. Dazed and embittered by what he saw as critical 'abuse', frantically trying to draw on inner resources of fortitude long since depleted and perhaps always scant, he retreated further into what he called the 'self murder' of alcoholism and despair, railing against Jews, communists and hippies; his young fans who, in his words, seemed to 'want somebody to ... tear apart limb from limb like some sort of sacrificial hero', scared him as much as his critics. By the mid-1960s, most of his books were remaindered, and he calculated his weekly income at $65. On 21 October 1969, Kerouac died; twenty-six blood transfusions had failed to stop the internal haemorrhaging caused by his drinking. He wrote steadily until the end. He 'stay[ed] on the job', his friend Robert Creeley noted, 'long after anyone seemed to be listening'.

Although Kerouac is only now, decades after his death, beginning to gain respectful attention, he was very much a creature of his own time; his critics in the early Cold War years were not altogether mistaken in perceiving his presence as a threat. He told his first biographer, Ann Charters, that he kept 'the neatest records you ever saw', filing away thousands of old letters, news clippings and photographs; he meant his work to be in some sense verifiable. His thirteen 'true story novels' were a vast, continuous Balzacian epic offering a 'contemporary history record [of] ... what really happened and what people really thought'. This was auto-history as well as auto-biography, an investigation of a historical era through the lens of a private life: the self explored, in Antonio Gramsci's apt words, as the 'product of the historical process to date, which has deposited in [it] an infinity of traces without leaving an inventory'.

Kerouac's belief in heroically uncensored subjectivity, his insistence that he came before his reader totally unarmed, unprepared and unguarded, was in part a response to a particular moment of US history, a time when military preparedness, and the security measures it was thought to require, reached unprecedented extremes. In the wake of Hiroshima, as hostilities between the United States and the

Soviet Union, its recent ally, intensified into a staged battle between the putative forces of good and evil, the bomb was defined as 'the property of the American people', its composition a secret that must be kept. Policy-makers formulated the doctrine of 'plausible deniability'; the covert actions of the CIA, itself new in 1947, its assassination plots and 'roll back' strategies, were to be conducted in such a way that no one in the top echelons of the US government could be held accountable if they were exposed.

Knowledge was viewed not as the result of discovery and collaboration, of tapping into a free-flowing source that predated and exceeded the individual mind, but as a commodity owned by a particular set of minds in a particular nation. The category of 'classified information' covered ever-greater portions of the national experience, though no private individual was safe from public investigation. Everyone was under surveillance, it seemed, by neighbours and fellow citizens, if not the FBI. Thousands of people were compelled to tell their stories to their employers or even the House Committee on Un-American Activities, but the ending of the tale was foreknown and predetermined; they were to confess, renounce their leftist pasts and inform on their left-wing collaborators, or suffer the consequences.

In the age that invented the idea of classified information, Kerouac's effort was to *de*classify the secrets of the human body and soul. '100% personal honesty' countered 'plausible deniability'; improvisation replaced planning; fluidity defied boundaries and compartmentalization; sheer radically intimate expressiveness undid collective programming. The absence of conventional plotting in Kerouac's narratives that made the critic Norman Podhoretz fume in 1958 that there was 'no dramatic reason' for anything that happened in Kerouac's fiction, offered an alternative model to a world in which events felt overdetermined, and cues to the unexpected were no longer heard. Drama is about choice – will-he-or-won't-he? – about control threatened and regained; it's part of the special effects of power. Kerouac, however, meant to slip the leash of the preconditioned and hyper-controlled. As Mardou Fox asks in *The Subterraneans*, 'What's in store for me in the direction I *don't* take?' – a question that refuses the distinction between offstage and onstage on which drama depends.

The America Kerouac describes in *The Subterraneans* is less a country than a continent, full of the ghosts of prior, displaced inhabitants; they signal the directions the nation itself did not take that nonetheless still lie open, waiting to be reimagined. As Mardou tells Leo Percepied (Kerouac's stand-in in the novel) about her life, he sees her Native American ancestors, 'wraiths of humanity treading lightly the surface of the ground so deeply suppurated with the stock of their suffering you have only to dig a foot down to find a baby's hand'. Mardou's ancestors, of whom she is not at this moment talking or thinking, bleed into her narrative, recolouring its figures, shifting its key; to Leo, she is not one person but many. The unknown is as real as the known; what has not happened, what has not been told, isn't obliterated by what has. In a similar fashion, the 'clash of the streets beyond the window's bare soft sill' provides the soundtrack to Mardou's narrative; the presumably unrelated activities and noises of outside filter inside, into the room in which the lovers are sitting – words themselves exist in close proximity to the sounds that predate, accompany and succeed their formulations.

From the opening page of *The Subterraneans*, Kerouac has been pulling the reader inside the story as well. 'I must explain,' he says, how he was feeling when he was introduced to Mardou; further 'confessions must be made' about his boastful image of himself as 'phallus, ... of women as wells', and the racial prejudices that make him recoil when he wakes up to see a 'Negro woman' asleep at his side, even as he realizes 'what a beast I am for feeling anything near it'. On yet another track of the multiple mix that is his narrative, Kerouac is hypothesizing the reader's responses as extensions and alternatives to his own; he feels his audience out there transforming and modifying what he writes. The reader is the future of the text, a future just becoming visible in its present, as surely as Mardou's ancestors are the past into which its present disappears.

Kerouac's presentation of his sexuality follows the same logic; the love story of Leo and Mardou is interrupted, overlaid with a secondary tale about Leo's sycophantic overtures to the successful, homosexual author Arial Lavalina (based on Gore Vidal). Yet neither the biographical Kerouac or his fictive stand-in here are homosexual or even bisexual in any conventional sense. It's rather that Kerouac won't shut off an alternative script – inevitably the contours of his homosexual impulses surface through the heterosexual patterns that in actual fact dominate them.

Nor will Kerouac choose between apparently conflicting temporal modes or points of view. Telling the reader about the day, a few months prior to the writing of the story, on which he first met Mardou as he was walking down the street with Larry O'Hara, he simultaneously alludes to the actual moment at which he writes this account of it, sitting in the 'sadglint of my wallroom,' listening to Sarah Vaughan on the radio. Destablizing the self, unmooring the story, as Kerouac does here, is to maximize his own vulnerability, but as Charlie Parker advised his backup musicians, if you 'act just a little bit foolish and let yourself go, better ideas will come [to you]'. Embarrassment and failure may attend a readiness to loose the self from its conventional frame, yet to entertain alternative selves, to go out of character, letting accident usurp the role of decision, putting the guest in the chair of the host, the child in the place usually reserved for the adult, is the key to the kind of art that both Kerouac and Parker sought to create; an art in which anarchic simultaneity rather than sequence is the principle of order, leaching over borders, reversing outsides and insides, and returning us to a state of mental and physical flux. Differentiation here is but one of the forms that undifferentiation takes.

Kerouac tells the reader all those 'secrets, which are so necessary to tell, or why write or live?' To leave this life without recording the things only he remembered would have been for Kerouac the unpardonable sin. But he is not comfortable with his revelations. How can he love Mardou, he openly wonders, yet speak of her thighs and 'what the thighs contain', hanging her private life on 'the washline of the world'? In *A Lover's Discourse*, Roland Barthes says that love is about giving up control, being compelled or seduced to trust something or someone not ourselves because we believe that the rewards of exposure justify the risk. Once we tell a third party about our experience of love, however, as we inevitably do, we begin to revise it, because in any narrative we fashion, we ourselves, not the beloved, emerge as the hero.

Kerouac wrote about his experiences in one form or another almost as soon as they happened – *The Subterraneans* was written within days of the break with Alene Lee – precisely in order to evade as far as humanly possible the tempting powers of reinterpretation that distance provides; but he, too, knew that it is well-nigh impossible to tell a story without putting oneself in charge. Narratives are always involved with mastery, with self-promotion. 'It's difficult to make a real confession,' he tells the reader early in *The Subterraneans*, when 'all you can do is take off on long paragraphs about minor details about yourself'. He can't narrate the story of this love affair without getting involved in big 'word constructions' that 'betray' it.

Had his libel-suit-conscious publishers not forbidden it, Kerouac, as a matter of artistic principle, would have used actual names in all his books, but even he knew that in *The Subterraneans* he was dealing with highly delicate and inflammable subject matter. He based Dean Moriarty openly on Neal Cassady, but much as he loved Cassady, he had not been to bed with him; he could not write his full sexual history or describe his most intimate anatomy as he does Alene Lee's in *The Subterraneans*. He was also writing about interracial sex, a subject till then explored in depth by only one major American writer, the African-American novelist Chester Himes, in *Lonely Crusade* (1947).

In 1955, Kerouac wrote *Tristessa* (not published until 1960), another novel about a woman of colour, but Esperanza Villaneuva, the real person on whom the central character is based, was illiterate, lived in Mexico and spoke no language but Spanish. There was scant chance that she or her intimates would read his book. Alene Lee, a woman who, by Kerouac's own account, read *The Portable William Faulkner* in one sitting, a trendsetter at ease with the most contemporary jazz, the companion as well as (in Kerouac's words) the 'playdoll' of the sophisticated, hip and 'cool' group that Allen Ginsberg dubbed the Subterraneans, was Kerouac's peer as well as his subject.

In a rare interview of the 1970s, Alene Lee described her discontent with the Eisenhower era in which the events of *The Subterraneans* occurred; Americans were settling for 'the way things were, and were making money, or trying to'. When she met Kerouac, she was working as an assistant for a health book company with radical origins and literary ambitions; the office manager edited books like *Urine: Water of Life* by day and wrote a biography of Virginia Woolf by night. Wondering, 'why am I in this office, typing up these bills, answering this correspondence?', Lee was also typing two of Burroughs's unpublished manuscripts, *Queer* and *The Yage Letters*. Although, according to Gregory Corso ('Yuri'), Alene's affair with him was a one-time encounter, she had also slept with Ginsberg (during his brief attempt to be heterosexual) and become his friend; later, she had a serious relationship with Lucien Carr ('Sam Vedder'), perhaps the most beloved of all Kerouac's male friends.

Alene Lee fiercely guarded her privacy – no Kerouac biographer gave her real name until after her death in 1995. When Kerouac brought the manuscript of *The Subterraneans* to her not long after he finished it, in her words, she 'went into shock. A lot of it was still raw.' These, she insisted, 'were not the times as I knew them'; he had gotten his friends right, but not hers. She said little more, only describing both of them at this time as incapable of a real attachment to anyone, 'helpless . . ., [and] play-acting at serious life'. She admired Kerouac's writing but grew weary of his 'drinking and barging in on people and going this place or that', behaviour inappropriate and detrimental to his own literary standing, a description of his conduct wholly consistent with the picture Kerouac draws in his novel.

Contact between Kerouac and Lee did not cease after they officially broke up in the fall of 1953. Writing to a friend in 1954, Kerouac alludes to getting a letter from her as if it were not an unusual event. As late as 1958, drunk and dishevelled after a reading, he dragged his then girlfriend, the writer Joyce Johnson, over to meet her. Johnson describes the encounter in *Minor Characters* (1983), her evocative memoir of Beat New York. Lee had a baby, and 'she lived alone with it in a cold-water flat that smelled of milk and diapers and Johnson's oil; she supported the two of them with odd typing jobs . . . She didn't seem angry or excited to see Jack – she only seemed weary,' talking to him with 'the caustic affection of someone whom hard times had made bitterly wise, while others, such as he, were running in circles making idiots of themselves.' Johnson had already heard too much about Alene's importance to Jack; on this occasion, she couldn't get him to leave. 'Want to stay,' he drunkenly insisted. 'Not this time, baby,' Alene said, and laughed. Johnson was surprised that Alene 'had taken no notice of the tenderness expressed in [*The Subterraneans*]', but Lee's open awareness of the difference between Jack's troubles, however real, and her own difficulties as a young, intelligent single mother of colour in the United States in the 1950s seems amply justified.

Kerouac made what efforts he could to protect and empower Lee. He shifted the locale of his novel from Manhattan, where it actually occurred, to San Francisco. The 'Black Mask' and 'Dante's', the bars at which the Subterranean group gathers, were actually two New York hot spots, Fugazzi's a jukebox joint on 6th Avenue, and the San Remo on Bleecker and Macdougal streets, both frequented by poets and painters, including Dylan Thomas, Gore Vidal, Willem de Kooning and Kerouac's friend Franz Kline. Alene Lee did indeed live in Paradise Alley, but it was a small courtyard located in the East Village (on 11th Street) near the apartment of Allen Ginsberg. People who knew San Francisco were puzzled by the pushcart in which Yuri pulls Leo and Mardou to Adam's door; a series of steep hills quite unlike the small flat island of Manhattan, San Francisco had no pushcarts.

Far more important, Kerouac undercuts his own story, the way he saw and felt about the relationship, by insistently presenting Mardou's resistance to it. As a woman, Mardou is 'made to bend', Leo confidently tells the reader, describing himself as 'smug and snug in the rug of myself', just, moments before Mardou breaks off their affair. She has told him from the first that she wanted to be 'independent', a word never far from her lips, and he realizes too late that she meant it. When Leo mythologizes the two of them as Adam and Eve, she cuts him off: 'don't call me Eve'. To him, she is the spirit of bebop incarnate, but, much as she cares for the music, it troubles her, too, because 'many junkies are bop men, and I hear the junk [heroin] in it'. Even as he doubts that he is capable of sacrificing his 'white ambitions' or displeasing his Southern relations by a long-term commitment to her, he thinks he can brush off her nervousness about appearing openly in public with him as evidence of her 'Negro fear of American society', a fear he thinks should be automatically allayed by his own protective presence. 'You don't understand,' is her all-encompassing answer.

Although Leo notes that Mardou has been passed among the Subterreanneans in a classic pattern of sexual exchange among men, he admits that he and Leroy (Neal Cassady) 'in the old days ... [were] always swapping [women]', and he is patently titillated to inherit her from Julien Alexander (based on Anton Rosenberg) and Adam Moorad. It is left to Mardou, not Leo, to expose this masculine ritual. Once Leo learns that she has indeed slept with Yuri, a betrayal quite literally dreamed into existence by himself, he retreats with alarming speed into a visibly well-worn misogyny. 'I should have paid more attention to the old junky ... who said ... they're all the same, boy, don't get hung up on one,' he tells her. But Mardou knows that such talk is 'just what Yuri wants'. Now the two of them can go to the bar and 'talk me over and agree that women are good lays and there are a lot of them', celebrating the permanence of men-relating-to-men while relegating their relationships with women to sideshow status.

Kerouac's pathological dependence on his mother was noted by all his friends, and Mardou's understated comment to Leo, 'I don't think it's good for you to live with your mother always,' though he tries to dismiss it as jealousy, reminds him that his mother has told him much the same thing. Later, he admits to himself that he lives at home because he is incapable of making a living on his own, of holding the love of another woman. The name Kerouac gave his stand-in, 'Leo', which was the name of his father, and 'Percepied', or 'pierced foot', an allusion to Oedipus, bespeaks Leo's recognition of the accuracy of Mardou's diagnosis.

The Beats were an ethnically diverse group but, with the exception of the poets Bob Kaufman and Amiri Baraka, an all-white one. In 1959, at a conference for black writers, Langston Hughes asked, 'Who wants to be Beat?', and answered promptly, 'Not Negroes,' a conclusion which Baraka would soon share. Kerouac wrote *The Subterraneans*, in any case, before the Civil Rights movement achieved national recognition, when black–white liaisons were still illegal in some states and condoned virtually nowhere, when a defence of the 'underdog' or support for a Negro organization was automatic grounds for suspicion of Communist sympathies. It is none the less troubling that certain questions seem not to have occurred to him.

Why, for instance, is this young woman of colour passing her time in almost exclusively white company? Kerouac tacitly assumes that she associates with whites because she is beautiful and talented enough to be able to do what all blacks want to do. What, then, about her date with a black man, mentioned in passing by Leo, her desire to 'make it with a Negro boy again'? Kerouac is far more interested in Mardou's Cherokee father than the black mother who died giving her birth – was this Alene Lee's emphasis? But Kerouac's honest exploration of his own racial bias was real and daring, if limited. In the book's most shocking scene, Leo confesses to Mardou his anxiety over black difference as a fear of her genitals. She allows him to look at her, to 'actually see and make the study with her'; he is reassured, and she feels closer to him, realizing, he says, that 'I would never snake-like hide the furthest [thought] from her'. We will never know Alene Lee's interpretation of this incident, but by her own telling, as well as Kerouac's, it was not race which finally divided them.

Gabrielle Kerouac (whose home was in Queens, New York, rather then Oakland, California) did, as Leo claims, provide her son with a safe place where he could write: exposure and retreat, living it up to write it down, were the twin poles of his life and art. This fortress, too, however, is penetrated not only by Mardou's psychoanalytically informed scepticism but by her own claims as a writer. Kerouac said that *The Subterraneans* was written 'like a long letter to a friend'; the epistolary mode was central to his enterprise. But the only long letter in the novel is the one written by Mardou and sent, as Ami Shah has pointed out, to his mother's house, boldly transgressing the barrier Leo has placed between his love life and his writing life. Hers is a 'beauty' of a letter, a 'masterpiece', Leo tells us, quoting it in full; his response, of which he gives us only a few lines, is an 'inane-if-at-all confession', 'dull baloney bullshit'.

As he transcribes it, however, Leo keeps interrupting Mardou's letter with his own lengthy riffs on it; he finds it impossible to let her have the spotlight by herself. Yet Kerouac/Leo is aware of what he's doing. At his angriest, he tell us, 'I finally paid her back for what she done to me – it had to come and this is it.' What follows is a radically altered, much shorter version of Mardou's letter – just the kind of censoring and editing, of course, that Kerouac crusaded against – retaining only the parts of the letter alluding (in favourable terms) to himself. Leo tells us repeatedly that when it comes to Mardou, 'I question my motives'; 'maybe I wasn't seeing, interpreting right, as so oft I do'. Such lines are an open invitation extended by Kerouac to the reader to interrogate, even discredit, his text.

Kerouac described *The Subterraneans* as 'a full confession of [his] most wretched and hidden agonies'; he meant to leave no corner of his heart unexamined or free of guilt. But the French philosopher Michel Foucault has underlined the ways in which a confessional discourse like Kerouac's tries to free itself of the constraints of official power by 'extracting from the very depths of the [self] ... a truth' which is believed to predate and outlast it, yet all the while, the authority apparently being defied simply uses the act of confession as a means of offering the individual the release of self-expression while withholding the power radically to change himself or the world around him. Kerouac's revelations about himself in *The Subterraneans*, even his empowering of Mardou's disruptive voice, serve finally to give him what he perhaps most wanted from the affair in the first place, a novel. The narrative concludes with two short sentences quite unlike the popping-and-parenthesizing-in-all-directions style that dominates the rest of the text. 'I go home having lost her love. And write this book,' lines plain as self-interest or money, bespeaking gain as well as loss.

This analysis, however, situates Kerouac within a relativist, relentlessly deconstructive postmodern critique, one that Kerouac both acknowledged and protested. Postmodernism has no special claims to universal insight. Like all intellectual styles, it is the product of a particular time and place, in this case, the United States in the 1950s and 1960s. With Bebop, Abstract Expressionism, and the Actors Studio, the Beat Generation represented a final, explosive transformation of modernism on the cusp of its postmodern future. Both Ginsberg and Burroughs in their different ways made the transition to the 1960s with their cultural leadership intact, even enhanced, but Kerouac saw the future and hated it. The 'cool' Subterraneans with their deliberate withholding of emotional emphasis, who are, Leo realizes, 'the most unputdownable [people] in this ... new culture', represent that postmodern future; so does the 'successful young author', the ' "ironic" looking' – note the postmodern quotes – Harold Sand, a character modelled on William Gaddis, who would shortly emerge as one of the leaders of the new postmodern fiction.

Ginsberg and Cassady allied themselves closely with Ken Kesey's irreverent, technologically avant-garde, acid-dropping Merry Pranksters in the 1960s, but Kerouac was appalled by the whole show. He tried LSD only to report that 'walking on water wasn't built in a day'. He had pledged undying allegiance to what Roland Barthes calls 'the impossible science of the unique being'; he belonged irrevocably to the group Amiri Baraka described in 1963 as the 'last romantics of our age'. Kerouac was part of a Cold War spiritual underground, filled with danger and magic, that propagated a new and exacting version of unworldliness expressly designed for a time when the world meant the Holocaust, Hiroshima, the Soviet Union's show trials and genocidal purges, and the ugly postwar antics of the Western imperial powers.

By the mid-1960s, Kerouac knew that his cultural moment had passed. In *Vanity of Duluoz* (1968), his last major novel, he tied the shift to the advent of the phrase 'You're putting me on.' What was new, he thought, was not that people lied, but that people now assumed that everyone else was lying too; the adversarial position had disappeared, truth-telling was not recognized except as another form of deceit. He was especially upset by a letter from a woman, a proto-deconstructionist apparently, who claimed that Kerouac had not written his books, that there were, in fact, no books, no 'Jack

Kerouac' at all. Did she think his books 'just suddenly appeared on a computer?', he fumed. He was still sure that 'lying is a sin ... and being a false witness is a mortal sin'.

Kerouac could not altogether overcome his prejudices; the love affair with Alene Lee served him best as the impetus and material for his book. Does this mean he didn't love her as far as he was able, that he didn't mourn her loss even as he engineered it? In *The Subterraneans*, Kerouac is recording the second-to-second, back-and-forth, almost somatic fluctuations of the psyche, that stage of consciousness when thoughts and feelings have acquired their power but not yet their authority, when the mind is still too close to its sources to impose the censorship of choice. He described his young companions in the early days of the Beat Generation as elated and excited one day, 'bushed and ... brooding' the next, but, to his mind, the downswing was also a preparation for something else. They were '*storing* up for more belief'. It is still possible to find 'the key / out of this dark corridor, / the effulgent door, / the mysterious knob, / the bright room gained'.

Suggested Reading

Beaulieu, Victor-Lévy. *Jack Kerouac: A Chicken Essay*, trans. Sheila Fischman. Toronto: Coach House Press, 1975.

Bird: The Legend of Charlie Parker, ed. Robert Reisner. 1962; reprinted, New York: DaCapo Press, 1991.

Brinkley, Douglas. 'In the Kerouac Archive'. *Atlantic Monthly* (November 1998): 49–76.

Creeley, Robert. 'Thinking of Jack: A Preface', in Jack Kerouac, *Good Blonde & Others*. San Francisco: Grey Fox Press, 1994.

Eburne, Jonathan Paul. 'Trafficking in the Void: Burroughs, Kerouac, and the Consumption of Otherness'. *Modern Fiction Studies* 43: 1 (1997): 53–92.

Gifford, Barry, and Lawrence Lee. *Jack's Book: An Oral History of Jack Kerouac*. New York: St Martin's Press, 1978.

Johnson, Joyce. *Minor Characters: A Beat Memoir*. 1983; reprinted, New York: Viking, 1999.

Kerouac, Jack. 'On the Road Again'. *New Yorker* (22 and 29 June 1998): 46–59.

—. *The Portable Jack Kerouac*, ed. Ann Charters. New York: Viking, 1995.

—. *Jack Kerouac: Selected Letters, 1940–1956*, ed. Ann Charters. New York: Viking, 1995.

—. *Jack Kerouac: Selected Letters, 1957–1969*, ed. Ann Charters. New York: Viking, 1999.

Lhamon, Jr, W. T. *Deliberate Speed: The Origins of a Cultural Style in the 1950s*. Washington: Smithsonian Institute Press, 1990.

Moderns: An Anthology of New Writing in America, The, ed. Leroi Jones (Amiri Baraka). New York: Corinth Books, 1963.

Nicosia, Gerald. *Memory Babe: A Critical Biography of Jack Kerouac*. New York: Grove Press, 1983.

Podhoretz, Norman. 'The Know-Nothing Bohemians' in *Doings and Undoings: The Fifties and After in American Writing*. New York: Farrar, Straus, and Giroux, 1964.

Tallman, Warren. 'Kerouac's Sound', *Evergreen Review* 4 (1960), 153–69.

Tytell, John. *Naked Angels: Kerouac, Ginsberg, Burroughs*. New York: Grove Weidenfeld, 1976.

Vidal, Gore. 'Now You Owe Me a Dollar' in *Palimpsest*. New York: Random House, 1995.

Watson, Steven. *The Birth of the Beat Generation: Visionaries, Rebels and Hipsters 1944–1960*. New York: Pantheon, 1995.

The Subterraneans

1

Once I was young and had so much more orientation and could talk with nervous intelligence about everything and with clarity and without as much literary preambling as this; in other words this is the story of an unselfconfident man, at the same time of an egomaniac, naturally, facetious won't do – just to start at the beginning and let the truth seep out, that's what I'll do –. It began on a warm summer-night – ah, she was sitting on a fender with Julien Alexander who is . . . let me begin with the history of the subterraneans of San Francisco . . .

Julien Alexander is the angel of the subterraneans, the subterraneans is a name invented by Adam Moorad who is a poet and friend of mine who said 'They are hip without being slick, they are intelligent without being corny, they are intellectual as hell and know all about Pound without being pretentious or talking too much about it, they are very quiet, they are very Christlike.' Julien certainly is Christlike. I was coming down the street with Larry O'Hara old drinking buddy of mine from all the times in San Francisco in my long and nervous and mad careers I've gotten drunk and in fact cadged drinks off friends with such 'genial' regularity nobody really cared to notice or announce that I am developing or was developing, in my youth, such bad free-loading habits though of course they did notice but liked me and as Sam said 'Everybody comes to you for your gasoline boy, that's some filling station you got there' or say words to that effect – old Larry O'Hara always nice to me, a crazy Irish young businessman of San Francisco with Balzacian backroom in his bookstore where they'd smoke tea and talk of the old days of the great Basie band or the days of the great Chu Berry – of whom more anon since she got involved with him too as she had to get involved with everyone because of knowing me who am nervous and many levelled and not in the least one-souled –

3

not a piece of my pain has showed yet – or suffering – Angels, bear with me – I'm not even looking at the page but straight ahead into the sadglint of my wallroom and at a Sarah Vaughan Gerry Mulligan Radio KROW show on the desk in the form of a radio, in other words, they were sitting on the fender of a car in front of the Black Mask bar on Montgomery Street, Julien Alexander the Christlike unshaved thin youthful quiet strange almost as you or as Adam might say apocalyptic angel or saint of the subterraneans, certainly star (now), and she, Mardou Fox, whose face when first I saw it in Dante's bar around the corner made me think, 'By God, I've got to get involved with that little woman' and maybe too because she was Negro. Also she had the same face that Rita Savage a girlhood girlfriend of my sister's had, and of whom among other things I used to have daydreams of her between my legs while kneeling on the floor of the toilet, I on the seat, with her special cool lips and Indian-like hard high soft cheekbones – same face, but dark, sweet, with little eyes honest glittering and intense she Mardou was leaning saying something extremely earnestly to Ross Wallenstein (Julien's friend) leaning over the table, deep – 'I got to get involved with her' – I tried to shoot her the glad eye the sex eye she never had a notion of looking up or seeing – I must explain, I'd just come off a ship in New York, paid off before the trip to Kobe Japan because of trouble with the steward and my inability to be gracious and in fact human and like an ordinary guy while performing my chores as saloon messman (and you must admit now I'm sticking to the facts), a thing typical of me, I would treat the first engineer and the other officers with backwards-falling politeness, it finally drove them angry, they wanted me to say something, maybe gruff, in the morning, while setting their coffee down and instead of which silently on crepefeet I rushed to do their bidding and never cracked a smile or if so a sick one, a superior one, all having to do with that loneliness angel riding on my shoulder as I came down warm Montgomery Street that night and saw Mardou on the fender with Julien, remembering, 'O there's the girl I gotta get involved with, I wonder if she's going with any of these boys' – dark, you could barely see her in the dim street – her feet in thongs of sandals of such sexuality-looking greatness I wanted to kiss her, them – having no notion of anything though.

The subterraneans were hanging outside the Mask in the warm

4

night, Julien on the fender, Ross Wallenstein standing up, Roger Beloit the great bop tenorman, Walt Fitzpatrick who was the son of a famous director and had grown up in Hollywood in an atmosphere of Greta Garbo parties at dawn and Chaplin falling in the door drunk, several other girls, Harriet the ex-wife of Ross Wallenstein a kind of blonde with soft expressionless features and wearing a simple almost housewife-in-the-kitchen cotton dress but softly bellysweet to look at – as another confession must be made, as many I must make ere time's sup – I am crudely malely sexual and cannot help myself and have lecherous and so on propensities as almost all my male readers no doubt are the same – confession after confession. I am a Canuck, I could not speak English till I was 5 or 6, at 16 I spoke with a halting accent and was a big blue baby in school though varsity basketball later and if not for that no one would have noticed I could cope in any way with the world (underselfconfidence) and would have been put in the madhouse for some kind of inadequacy –

But now let me tell Mardou herself (difficult to make a real confession and show what happened when you're such an egomaniac all you can do is take off on big paragraphs about minor details about yourself and the big soul details about others go sitting and waiting around) – in any case, therefore, also there was Fritz Nicholas the titular leader of the subterraneans, to whom I said (having met him New Year's Eve in a Nob Hill swank apartment sitting crosslegged like a peote Indian on a thick rug wearing a kind of clean white Russian shirt and a crazy Isadora Duncan girl with long blue hair on his shoulder smoking pot and talking about Pound and peote) (thin also Christlike with a faun's look and young and serious and like the father of the group, as, say, suddenly you'd see him in the Black Mask sitting there with head thrown back thin dark eyes watching everybody as if in sudden slow astonishment and 'Here we are little ones and now what my dears,' but also a great dope man, anything in the form of kicks he would want at any time and very intense) I said to him, 'Do you know this girl, the dark one?' – 'Mardou?' – 'That her name? Who she go with?' – 'No one in particular just now, this has been an incestuous group in its time,' a very strange thing he said to me there, as we walked to his old beat '36 Chevvy with no backseat parked across from the bar for the purpose of picking up some tea for the group to get all together, as, I told Larry, 'Man, let's get

5

some tea' – 'And what for you want all those people?' – 'I want to dig them as a group,' saying this, too, in front of Nicholas so perhaps he might appreciate my sensitivity being a stranger to the group and yet immediately, etc., perceiving their value – facts, facts, sweet philosophy long deserted me with the juices of other years fled – incestuous – there was another final great figure in the group who was however now this summer not here but in Paris, Jack Steen, very interesting Leslie-Howard-like little guy who walked (as Mardou later imitated for me) like a Viennese philosopher with soft arms swinging slight side flow and long slow flowing strides, coming to a stop on corner with imperious soft pose – he too had had to do with Mardou and as I learned later most weirdly – but now my first crumb of information concerning this girl I was SEEKING to get involved with as if not enough trouble already or other old romances hadn't taught me that message of pain, keep asking for it, for life –

Out of the bar were pouring interesting people, the night making a great impression on me, some kind of Truman-Capote-haired dark Marlon Brando with a beautiful thin birl or girl in boy slacks with stars in her eyes and hips that seemed so soft when she put her hands in her slacks I could see the change – and dark thin slackpant legs dropping down to little feet, and that face, and with them a guy with another beautiful doll, the guy's name Rob and he's some kind of adventurous Israeli soldier with a British accent whom I suppose you might find in some Riviera bar at 5 a.m. drinking everything in sight alphabetically with a bunch of interesting crazy international-set friends on a spree – Larry O'Hara introducing me to Roger Beloit (I did not believe that this young man with ordinary face in front of me was that great poet I'd revered in my youth, my youth, my youth, that is, 1948, I keep saying my youth) – 'This is Roger Beloit? – I'm Bennett Fitzpatrick' – (Walt's father) which brought a smile to Roger Beloit's face – Adam Moorad by now having emerged from the night was also there and the night would open –

So we all did go to Larry's and Julien sat on the floor in front of an open newspaper in which was the tea (poor quality L.A. but good enough) and rolled, or 'twisted' as Jack Steen, the absent one, had said to me the previous New Year's and that having been my first contact with the subterraneans, he'd asked to roll a stick for me and I'd said really coldly· 'What for? I roll my own' and

6

immediately the cloud crossed his sensitive little face, etc., and he hated me – and so cut me all the night when he had a chance – but now Julien was on the floor, crosslegged, and himself now twisting for the group and everybody droned the conversations which I certainly won't repeat, except, it was like, 'I'm looking at this book by Percepied – who's Percepied, has he been busted yet?' and such small talk, or, while listening to Stan Kenton talking about the music of tomorrow and we hear a new young tenorman come on, Ricci Comucca, Roger Beloit says, moving back expressive thin purple lips, 'This is the music of tomorrow?' and Larry O'Hara telling his usual stock repertoire anecdotes. In the '36 Chevvy on the way, Julien, sitting beside me on the floor, had stuck out his hand and said, 'My name's Julien Alexander, I have something, I conquered Egypt,' and then Mardou stuck her hand out to Adam Moorad and introduced herself, saying, 'Mardou Fox,' but didn't think of doing it to me which should have been my first inkling of the prophecy of what was to come, so I had to stick my hand at her and say, 'Leo Percepied my name' and shake – ah, you always go for the ones who don't really want you – she really wanted Adam Moorad, she had just been rejected coldly and subterraneanly by Julien – she was interested in thin ascetic strange intellectuals of San Francisco and Berkeley and not in big paranoiac bums of ships and railroads and novels and all that hatefulness which in myself is to myself so evident and so to others too – though and because ten years younger than I seeing none of my virtues which anyway had long been drowned under years of drugtaking and desiring to die, to give up, to give it all up and forget it all, to die in the dark star – it was I stuck out my hand, not she – ah time.

But in eyeing her little charms I only had the foremost one idea that I had to immerse my lonely being ('A big sad lonely man,' is what she said to me one night later, seeing me suddenly in the chair) in the warm bath and salvation of her thighs – the intimacies of young lovers in a bed, high, facing eye to eye, breast to breast naked, organ to organ, knee to shivering goose-pimpled knee, exchanging existential and lover-acts for a crack at making it – 'making it' the big expression with her, I can see the little out-pushing teeth through the little redlips seeing 'making it' – the key to pain – she sat in the corner, by the window, she was being 'separated' or 'aloof' or 'prepared to cut out from this group' for

7

her own reasons. – In the corner I went, not leaning my head on her but on the wall and tried silent communication, then quiet words (as befit party) and North Beach words, 'What are you reading?' and for the first time she opened her mouth and spoke to me communicating a full thought and my heart didn't exactly sink but wondered when I heard the cultured funny tones of part Beach, part I. Magnin model, part Berkeley, part Negro highclass, something, a mixture of *langue* and style of talking and use of words I'd never heard before except in certain rare girls of course *white* and so strange even Adam at once noticed and commented with me that night – but definitely the new bop generation way of speaking, you don't say *I*, you say 'ahy' or 'Oy' and long ways, like oft or erst-while 'effeminate' way of speaking so when you hear it in men at first it has a disagreeable sound and when you hear it in women it's charming but much too strange, and a sound I had already definitely and wonderingly heard in the voice of new bop singers like Jerry Winters especially with Kenton band on the record *Yes Daddy Yes* and maybe in Jeri Southern too – but my heart sank for the Beach has always hated me, cast me out, overlooked me, shat on me, from the beginning in 1943 on in – for look, coming down the street I am some kind of hoodlum and then when they learn I'm not a hoodlum but some kind of crazy saint they don't like it and moreover they're afraid I'll suddenly become a hoodlum anyway and slug them and break things and this I have almost done anyway and in my adolescence did so, as one time I roamed through North Beach with the Stanford basketball team, specifically with Red Kelly whose wife (rightly?) died in Redwood City in 1946, the whole team behind us the Garetta brothers besides, he pushed a violinist a queer into a doorway and I pushed another one in, he slugged his, I glared at mine, I was 18, I was a nannybeater and fresh as a daisy too – now, seeing this past in the scowl and glare and horror and the beat of my brow-pride they wanted nothing to do with me, and so I, of course also knew that Mardou had real genuine distrust and dislike of me as I sat there 'trying to (not make IT) but make her' – unhiplike, brash, smiling, the false hysterical 'compulsive' smiling they call it – me hot – them cool – and also I had on a very noxious unbeachlike shirt, bought on Broadway in New York when I thought I'd be cutting down the gangplanks in Kobe, a foolish Crosby Hawaiian shirt with designs, which malelike and vain after the original

8

honest humilities of my regular self (really) with the smoking of two drags of tea I felt constrained to open an extra button down and so show my tanned, hairy chest – which must have disgusted her – in any case she didn't look, and spoke little and low – and was intent on Julien who was squatting with his back to her – and she listened and murmured the laughter in the general talk – most of the talk being conducted by O'Hara and loudspeaking Roger Beloit and that intelligent adventurous Rob and I, too silent, listening, digging, but in the tea vanity occasionally throwing in 'perfect' (I thought) remarks which were 'too perfect' but to Adam Moorad who'd known me all the time clear indication of my awe and listening and respect of the group in fact, and to them this new person throwing in remarks intended to show his hipness – all horrible, and unredeemable. – Although at first, before the puffs, which were passed around Indian style, I had the definite sensation of being able to come close with Mardou and involved and making her that very first night, that is taking off with her alone if only for coffee but with the puffs which made me pray reverently and in serious secrecy for the return of my pre-puff 'sanity' I became extremely unselfconfident, overtrying, positive she didn't like me, hating the facts – remembering now the first night I met my Nicki Peters love in 1948 in Adam Moorad's pad in (then) the Fillmore, I was standing unconcerned and beer-drinking in the kitchen as ever (an at home working furiously on a huge novel, mad, cracked, confident, young, talented as never since) when she pointed to my profile shadow on the pale green wall and said, 'How beautiful your profile is,' which so nonplussed me and (like the tea) made me unselfconfident, attentive, attempting to 'begin to make her', to act in that way which by her almost hypnotic suggestion now led to the first preliminary probings into pride vs. pride and beauty or beatitude or sensitivity *versus* the stupid neurotic nervousness of the phallic type, forever conscious of his phallus, his tower, of women as wells – the truth of the matter being there, but the man unhinged, unrelaxed, and now it is no longer 1948 but 1953 with cool generations and I five years older, or younger, having to make it (or make the women) with a new style and stow the nervousness – in any case, I gave up consciously trying to make Mardou and settled down to a night of digging the great new perplexing group of subterraneans Adam had discovered and named on the Beach.

But from the first Mardou was indeed self-dependent and independent announcing she wanted no one, nothing to do with anyone, ending (after me) with same – which now in the cold unblessing night I feel in the air, this announcement of hers, and that her little teeth are no longer mine but probably my enemy's lapping at them and giving her the sadistic treatment she probably loves as I had given her none – murders in the air – and that bleak corner where a lamp shines, and winds swirl, a paper, fog, I see the great discouraged face of myself and my so-called love drooping in the lane, no good – as before it had been melancholy droopings in hot chairs, downcast by moons (though tonight's the great night of the harvest moon) – as where then, before, it was the recognition of the need for my return to world-wide love as a great writer should do, like a Luther, a Wagner, now this warm thought of greatness is a big chill in the wind – for greatness dies too – ah and who said I was great – and supposing one were a great writer, a secret Shakespeare of the pillow night? or really so – a Baudelaire's poem is not worth his grief – his grief – (It was Mardou finally said to me, 'I would have preferred the happy man to the unhappy poems he's left us,' which I agree with and I am Baudelaire, and love my brown mistress and I too leaned to her belly and listened to the rumbling underground) – but I should have known from her original announcement of independence to believe in the sincerity of her distaste for involvement, instead hurling on at her as if and because in fact I wanted to be hurt and 'lacerate' myself – one more laceration yet and they'll pull the blue sod on, and make my box plop boy – for now death bends big wings over my window, I see it, I hear it, I smell it, I see it in the limp hang of my shirts destined to be not worn, new-old, stylish-out-of-date, neckties snakelike behung I don't even use any more, new blankets for autumn peace beds now writhing rushing cots on the sea of self-murder – loss – hate – paranoia – it was her little face I wanted to enter, and did –

That morning when the party was at its pitch I was in Larry's bedroom again admiring the red light and remembering the night we'd had Micky in there the three of us, Adam and Larry and myself, and had benny and a big sex-ball amazing to describe in itself – when Larry ran in and said, 'Man you gonna make it with her tonight?'– 'I'd shore like to – I dunno – ' – 'Well man find out, ain't much time left, whatsamatter with you, we bring all these people to the house and give em all that tea and now all my beer from the icebox, man we gotta get something out of it, work on it –.' 'Oh, you like her?' – 'I like anybody as far as that goes man – but I *mean*, after all.' – Which led me to a short unwillful abortive fresh effort, some look, glance, remark, sitting next to her in corner, I gave up and at dawn she cut out with the others who all went for coffee and I went down there with Adam to see her again (following the group down the stairs five minutes later) and they were there but she wasn't, independently darkly brooding, she'd gone off to her stuffy little place in Heavenly Lane on Telegraph Hill.

So I went home and for several days in sexual phantasies it was she, her dark feet, thongs of sandals, dark eyes, little soft brown face, Rita-Savage-like cheeks and lips, little secretive intimacy and somehow now softly snakelike charm as befits a little thin brown woman disposed to wearing dark clothes, poor beat subterranean clothes . . .

A few nights later Adam with an evil smile announced he had run into her in a Third Street bus and they'd gone to his place to talk and drink and had a big long talk which Leroy-like culminated in Adam sitting naked reading Chinese poetry and passing the stick and ending up laying in the bed, 'And she's very affectionate, God, the way suddenly she wraps her arms around you as if for no other reason but pure sudden affection' – 'Are you going to make it? have an affair with her?' – 'Well now let me – actually I tell you – she's a whole lot and not a little crazy – she's having therapy, has apparently very seriously flipped only very recently, something to do with Julien, has been having therapy but not showing up, sits or lies down reading or doing nothing but staring at the ceiling all day long in her place, eighteen dollars a month in Heavenly Lane, gets, apparently, some kind of allowance tied up somehow by her doctors or somebody with her inadequacy to work or something – is always talking about it and really too much for my likings – has apparently real hallucinations concerning nuns in the orphanage where she was raised and has seen them and felt actual threat – and also other things, like the sensation of taking junk although she's never had junk but only known junkies.' – 'Julien?' – 'Julien takes junk whenever he can which is not often because he has no money and his ambition like is to be a real junkey – but in any case she had hallucinations of not being properly contact high but actually somehow secretly injected by someone or something, people who follow her down the street, say, and is really crazy – and it's too much for me – and finally being a Negro I don't want to get all involved.' – 'Is she pretty?' – 'Beautiful – but I can't make it.' – 'But boy I sure dig her looks and everything else.' – 'Well alright man then you'll make it – go over there, I'll give you the address, or better yet when, I'll invite her here and we'll talk, you can try if you want but although I have a hot feeling sexually and all that for her I really don't want to get any further into her not only for these reasons but finally, the big one, if I'm going to get involved with a girl now I want to be permanent like permanent and serious and long termed and I can't do that with her.' – 'I'd like a long permanent, et cetera.' – 'Well we'll see.'

He told me of a night she'd be coming for a little snack dinner he'd cook for her so I was there, smoking tea in the red living-room, with a dim red bulb light on, and she came in looking the same but now I was wearing a plain blue silk sports shirt and fancy slacks and I sat back cool to pretend to be cool hoping she would notice this with the result, when the lady entered the parlour I did not rise.

While they ate in the kitchen I pretended to read. I pretended to pay no attention whatever. We went out for a walk the three of us and by now all of us vying to talk like three good friends who want to get in and say everything on their minds, a friendly rivalry – we went to the Red Drum to hear the jazz which that night was Charlie Parker with Honduras Jones on drums and others interesting, probably Roger Beloit too, whom I wanted to see now, and that excitement of softnight San Francisco bop in the air but all in the cool sweet unexerting Beach – so we in fact ran, from Adam's on Telegraph Hill, down the white street under lamps, ran, jumped, showed off, had fun – felt gleeful and something was throbbing and I was pleased that she was able to walk as fast as we were – a nice thin strong little beauty to cut along the street with and so striking everyone turned to see, the strange bearded Adam, dark Mardou in strange slacks, and me, big gleeful hood.

So there we were at the Red Drum, a tableful of beers a few that is and all the gangs cutting in and out, paying a dollar quarter at the door, the little hip-pretending weasel there taking

12

tickets, Paddy Cordavan floating in as prophesied (a big tall blond brakeman type subterranean from the Eastern Washington cowboy-looking in jeans coming in to a wild generation party all smoky and mad and I yelled 'Paddy Cordavan?' and 'Yeah?' and he'd come over) – all sitting together, interesting groups at various tables, Julien, Roxanne (a woman of 25 prophesying the future style of America with short almost crewcut but with curls black snaky hair, snaky walk, pale pale junkey anaemic face and we say junkey when once Dostoevsky would have said what? if not ascetic or saintly? but not in the least? but the cold pale booster face of the cold blue girl and wearing a man's white shirt but with the cuffs undone untied at the buttons so I remember her leaning over talking to someone after having slinked across the floor with flowing propelled shoulders, bending to talk with her hand holding a short butt and the neat little flick she was giving it to knock ashes but repeatedly with long long fingernails an inch long and also orient and snakelike) – groups of all kinds, and Ross Wallenstein, the crowd, and up on the stand Bird Parker with solemn eyes who'd been busted fairly recently and had now returned to a kind of bop dead Frisco but had just discovered or been told about the Red Drum, the great new general gang wailing and gathering there, so here he was on the stand, examining them with his eyes as he blew his now-settled-down-into-regulated-design 'crazy' notes – the booming drums, the high ceiling – Adam for my sake dutifully cutting out at about 11 o'clock so he could go to bed and get to work in the morning, after a brief cutout with Paddy and myself for a quick ten-cent beer at roaring Pantera's, where Paddy and I in our first talk and laughter together pulled wrists – now Mardou cut out with me, glee eyed, between sets, for quick beers, but at her insistence at the Mask instead where they were fifteen cents, but she had a few pennies herself and we went there and began earnestly talking and getting hightingled on the beer and now it was the beginning – returning to the Red Drum for sets, to hear Bird, whom I saw distinctly digging Mardou several times also myself directly into my eye looking to search if really I was that great writer I thought myself to be as if he knew my faults and ambitions or remembered me from other night clubs and other coasts, other Chicagos – not a challenging look but the king and founder of the bop generation at least the sound of it in digging his audience digging the eyes, the secret eyes him-watching, as he just pursed his lips and let great lungs and immortal fingers work, his eyes separate and interested and humane, the kindest jazz musician there could be while being and therefore naturally the greatest – watching Mardou and me in the infancy of our love and probably wondering why, or knowing it wouldn't last, or seeing who it was would be hurt, as now, obviously, but not quite yet, it was Mardou whose eyes were shining in my direction, though I could not have known and now do not definitely know – except the one fact, on the way home, the session over the beer in the Mask drunk we went home on the Third Street bus sadly through night and throb knock neons and when I suddenly leaned over her to shout something further (in her secret self as later confessed) her heart leapt to smell the 'sweetness of my breath' (quote) and suddenly she almost loved me – I not knowing this, as we found the Russian dark sad door of Heavenly Lane a great iron gate rasping on the sidewalk to the pull, the insides of smelling garbage cans sad-leaning together, fish heads, cats, and then the Lane itself, my first view of it (the long history and hugeness of it in my soul, as in 1951 cutting along with my sketchbook on a wild October evening when I was discovering my own writing soul at last I saw the subterranean Victor who'd come to Big Sur once on a motor-cycle, was reputed to have gone to Alaska on same, with little subterranean chick Dorie Kiehl, there he was in striding Jesus coat heading north to Heavenly Lane to his pad and I followed him awhile, wondering about Heavenly Lane and all the long talks I'd been having for years with people like Mac Jones about the mystery, the silence of the subterraneans, 'urban Thoreaus' Mac called them, as from Alfred Kazin in New York New School lectures back East commenting on all the students being interested in Whitman from a sexual revolution standpoint and in Thoreau from a contemplative mystic and antimaterialistic as if existentialist or whatever standpoint, the *Pierre*-of-Melville goof and wonder of it, the dark little beat burlap dresses, the stories you'd heard about great tenormen shooting junk by broken windows and starting at their horns, or great young poets with bears lying high in Rouault-like saintly obscurities, Heavenly Lane the famous Heavenly Lane where they'd all at one time or another the bat subterraneans lived, like Alfred and his little sickly wife something straight out of Dostoevsky's

Petersburg slums you'd think but really the American lost bearded idealistic – the whole thing in any case), seeing it for the first time, but with Mardou, the wash hung over the court, actually the back courtyard of a big 20-family tenement with bay windows, the wash hung out and in the afternoon the great symphony of Italian mothers, children, fathers BeFinneganing and yelling from stepladders, smells, cats mewing, Mexicans, the music from all the radios whether bolero of Mexican or Italian tenor of spaghetti eaters or loud suddenly turned-up KPEA symphonies of Vivaldi harpsichord intellectuals performances boom blam the tremendous sound of it which I then came to hear all the summer wrapt in the arms of my love – walking in there now, and going up the narrow musty stairs like in a hovel, and her door.

Plotting I demanded we dance – previously she'd been hungry so I'd suggested and we'd actually gone and bought egg foo young at Jackson and Kearny and now she heated this (later confession she'd hated it tho it's one of my favourite dishes and typical of my later behaviour I was already forcing down her throat that which she in subterranean sorrow wanted to endure alone if at all ever), ah. – Dancing, I had put the light out, so, in the dark, dancing, I kissed her – it was giddy, whirling to the dance, the beginning, the usual beginning of lovers kissing standing in a dark room the room being the woman's the man all designs – ending up later in wild dances she on my lap or thigh as I danced her around bent back for balance and she around my neck her arms that came to warm so much the *me* that then was only hot –

And soon enough I'd learn she had no belief and had had no place to get it from – Negro mother dead for birth of her – unknown Cherokee-halfbreed father a hobo who'd come throwing torn shoes across grey planes of fall in black sombrero and pink scarf squatting by hotdog fires casting Tokay empties into the night 'Yaa Calexico!'

Quick to plunge, bite, put the light out, hide my face in shame, make love to her tremendously because of lack of love for a year almost and the need pushing me down – our little agreements in the dark, the really should-not-be-tolds – for it was she who later said 'Men are so crazy, they want the essence, the woman is the essence, there it is right in their hands but they rush off erecting big abstract constructions' – 'You mean they should just stay home with the essence, that is lie under a tree all day with

15

the woman but Mardou that's an old idea of mine, a lovely idea,
I never heard it better expressed and never dreamed.' – 'Instead
they rush off and have big wars and consider women as prizes
instead of human beings, well man I may be in the middle of all
this shit but I certainly don't want any part of it' (in her sweet
cultured hip tones of new generation). – And so having had the
essence of her love now I erect big word constructions and thereby
betray it really – telling tales of every gossip sheet the washline of
the world – and hers, ours, in all the two months of our love (I
thought) only once-washed as she being a lonely subterranean
spent mooningdays and would go to the laundry with them but
suddenly it's dank late afternoon and too late and the sheets are
grey, lovely to me – because soft. – But I cannot in this confession
betray the innermosts, the thighs, what the thighs contain – and
yet why write? – the thighs contain the essence – yet tho there
I should stay and from there I came and'll eventually return,
still I have to rush off and construct construct – for nothing –
for Baudelaire poems –

Never did she use the word love, even that first moment after
our wild dance when I carried her still on my lap and hanging
clear to the bed and slowly dumped her, suffered to find her, which
she loved, and being unsexual in her entire life (except for the first
15-year-old conjugality which for some reason consummated her
and never since) (O the pain of telling these secrets which are so
necessary to tell, or why write or live) now *casus in eventu est* but
glad to have me losing my mind in the slight way egomaniacally
I might on a few beers. – Lying then in the dark, soft, tentacled,
waiting, till sleep – so in the morning I wake from the scream of
beermares and see beside me the Negro woman with parted lips
sleeping, and little bits of white pillow stuffing in her black hair,
feel almost revulsion, realize what a beast I am for feeling anything
near it, grape little sweetbody naked on the restless sheets of the
night-before excitement, the noise in Heavenly Lane sneaking in
through the grey window, a grey doomsday in August so I feel
like leaving at once to get 'back to my work' the chimera of not the
chimera but the orderly advancing sense of work and duty which
I had worked up and developed at home (in South City) humble
as it is, the comforts there too, the solitude which I wanted and
now can't stand. – I got up and began to dress, apologize, she lay
like a little mummy in the sheet and cast the serious brown eyes

16

on me, like eyes of Indian watchfulness in a wood, like with the brown lashes suddenly rising with black lashes to reveal sudden fantastic whites of eye with the brown glittering iris centre, the seriousness of her face accentuated by the slightly Mongoloid as if of a boxer nose and the cheeks puffed a little from sleep, like the face on a beautiful porphyry mask found long ago and Aztecan. – 'But why do you have to rush off so fast, as though almost hysterical or worried?' – 'Well I do I have work to do and I have to straighten out – hangover –' and she barely awake, so I sneak out with a few words in fact when she lapses almost into sleep and I don't see her again for a few days –

The adolescent cocksman having made his conquest barely broods at home the loss of the love of the conquered lass, the blacklash lovely – no confession there. – It was on a morning when I slept at Adam's that I saw her again, I was going to rise, do some typing and coffee drinking in the kitchen all day since at that time work, work was my dominant thought, not love – not the pain which impels me to write this even while I don't want to, the pain which won't be eased by the writing of this but heightened, but which will be redeemed, and if only it were a dignified pain and could be placed somewhere other than in this black gutter of shame and loss and noisemaking folly in the night and poor sweat on my brow – Adam rising to go to work, I too, washing, mumbling talk, when the phone rang and it was Mardou, who was going to her therapist, but needed a dime for the bus, living around the corner, 'Okay come on over but quick I'm going to work or I'll leave the dime with Leo.' – 'O is he there?' – 'Yes.' – In my mind man-thoughts of doing it again and actually looking forward to seeing her suddenly, as if I'd felt she was displeased with our first night (no reason to feel that, previous to the balling she'd lain on my chest eating the egg foo young and dug me with glittering glee eyes) (that tonight my enemy devour?) the thought of which makes me drop my greasy hot brow into a tired hand – O love, fled me – or do telepathies cross sympathetically in the night? Such cacoëthes him befalls – that the cold lover of lust will earn the warm bleed of spirit – so she came in, 8 a.m., Adam went to work and we were alone and immediately she curled up in my lap, at my invite, in the big stuffed chair and we began to talk, she began to tell her story and I turned on (in the grey day) the dim red bulb-light and thus began our true love –

17

She had to tell me everything – no doubt just the other day she'd already told her whole story to Adam and he'd listened tweaking his beard with a dream in his far-off eye to look attentive and loverman in the bleak eternity, nodding – now with me she was starting all over again but as if (as I thought) to a brother of Adam's a greater lover and bigger, more awful listener and worrier. – There we were in all grey San Francisco of the grey West, you could almost smell rain in the air and far across the land, over the mountains beyond Oakland and out beyond Donner and Truckee was the great desert of Nevada, the wastes leading to Utah, to Colorado, to the cold cold come fall plains where I kept imagining that Cherokee-halfbreed hobo father of hers lying bellydown on a flatcar with the wind furling back his rags and black hat, his brown sad face facing all that land and desolation. – At other moments I imagined him instead working as a picker around Indio and on a hot night he's sitting on a chair on the sidewalk among the joking shirtsleeved men, and he spits and they say, 'Hey Hawk Taw, tell us that story agin about the time you stole a taxicab and drove it clear to Manitoba, Canada – d'jever hear him tell that one, Cy?' – I saw the vision of her father, he's standing straight up, proudly, handsome, in the bleak dim red light of America on a corner, nobody knows his name, nobody cares –

Her own little stories about flipping and her minor fugues, cutting across boundaries of the city, and smoking too much marijuana, which held so much terror for her (in the light of my own absorptions concerning her father the founder of her flesh and predecessor terror-ee of her terrors and knower of much greater flips and madness than she in psychoanalytic-induced anxieties could ever even summon up to just imagine), formed just the background for thoughts about the Negroes and Indians and America in general but with all the overtones of 'new generation' and other historical concerns in which she was now swirled just like all of us in the Wig and Europe Sadness of us all, the innocent seriousness with which she told her story and I'd listened to so often and myself told – wide eyed hugging in heaven together – hipsters of America in the 1950s sitting in a dim room – the clash of the streets beyond the window's bare soft sill. – Concern for her father, because I'd been out there and sat down on the ground and seen the rail and steel of America covering the ground filled with the bones of old Indians and Original Americans. – In the cold grey fall in Colorado and Wyoming I'd worked on the land and watched Indian hoboes come suddenly out of brush by the track and move slowly, hawk lipped, rill-jawed and wrinkled, into the great shadow of the light bearing burdenbags and junk talking quietly to one another and so distant from the absorptions of the field hands, even the Negroes of Cheyenne and Denver streets, the Japs, the general minority Armenians and Mexicans of the whole West that to look at a three-or-foursome of Indians crossing a field and a railroad track is to the senses like something unbelievable as a dream – you think, 'They must be Indians – ain't a soul looking at 'em – they're goin' that way – nobody notices – doesn't matter much which way they go – reservation? What have they got in those brown paper bags?' and only with a great amount of effort you realize 'But they were the inhabitors of this land and under these huge skies they were the worriers and keeners and protectors of wives in whole nations gathered around tents – now the rail that runs over their forefathers' bones leads them onward pointing into infinity, wraiths of humanity treading lightly the surface of the ground so deeply suppurated with the stock of their suffering you only have to dig a foot down to find a baby's hand. – The hotshot passenger train with grashing diesel balls, by browm, browm, the Indians just look up – I see them vanishing like spots – ' and sitting in the redbulb room in San Francisco now with sweet Mardou I think, 'And this is your father I saw in the grey waste, swallowed by night – from his juices came your lips, your eyes full of suffering and sorrow, and we're not to know his name or name his destiny?' – Her little brown hand is curled in mine, her fingernails are paler than her skin, on her toes too and with her shoes off she has one foot curled in between my thighs for warmth and we talk, we begin our romance on the deeper level of love and histories of respect and shame. – For the greatest key to courage is shame and the blurfaces in the passing train see nothing out on the plain but figures of hoboes rolling out of sight –

'I remember one Sunday, Mike and Rita were over, we had some very strong tea – they said it had volcanic ash in it and it was the strongest they'd ever had.' – 'Came from L. A.?' – 'From Mexico – some guys had driven down in the station wagon and pooled their money, or Tijuana or something, I dunno – Rita was flipping at the time – when we were practically stoned she rose very dramatically and stood there in the middle of the room man saying she felt her nerves burning thru her bones – To see her *flip* right before my eyes – I got nervous and had some kind of idea about Mike, he kept *looking* at me like he wanted to kill me – he has such a funny look anyway – I got out of the house and walked along and didn't know which way to go, my mind kept turning into the several directions that I was thinking of going but my body kept walking straight along Columbus altho I felt the sensation of each of the directions I mentally and emotionally turned into, amazed at all the possible directions you can take with different motives that come in, like it can make you a different *person* – I've often thought of this since childhood, of suppose instead of going up Columbus as I usually did I'd turn into Filbert would something happen that at the time is insignificant enough but would be like enough to influence my whole life in the end? – What's in store for me in the direction I *don't* take? – and all that, so if this had not been such a constant preoccupation that accompanied me in my solitude which I played upon in as many different ways as possible I wouldn't bother now except but seeing the horrible roads this pure *supposing* goes to it took me to *frights*, if I wasn't so damned *persistent* – ' and so on deep into the day, a long confusing story only pieces of which and imperfectly I remember, just the mass of the misery in connective form –

Flips in gloomy afternoons in Julien's room and Julien sitting paying no attention to her but staring in the grey moth void stirring only occasionally to close the window or change his knee crossings, eyes round staring in a meditation so long and so mysterious and as I say so Christlike really outwardly lamby it was enough to drive anybody crazy I'd say to live there even one day with Julien or Wallenstein (same type) or Mike Murphy (same type), the subterraneans their gloomy longthoughts enduring. – And the meekened girl waiting in a dark corner, as I remembered so well the time I was at Big Sur and Victor arrived on his literally homemade motorcycle with little Dorie Kiehl, there was a party in Patsy's cottage, beer, candlelight, radio, talk, yet for the first hour the newcomers in their funny ragged clothes and he with that beard and she with those sombre serious eyes had sat practically out of sight behind the candlelight shadows so no one could see them and since they said nothing whatever but just (if not listened) meditated, gloomed, endured, finally I even forgot they were there

– and later that night they slept in a pup tent in the field in
the foggy dew of Pacific Coast Starry Night and with the same
humble silence mentioned nothing in the morn – Victor so much
in my mind always the central exaggerator of subterranean hip
generation tendencies to silence, bohemian mystery, drugs, beard,
semi-holiness and, as I came to find later, insurpassable nastiness
(like George Sanders in *The Moon and Sixpence*) – so Mardou a
healthy girl in her own right and from the windy open ready
for love now hid in a musty corner waiting for Julien to speak.
– Occasionally in the general 'incest' she'd been slyly silently by
some consenting arrangement or secret statesmanship shifted or
probably just 'Hey Ross you take Mardou home tonight I wanta
make it with Rita for a change,' – and staying at Ross's for a week,
smoking the volcanic ash, she was flipping – (the tense anxiety
of improper sex additionally, the premature ejaculations of these
anaemic *maquereaux* leaving her suspended in tension and wonder).
– 'I was just an innocent chick when I met them, independent and
like well not happy or anything but feeling that I had something to
do, I wanted to go to night school, I had several jobs at my trade,
binding in Olstad's and small places down around Harrison, the
art teacher the old gal at school was saying I could become a great
sculptress and I was living with various roommates and buying
clothes and making it' – (sucking in her little lip, and that slick
'cuk' in the throat of drawing in breath quickly in sadness and
as if with a cold, like in the throats of great drinkers, but she not
a drinker but saddener of self) (supreme, dark) – (twining warm
arm farther around me) 'and he's lying there saying whatsamatter
and I can't understand – .' she can't understand suddenly what
has happened because she's lost her mind, her usual recognition
of self, and feels the eerie buzz of mystery, she really does not
know who she is and what for and where she is, she looks out the
window and this city San Francisco is the big bleak bare stage of
some giant joke being perpetrated on her. – 'With my back turned
I didn't know what Ross was thinking – even doing.' – She had
no clothes on, she'd risen out of his satisfied sheets to stand in
the wash of grey gloom-time thinking what to do, where to go. –
And the longer she stood there finger-in-mouth and the more the
man said, 'What's the matter ba-by' (finally he stopped asking and
just let her stand there) the more she could feel the pressure from
inside towards bursting and explosion coming on, finally she took

21

a giant step forward with a gulp of fear – everything was clear: danger in the air – it was writ in the shadows, in the gloomy dust behind the drawing table in the corner, in the garbage bags, the grey drain of day seeping down the wall and into the window – in the hollow eyes of people – she ran out of the room. – 'What'd he say?'

'Nothing – he didn't move but was just with his head off the pillow when I glanced back in closing the door – I had no clothes on in the alley, it didn't disturb me, I was so intent on this realization of everything I knew I was an innocent child.' – 'The naked babe, wow.' – (And to myself: 'My God, this girl, Adam's right she's crazy, like I'd do that, I'd flip like I did on Benzedrine with Honey in 1945 and thought she wanted to use my body for the gang car and the wrecking and flames but I'd certainly never run out into the streets of San Francisco naked tho I might have maybe if I really felt there was need for action, yah') and I looked at her wondering if she, was she telling the truth. – She was in the alley, wondering who she was, night, a thin drizzle of mist, silence of sleeping Frisco, the B-O boats in the bay, the shroud over the bay of great clawmouth fogs, the aureola of funny eerie light being sent up in the middle by the Arcade Hood Droops of the Pillar-templed Alcatraz – her heart thumping in the stillness, the cool dark peace. – Up on a wood fence, waiting – to see if some idea from outside would be sent telling her what to do next and full of import and omen because it had to be right and just once –'One slip in the wrong direction . . .' her direction kick, should she jump down on one side of fence or other, endless space reaching out in four directions, bleak-hatted men going to work in glistening streets uncaring of the naked girl hiding in the mist or if they'd been there and seen her would in a circle stand not touching her just waiting for the cop-authorities to come and cart her away and all their uninterested weary eyes flat with blank shame watching every part of her body – the naked babe. – The longer she hangs on the fence the less power she'll have finally to really get down and decide, and upstairs Ross Wallenstein doesn't even move from that junk-high bed, thinking her in the hall huddling, or he's gone to sleep anyhow in his own skin and bone. – The rainy night blooping all over, kissing everywhere men women and cities in one wash of sad poetry, with honey lines of high-shelved Angels trumpet-blowing up above the final Orient-shroud Pacific-huge songs of Paradise, an end to fear below. – She squats on the fence, the thin drizzle making beads on her brown shoulders, stars in her hair, her wild now-Indian eyes now staring into the Black with a little fog emanating from her brown mouth, the misery like ice crystals on the blankets on the ponies of her Indian ancestors, the drizzle on the village long ago and the poorsmoke crawling out of the underground and when a mournful mother pounded acorns and made mush in hopeless millenniums – the song of the Asia hunting gang clanking down the final Alaskan rib of earth to New World Howls (in their eyes and in Mardou's eyes now the eventual Kingdom of Inca Maya and vast Azteca shining of gold snake and temples as noble as Greek, Egypt, the long sleek crack jaws and flattened noses of Mongolian geniuses creating arts in temple rooms and the leap of their jaws to speak, till the Cortez Spaniards, the Pizarro weary old-world sissified pantalooned Dutch bums came smashing canebrake in savannahs to find shining cities of Indian Eyes high, landscaped, boulevarded, ritualled, heralded, beflagged in that selfsame New World Sun the beating heart held up to it) – her heart beating in the Frisco rain, on the fence, facing last facts, ready to go run down the land now and go back and fold in again where she was and where was all – consoling herself with visions of truth – coming down off the fence, on tiptoe, moving ahead, finding a hall, shuddering, sneaking –

'I'd made up my mind, I'd erected some structure, it was like, but I can't –.' Making a new start, starting from flesh in the rain, 'Why should anyone want to harm my little heart, my feet, my little hands, my skin that I'm wrapt in because God wants me warm and Inside, my toes – why did God make all this all so decayable and dieable and harmable and wants to make me realize and scream – why the wild ground and bodies bare and breaks – I quaked when the giver creamed, when my father screamed, my mother dreamed – I started small and ballooned up and now I'm big and a naked child again and only to cry and fear. – Ah – Protect yourself, angel of no harm, you who've never and could never harm and crack another innocent its shell and thin veiled pain – wrap a robe around you, honeylamb – protect yourself from rain and wait, till Daddy comes again, and Mama throws you warm inside her valley of the moon, loom at the loom of patient time, be happy in the mornings.' – Making a new start, shivering, out of the alley night naked in the skin and on wood feet to the stained door of some neighbour – knocking – the woman coming to the door in answer to the frightened butter knock knuckles, sees the naked browngirl, frightened – ('Here is a woman, a soul in my rain, she looks at me, she is frightened.') – 'Knocking on this perfect stranger's door, sure.' – 'Thinking I was just going down the street to Betty's and back, promised her *meaning* it deeply I'd bring the clothes back and she did let me in and she got a blanket and wrapped it around me, then the clothes, and luckily she was alone – an Italian woman. – And in the alley I'd all come out and *on*, it was now first clothes, then I'd go to Betty's and get two bucks – then buy this brooch I'd seen that afternoon at some place with old seawood in the window, at North Beach, art handicraft ironwork like, a shoppey, it was the first symbol I was going to allow myself.' – 'Sure.' – Out of the naked rain to a robe, to innocence shrouding in, then the decoration of God and religious sweetness. – 'Like when I had that fist fight with Jack Steen it was in my mind strongly.' – 'Fist fight with Jack Steen?' – 'This was earlier, all the junkies in Ross's room, tying up and shooting with Pusher, you know Pusher, well I took my clothes off there too – it was . . . all . . . part of the same . . . flip . . .' – 'But this *clothes*, this *clothes*!' (to myself). – 'I stood in the middle of the room flipping and Pusher was plucking at the guitar, just one string, and I went up to him and said, "Man don't pluck those dirty notes at ME," and like he just got up without a word and left.' – And Jack Steen was furious at her and thought if he hit her and knocked her out with his fists she'd come to her senses so he slugged at her but she was just as strong as he (anaemic pale 110 lb junkey ascetics of America), blam, they fought it out before the weary others. – She'd pulled wrists with Jack, Julien, beat them practically – 'Like Julien finally won at wrists but he really furiously had to put me down to do it and hurt me and was really upset' (gleeful little shniffle thru the little out-teeth) – so there she'd been fighting it out with Jack Steen and really almost licking him but he was furious and neighbours downstairs called cops who came and had to be explained to – 'dancing'. – 'But that day I'd seen this iron thing, a little brooch with a beautiful dull sheen, to be worn around the neck, you know how nice that would look on my breast.' – 'On your brown breastbone a dull gold

24

beautiful it would be baby, go on with your amazing story.' – 'So I immediately needed this brooch in spite of the time, 4 a.m. now, and I had that old coat and shoes and an old dress she gave me, I felt like a streetwalker but I felt no one could tell – I ran to Betty's for the two bucks, woke her up –.' She demanded the money, she was coming out of death and money was just the means to get the shiny brooch (the silly means invented by inventors of barter and haggle and styles of who owns who, who owns what –). Then she was running down the street with her $2, going to the store long before it opened, going for a coffee in the cafeteria, sitting at the table alone, digging the world at last, the gloomy hats, the glistening sidewalks, the signs announcing baked flounder, the reflections of rain in paneglass and in pillar mirror, the beauty of the food counters displaying cold spreads and mountains of crullers and the steam of the coffee urn. – 'How warm the world is, all you gotta do is get little symbolic coins – they'll let you in for all the warmth and food you want – you don't have to strip your skin off and chew your bone in alleyways – these places were designed to house and comfort bag-and-bone people come to cry for consolation.' – She is sitting there staring at everyone, the usual sexfiends are afraid to stare back because the vibration from her eyes is wild, they sense some living danger in the apocalypse of her tense avid neck and trembling wiry hands. – 'This ain't no woman.' – 'That crazy Indian she'll kill somebody.' – Morning coming, Mardou hurrying gleeful and mind-swum, absorbed, to the store, to buy the brooch – standing then in a drugstore at the picture postcard swiveller for a solid two hours examining each one over and over again minutely because she only had ten cents left and could only buy two and those two must be perfect private talismans of the new important meaning, personal omen emblems – her avid lips slack to see the little corner meanings of the cable-car shadows, Chinatown, flower stalls, blue, the clerks wondering: 'Two hours she's been in here, no stockings on, dirty knees, looking at cards, some Third Street Wino's wife run away, came to the big whiteman drugstore, never saw a shiny sheen postcard before –.' In the night before they would have seen her up Market Street in Foster's with her last (again) dime and a glass of milk, crying into her milk, and men always looking at her, always trying to make her but now doing nothing because frightened, because she was like a child – and because: 'Why didn't Julien or Jack Steen or Walt Fitzpatrick give you a place to stay and leave you alone in the corner, or lend you a couple bucks?' – 'But they didn't care, they were frightened of me, they *really* didn't want me around they had like distant objectivity, watching me, asking *nasty* questions – a couple times Julien went into his head-against-mine act like you know "Whatsamatter, Mardou", and his routines like that and phony sympathy but he really just was curious to find out why I was flipping – none of them'd ever give me *money*, man.' – 'Those guys really treated you bad, do you know that?' – 'Yeah well they never treat anyone – like they never do anything – you take care of yourself, I'll take care of me.' – 'Existentialism.' – 'But American worse cool existentialism and of junkies man, I hung around with them, it was for almost a year by then and I was getting, every time they turned on, a kind of a contact high.' – She'd sit with them, they'd go on the nod, in the dead silence she'd wait, sensing the slow snake-like waves of vibration struggling across the room, the eyelids falling, the heads nodding and jerking up again, someone mumbling some disagreeable complaint, 'Ma-a-n, I'm drug by that son of a bitch MacDoud with all his routines about how he ain't got enough money for one cap, could he get a half a cap or pay a half – m-a-a-n, I never seen such nowhereness, no s-h-i-t, why don't he just go somewhere and *fade*, um.' (That junkey 'um' that follows any out-on-the-limb, and anything one says is out-on-the-limb, statement, *um, be-um*, the self-indulgent baby sob inkept from exploding to the big bawl mawk crackfaced W A A A they feel from the junk regressing their systems to the crib.) – Mardou would be sitting there, and finally high on tea or benny she'd begin to feel like she'd been injected, she'd walk down the street in her flip and actually feel the electric contact with other human beings (in her sensitivity recognizing a fact) but some times she was suspicious because it was someone secretly injecting her and following her down the street who was really responsible for the electric sensation and so independent of any natural law of the universe. – 'But you really didn't believe that – but you did – when I flipped on benny in 1945 I really believed the girl wanted to use my body to burn it and put her boy's papers in my pocket so the cops'd think he was dead – I told her, too.' – 'Oh what did she do?' – 'She said, "Ooo daddy", and hugged me and took care of me, Honey was a wild bitch, she put

26

pancake makeup on my pale – I'd lost thirty, ten, fifteen pounds – but what happened?' – 'I wandered around with my brooch.' – She went into some kind of gift shop and there was a man in a wheel chair there. (She wandered into a doorway with cages and green canaries in the glass, she wanted to touch the beads, watch goldfish, caress the old fat cat sunning on the floor, stand in the cool green parakeet jungle of the store high on the green out-of-this-world dart eyes of parrots swivelling witless necks to cake and burrow in the mad feather and to feel that definite communication from them of birdy terror, the electric spasms of their notice, squawk, lawk, leek, and the man was extremely strange.) – 'Why?' – 'I dunno he was just very strange, he wanted, he talked with me very clearly and insisting – like intensely looking right at me and at great length but smiling about the simplest commonplace subjects but we both knew we meant everything else that we said – you know life – actually it was about the tunnels, the Stockton Street tunnel and the one they just built on Broadway, that's the one we talked of the most, but as we talked this a great electrical current of real understanding passed between us and I could feel the other levels of the infinite number of them of every intonation in his speech and mine and the world of meaning in every *word* – I'd never realized before how much is *happening* all the time, and people *know* it – in their eyes they show it, they *refuse* to show it by any other – I stayed a very long time.' – 'He must have been a weirdy himself.' – 'You know, balding, and queer like, and middleaged, and with that with-neck-cut-off look or head-on-air,' (witless, peaked) 'looking all over, I guess it was his mother the old lady with the Paisley shawl but my god it would take me all day' – 'Wow.' – 'Out on the street this beautiful old woman with white hair had come up to me and saw me, but was asking directions, but liked to talk –.' (On the sunny now lyrical Sunday morning after-rain sidewalk, Easter in Frisco and all the purple hats out and the lavender coats parading in the cool gusts and the little girls so tiny with their just whitened shoes and hopeful coats going slowly in the white hill streets, churches of old bells busy and downtown around Market where our tattered holy Negro Joan of Arc wandered hosannahing in her brown borrowed-from-night skin and heart, flutters of betting sheets at corner newsstands, watchers at nude magazines, the flowers on the corner in baskets and the old Italian in his apron with the newspapers kneeling to water, and the Chinese father in tight ecstatic suit wheeling the basket-carriaged baby down Powell with his pink-spot-cheeked wife of glitter brown eyes in her new bonnet rippling to flap in sun, there stands Mardou smiling intensely and strangely and the old eccentric lady not any more conscious of her Negroness than the kind cripple of the store and because of her out and open face now, the clear indications of a troubled pure innocent spirit just risen from a pit in pock-marked earth and by own broken hands self-pulled to safety and salvation, the two women Mardou and the old lady in the incredibly sad empty streets of Sunday after the excitements of Saturday night the great glitter up and down Market like wash gold dusting and the throb of neons at O'Farrell and Mason bars with cocktail glass cherrysticks winking invitation to the open hungering hearts of Saturday and actually leading only finally to Sunday-morning blue emptiness just the flutter of a few papers in the gutter and the long white view to Oakland Sabbath haunted, still – Easter sidewalk of Frisco as white ships cut in clean blue lines from Sasebo beneath the Golden Gate's span, the wind that sparkles all the leaves of Marin here laving the washed glitter of the white kind city, in the lostpurity clouds high above redbrick track and Embarcadero pier, the haunted broken hint of song of old Pomos the once only-wanderers of these eleven last American now white-behoused hills, the face of Mardou's father himself now as she raises her face to draw breath to speak in the streets of life materializing huge above America, fading –.) 'And like I told her but talked too and when she left she gave me her flower and pinned it on me and called me honey.' – 'Was she white?' – 'Yeah, like, she was very affectionate, very plea-*sant* she seemed to love me – like save me, bring me out – I walked up a hill, up California past Chinatown, someplace I came to a white garage like with a big garage wall and this guy in a swivel chair wanted to know what I wanted, I understand all of my moves as one obligation after another to communicate to whoever not accidentally but by *arrangement* was placed before me, communicate and exchange this news, the vibration and new meaning that I had, about everything happening to everyone all the time everywhere and for them not to worry, nobody as mean as you think or – a coloured guy, in the swivel chair, and we had a long confused talk and he was reluctant, I remember, to look in my eyes and really listen to what I was saying.' – 'But what were you saying?' – 'But it's all forgotten now – something as simple and like you'd never expect like those tunnels or the old lady and I hanging-up on streets and directions – but the guy wanted to make it with me, I saw him open his zipper but suddenly he got ashamed, I was turned around and could see it in the glass.' (In the white planes of wall garage morning, the phantom man and the girl turned slumped watching in the window that not only reflected the black strange sheepish man secretly staring but the whole office, the chair, the safe, the dank concrete back interiors of garage and dull sheen autos, showing up also unwashed specks of dust from last night's rainsplash and thru the glass the across-the-street immortal balcony of wooden bay-window tenement where suddenly she saw three Negro children in strange attire waving but without yelling at a Negro man four stories below in overalls and therefore apparently working on Easter, who waved back as he walked in his own strange direction that bisected suddenly the slow direction being taken by two men, two hatted, coated ordinary men but carrying one a bottle, the other a boy of three, stopping now and then to raise the bottle of Four Star California Sherry and drink as the Frisco a.m. All Morn Sun wind flapped their tragic top-coats to the side, the boy bawling, their shadows on the street like shadows of gulls the colour of hand-made Italian cigars of deep brown stores at Columbus and Pacific, now the passage of a fishtail Cadillac in second gear headed for hilltop houses bay-viewing and some scented visit of relatives bringing the funny papers, news of old aunts, candy to some unhappy little boy waiting for Sunday to end, for the sun to cease pouring thru the French blinds and paling the potted plants but rather rain and Monday again and the joy of the wood-fence alley where only last night poor Mardou'd almost lost.) – 'What'd the coloured guy do?' – 'He zipped up again, he wouldn't look at me, he turned away, it was strange he got ashamed and sat down – it reminded me too when I was a little girl in Oakland and this man would send us to the store and give us dimes then he'd open his bathrobe and show us himself.' – 'Negro?' – 'Yea, in my neighbourhood where I lived – I remember I used to never stay there but my girlfriend did and think she even did something with him one time.' – 'What'd you do about the guy in the swivel chair?' – 'Well, like I wandered out of there and it was a beautiful day, Easter, man.' – 'Gad, Easter where was I?' – 'The soft sun, the flowers and here I was going down the street and thinking "Why did I allow myself to be bored ever in the past" and to compensate for it got high or drunk or rages or all the tricks people have because they want anything but serene understanding of just what there is, which is after all so much, and thinking like angry social deals, – like angry – kicks – like hasseling over social problems and my race problem, it meant so little and I could feel that great confidence and gold of the morning would slip away eventually and had already started – I could have made my whole life like that morning just on the strength of pure understanding and willingness to live and go along, God it was all the most beautiful thing that ever happened to me in its own way – but it was all sinister.' – Ended when she got home to her sister's house in Oakland and they were furious at her anyway but she told them off and did strange things; she noticed for instance the complicated wiring her eldest sister had done to connect the TV and the radio to the kitchen plug in the ramshackle wood upstairs of their cottage near Seventh and Pine the railroad sooty wood and gargoyle porches like tinder in the sham scrapple slums, the yard nothing but a lot with broken rocks and black wood showing where hoboes Tokay'd last night before moving off across the meatpacking yard to the Mainline rail Tracy-bound thru vast endless impossible Brooklyn-Oakland full of telephone poles and crap and on Saturday nights the wild Negro bars full of whores and the Mexicans Ya–Yaaing in their own saloons and the cop car cruising the long sad avenue riddled with drinkers and the glitter of broken bottles (now in the wood house where she was raised in terror Mardou is squatting against the wall looking at the wires in the half dark and she hears herself speak and doesn't understand why she's saying it except that it must be said, come out, because that day earlier when in her wandering she finally got to wild Third Street among the lines of slugging winos and the bloody drunken Indians with bandages rolling out of alleys and the 10 cent movie house with three features and little children of skid row hotels running on the sidewalk and the pawnshops and the Negro chickenshack jukeboxes and she stood in drowsy sun suddenly listening to bop as if for the first time as it poured out, the intention of the musicians and of the horns and instruments suddenly a mystical unity expressing itself in waves like sinister and again electricity but screaming with palpable aliveness the direct *word* from the vibration, the interchanges of statement, the levels of waving intimation, the smile in sound, the same living insinuation in the way her sister'd arranged those wires wriggled entangled and fraught with intention, innocent looking but actually behind the mask of casual life completely by agreement the mawkish mouth almost sneering snakes of electricity purposely placed she'd been seeing all day and hearing in the music and saw now in the wires), 'What are you trying to do actually electrocute me?' so the sisters could see something was really wrong, worse than the youngest of the Fox sisters who was alcoholic and made the wild street and got arrested regularly by the vice squad, some nameless horrible yawning *wrong*, 'She smokes dope, she hangs out with all those queer guys with beards in the City.' – They called the police and Mardou was taken to the hospital – realizing now, 'God, I saw how awful what was really happening and about to happen to me and man I pulled out of it fast, and talked sanely with everyone possible and did everything right, they let me out in 48 hours – the other women were with me, we'd look out the windows and the things they said, they made me see the preciousness of really being *out* of those damn bathrobes and *out* of there and out on the street, the sun, we could see ships, out and FREE man to roam around, how great it really is and how we never appreciate it all glum inside our worries and skins, like *fools* really, or blind spoiled detestable children pouting because ... they can't get ... all ... the ... candy ... they want, so I talked to the doctors and told them –.' 'And you had no place to stay, where was your clothes?' – 'Scattered all over – all over the Beach – I had to do something – they let me have this place, some friends of mine, for the summer. I'll have to get out in October.' – 'In the Lane?' – 'Yah.' – 'Honey let's you and me – would you go to Mexico with me?' – 'Yes!' – 'If I go to Mexico? that is, if I get the money? altho I do have a hunnerd eighty now and we really actually could go tomorrow and make it – like Indians – I mean cheap and living in the country or in the slums.' – 'Yes – it would be so nice to get away now.' – 'But we could or should really wait till I get – I'm supposed to get five hundred see – and – ' (and that was when I would have whisked her off into the bosom of my own life) – she saying 'I really don't want anything more to do with the Beach or any of that gang, man, that's why — I guess I spoke or agreed too soon, you don't seem so sure now' (laughing to see me ponder). — 'But I'm only pondering practical problems.' — 'Nevertheless if I'd have said "may be" I bet — oooo that awright,' kissing me — the grey day, the red bulb-light, I had never heard such a story from such a soul except from the great men I had known in my youth, great heroes of America I'd been buddies with, with whom I'd adventured and gone to jail and known in raggedy dawns, the boys beat on kerbstones seeing symbols in the saturated gutter, the Rimbauds and Verlaines of America on Times Square, kids — no girl had ever moved me with a story of spiritual suffering and so beautifully her soul showing out radiant as an angel wandering in hell and the hell the selfsame streets I'd roamed in watching, watching for someone just like her and never dreaming the darkness and the mystery and eventuality of our meeting in eternity, the hugeness of her face now like the sudden vast Tiger head on a poster on the back of a woodfence in the smoky dumpyards Saturday no-school mornings, direct, beautiful, insane, in the rain. — We hugged, we held close — it was like love now, I was amazed — we made it in the living-room, gladly, in chairs, on the bed, slept entwined, satisfied — I would show her more sexuality —

We woke up late, she'd not gone to her psychoanalyst, she'd 'wasted' her day and when Adam came home and saw us in the chair again still talking and with the house belittered (coffee cups, crumbs of cakes I'd bought down on tragic Broadway in the grey Italianness which was so much like the lost Indianness of Mardou, tragic America-Frisco with its grey fences, gloomy sidewalks, doorways of dank, I from the small town and more recently from sunny Florida East Coast found so frightening). — 'Mardou, you wasted your visit to a therapist, really Leo you should be ashamed and feel a little responsible, after all — ' 'You mean I'm making her lay off her duties . . . I used to do it with all my girls . . . ah it'll be good for her to miss' (not knowing her need). — Adam almost joking but also most serious, 'Mardou you must write a letter or call — why don't you call him now?' — 'It's a she doctor, up at City & County.' — 'Well call now, here's a dime.' — 'But I can do it tomorrow, but it's too late.' — 'How do you know it's too late — no really, you really goofed today, and you too Leo you're awfully responsible you rat.' And then a gay

32

supper, two girls coming from outside (grey crazy outside) to join
us, one of them fresh from an overland drive from New York with
Buddy Pond, the doll an L.A. hip type with short haircut who
immediately pitched into the dirty kitchen and cooked everybody
a delicious supper of black bean soup (all out of cans) with a few
groceries while the other girl, Adam's, goofed on the phone and
Mardou and I sat around guiltily, darkly in the kitchen drinking
stale beer and wondering if Adam wasn't perhaps really right
about what should be done, how one should pull oneself together,
but our stories told, our love solidified, and something sad come
into both our eyes – the evening proceeding with the gay supper,
five of us the girl with the short haircut saying later that I was so
beautiful she couldn't look (which later turned out to be an East
Coast saying of hers and Buddy Pond's), 'beautiful' so amazing
to me, unbelievable, but must have impressed Mardou, who was
anyway during the supper jealous of the girl's attentions to me and
later said so – my position so airy, secure – and we all went driving
in her foreign convertible car, through now clearing Frisco streets
not grey but opening soft hot reds in the sky between the homes
Mardou and I laying back in the open backseat digging them, the
soft shades, commenting, holding hands – they up front like gay
young international Paris sets driving through town, the short hair
girl driving solemnly, Adam pointing out – going to visit some guy
on Russian Hill packing for a New York train and France-bound
ship where a few beers, small talk, later troopings on foot
with Buddy Pond to some literary friend of Adam's Aylward
So-and-So famous for the dialogues in *Current Review*, possessor
of a magnificent library, then around the corner to (as I told
Aylward) America's greatest wit, Charles Bernard, who had gin,
and an old grey queer, and others, and sundry suchlike parties,
ending late at night as I made my first foolish mistake in my life
and love with Mardou, refusing to go home with all the others at
3 a.m., insisting, tho at Charlie's invite, to stay till dawn studying
his pornographic (homo male sexual) pictures and listening to
Marlene Dietrich records, with Aylward – the others leaving,
Mardou tired and too much to drink looking at me meekly and not
protesting and seeing how I was, a drunk really, always staying
late, freeloading, shouting, foolish – but now loving me so not
complaining and on her little bare thronged brown feet padding
around the kitchen after me as we mix drinks and even when

33

Bernard claims a pornographic picture has been stolen by her (as she's in the bathroom and he's telling me confidentially, 'My dear, I saw her slip it into her pocket, her waist I mean her breast pocket') so that when she comes out of bathroom she senses some of this, the queers around her, the strange drunkard she's with, she complains not – the first of so many indignities piled on her, not on her capacity for suffering but gratuitously on her little female dignities. – Ah I shouldn't have done it, goofed, the long list of parties and drinkings and downcrashings and times I ran out on her, the final shocker being when in a cab together she's insisting I take her home (to sleep) and I can go to see Sam alone (in bar) but I jump out of cab, madly ('I never saw anything so maniacal'), and run into another cab and zoom off, leaving her in the night – so when Yuri bangs on her door the following night, and I'm not around, and he's drunk and insists, and jumps on her as he'd been doing, she gave in, she gave in – she gave up – jumping ahead of my story, naming my enemy at once – the pain, why should 'the sweet ram of their lunge in love' which has really nothing to do with me in time or space, be like a dagger in my throat?

Waking up, then, from the partying, in Heavenly Lane, again I have the beer nightmare (now a little gin too) and with remorse and again almost and now for no reason revulsion the little white woolly particles from the pillow stuffing in her black almost wiry hair, and her puffed cheeks and little puffed lips, the gloom and dank of Heavenly Lane, and once more 'I gotta go home, straighten out' – as tho never I was straight with her, but crooked – never away from my chimerical work room and comfort home, in the alien grey of the world city, in a state of WELL-BEING – ' 'But why do you always want to rush off so soon?' – 'I guess a feeling of well-being at home, that I need, to be straight – like –.' 'I know baby – but I'm I miss you in a way I'm jealous that you have a home and a mother who irons your clothes and all that and I haven't –.' 'When shall I come back, Friday night?' – 'But baby it's up to you – to say when.' – 'But tell me what YOU WANT.' – 'But I'm not supposed to.' – 'But what do you mean s'posed?' – 'It's like what they say – about – oh, I dunno' (sighing, turning over in the bed, hiding, burrowing little grape body around, so I go, turn her over, flop on bed, kiss the straight line that runs from her breastbone, a depression there, straight, clear down to her

34

belly-button where it becomes an infinitesimal line and proceeds like as if ruled with pencil on down and then continues just as straight underneath, and need a man get well-being from history and thought as she herself said when he has that, the essence, but still). – The weight of my need to go home, my neurotic fears, hangovers, horrors – 'I shouldna – we shouldn't a gone to Bernard's at all last night – at least we shoulda come home at three with the others.' – 'That's what I say baby – but God' (laughing the shnuffle and making little funny imitation voice of slurring) 'you never do what I ash you t'do.' – 'Aw I'm sorry – I love you – do you love me?' – 'Man,' laughing, 'what do you *mean*' – looking at me warily – 'I mean do you feel affection for me?' even as she's putting brown arm around my tense big neck. – 'Naturally baby.' – 'But what is the –?' I want to ask everything, can't, don't know how, what is the mystery of what I want from you, what is man or woman, love, what do I mean by love or why do I have to insist and ask and why do I go and leave you because in your poor wretched little quarters – 'It's the place depresses me – at home I sit in the yard under trees want.' – 'But I'm not supposed to.' – 'But what do you shall I open the blind?' – 'No everybody'll see you – I'll be so glad when the summer's over – when I get that dough and we go to Mexico.' – 'Well man, let's like you say go now on your money that you have now, you say we can really make it.' – 'Okay! Okay!' an idea which gains power in my brain as I take a few swigs of stale beer and consider a dobe hut say outside Texcoco at five dollars a month and we go to the market in the early dewy morning she in her sweet brown feet on sandals padding wifelike Ruthlike to follow me, we come, buy oranges, load up on bread, even wine, local wine, we go home and cook it up cleanly on our little cooker, we sit together over coffee writing down our dreams, analysing them, we make love on our little bed. – Now Mardou and I are sitting there talking all this over, daydreaming, a big phantasy – 'Well man,' with little teeth outlaughing, 'WHEN do we do this – like it's been a minor flip our whole relationship, all this indecisive clouds and planning – God.' – 'Maybe we should wait till I get that royalty dough – yep! really! it'll be better, cause like that we can get a typewriter and a three-speed machine and Gerry Mulligan records and clothes for you and everything we need, like the way it is now we can't do anything.' – 'Yeah – I dunno' (brooding)

35

'Man you know I don't have any eyes for that hysterical poverty deal' – (statements of such sudden pith and hip I get mad and go home and brood about it for days). 'When will you be back?' – 'Well okay, then we'll make it Thursday.' – 'But if you really want to make it Friday – don't let me interfere with your work, baby – maybe you'd like it better to be away longer times.' – 'After what you – O I love you – you –.' I undress and stay another three hours, and leave guiltily because the well-being, the sense of doing what I should has been sacrificed, but tho sacrificed to healthy love, something is sick in me, lost, fears – I realize too I have not given Mardou a dime, a loaf of bread literally, but talk, hugs, kisses, I leave the house and her unemployment cheque hasn't come and she has nothing to eat – 'What will you eat?' – 'O there's some cans – or I can go to Adam's maybe – but I don't wanta go there too often – I feel he resents me now, your friendship has been, I've come between that certain something you had sort of –.' 'No you didn't.' – 'But it's something else – I don't want to go out, I want to stay in, see no one' – 'Not even me?' – 'Not even you, sometimes God I feel that.' – 'Ah Mardou, I'm all mixed up – I can't make up my mind – we ought to do something together – I know what, I'll get a job on the railroad and we'll live together – ' this is the great new idea.

(And Charles Bernard, the vastness of the name in the cosmogony of my brain, a hero of the Proustian past in the scheme as I knew it, in the Frisco-alone branch of it, Charles Bernard who'd been Jane's lover, Jane who'd been shot by Frank, Jane whom I'd lived with, Marie's best friend, the cold winter rainy nights when Charles would be crossing the campus saying something witty, the great epics almost here sounding phantom like and uninteresting if at all believable but the true position and bigburn importance of not only Charles but a good dozen others in the light rack of my brain, so Mardou seen in this light, is a little brown body in a grey sheet bed in the slums of Telegraph Hill, huge figure in the history of the night yes but only one among many, the asexuality of the WORK – also the sudden gut joy of beer when the visions of great words in rhythmic order all in one giant archangel book go roaring thru my brain, so I lie in the dark also seeing also hearing the jargon of the future worlds – damajehe eleout ekeke dhdkdk dldoud, – d, ekeoeu dhdhdkehgyt – better not a more than lther ehe the macmurphy out of that dgardent that which

strangely he doth mdodudltkdip – baseeaatra – poor examples
because of mechanical needs of typing, of the flow of river sounds,
words, dark, leading to the future and attesting to the madness,
hollowness, ring and roar of my mind which blessed or unblessed
is where trees sing – in a funny wind – well-being believes he'll go
to heaven – a word to the wise is enough – 'Smart went Crazy,'
wrote Allen Ginsberg.)

Reason why I didn't go home at 3 a.m. – and example.

2

At first I had doubts, because she was Negro, because she was sloppy (always putting off everything till tomorrow, the dirty room, unwashed sheets – what do I really for Christ's sake care about sheets) – doubts because I knew she'd been seriously insane and could very well be again and one of the first things we did the first nights, she was going into the bathroom naked in the abandoned hall but the door of her place having a strange squeak it sounded to me (high on tea) like suddenly someone had come up and was standing in the stairwell (like maybe Gonzalez the Mexican sort of bum or hanger-on sort of faggish who kept coming up to her place on the strength of some old friendship she'd had with some Tracy Pachucos to bum little 7 centses from her or two cigarettes and all the time usually when she was at her lowest, sometimes even to take negotiable bottles away), thinking it might be him, or some of the subterraneans, in the hall asking 'Is anybody with you?' and she naked, unconcernedly, and like in the alley just stands there saying, 'No man, you better come back tomorrow I'm busy I'm not alone,' this my tea-reverie as I lay there, because the moan squeak of the door had that moan of voices in it, so when she got back from the toilet I told her this (reasoning honesty anyway) (and believing it had been really so, almost, and still believing her actively insane, as on the fence in the alley) but when she heard my confession she said she almost flipped again and was frightened of me and almost got up and ran out – for reasons like this, madness, repeated chances of more madness, I had my 'doubts' my male self- contained doubts about her, so reasoned, 'I'll just at some time cut out and get me another girl, white, white thighs, etc., and it'll have been a grand affair and I hope I don't hurt her tho.' – Ha! – doubts because she cooked sloppily and never cleaned up dishes right away, which at first I didn't like and then came to see she really didn't cook sloppily and did wash the dishes after a while and at the age of six (she later told me) she was forced to wash dishes for her tyrannical uncle's family and all the time on top of that forced to go out in alley in dark night with garbage pan every night same time where she was convinced the same ghost lurked for her – doubts, doubts – which I have not now in the luxury of time-past. – What a luxury it is to know that now I want her forever to my breast my prize my own woman whom I would defend from all Yuries and anybodies with my fists and anything else, *her* time has come to claim independence, announcing, only yesterday ere I began this tearbook, 'I want to be an independent chick with money and cuttin' around.' – 'Yeah, and knowing and screwing everybody, Wanderingfoot,' I'm thinking, wandering foot from when we – I'd stood at the bus stop in the cold wind and there were a lot of men there and instead of standing at my side she wandered·off in a little funny red raincoat and black slacks and went into a shoestore doorway (ALWAYS DO WHAT YOU WANT TO DO AIN'T NOTHIN' I LIKE BETTER THAN A GUY DOIN' WHAT HE WANTS, Leroy always said) so I follow her reluctantly thinking, 'She sure has wandering feet to hell with her I'll get another chick' (weakening at this point as reader can tell from tone) but turns out she knew I had only shirt no undershirt and should stand where no wind was, telling me later, the realization that she did not talk naked to anyone in the hall any more than it was wanderingfoot to walk away to lead me to a warmer waitingplace, that it was no more than shit, still making no impression on my eager impressionable ready to-create construct destroy and die brain – as will be seen in the great construction of jealousy which I later from a dream and for reasons of self-laceration recreated . . . Bear with me all lover readers who've suffered pangs, bear with me men who understand that the sea of blackness in a darkeyed woman's eyes is the lonely sea itself and would you ask the sea to explain itself, or ask woman why she crosseth hands on lap over rose? no –

Doubts, therefore, of, well, Mardou's Negro, naturally not only my mother but my sister whom I may have to live with some day and her husband a Southerner and everybody concerned, would be mortified to hell and have nothing to do with us – like it would preclude completely the possibility of living in the South, like in that Faulknerian pillar homestead in the Old Granddad moonlight I'd so long envisioned for myself and there

I am with Doctor Whitley pulling out the panel of my rolltop desk and we drink to great books and outside the cobwebs on the pines and old mules clop in soft roads, what would they say if my mansion lady wife was a black Cherokee, it would cut my life in half, and all such sundry awful American as if to say white ambition thoughts or white daydreams. – Doubts galore too about her body itself, again, and in a funny way really relaxing now to her love so surprising myself I couldn't believe it, I'd seen it in the light one playful night so I – walking through the Fillmore she insisted we confess everything we'd been hiding for this first week of our relationship, in order to see and understand and I gave my first confession, haltingly, 'I thought I saw some kind of black thing I've never seen before, hanging, like it *scared* me' (laughing) – it must have stabbed her heart to hear it, it seemed to me I felt some kind of shock in her being at my side as she walked as I divulged this secret thought – but later in the house with light on we both of us childlike examined said body and looked closely and it wasn't anything pernicious and pizen juices but just blue dark as in all kinds of women and I was really and truly reassured to actually see and make the study with her – but this being a doubt that, confessed, warmed her heart to me and made her see that fundamentally I would never snake-like hide the furthest, not the – but no need to defend, I cannot at all possibly begin to understand who I am or what I am any more, my love for Mardou has completely separated me from any previous phantasies valuable and otherwise – The thing therefore that kept these outburst doubts from holding upper sway in my activity in relating with her was the realization not only that she was sexy and sweet and good for me and I was cutting quite a figure with her on the Beach anyway (and in a sense too now cutting the subterraneans who were becoming progressively deeply colder in their looks towards me in Dante's and on street from natural reasons that I had taken over their play doll and one of their really if not the most brilliant gals in their orbit) – Adam also saying, 'You go well together and it's good for you,' he being at the time and still my artistic and paternal manager – not only this, but, hard to confess, to show how abstract the life in the city of the Talking Class to which we all belong, the Talking Class trying to rationalize itself I suppose out of a really base almost lecherous lustful materialism – it was the reading, the sudden illuminated glad wondrous discovery of Wilhelm Reich, his book *The Function of the Orgasm*, clarity as I had not seen in a long time, not since perhaps the clarity of personal modern grief of Céline, or, say, the clarity of Carmody's mind in 1945 when I first sat at his feet, the clarity of the poesy of Wolfe (at 19 it was clarity for me), the clarity here tho was scientific, Germanic, beautiful, true – something I'd always known and closely indeed connected to my 1948 sudden notion that the only thing that really mattered was love, the lovers going to and fro beneath the boughs in the Forest of Arden of the World, here magnified and at the same time microcosmed and pointed in and maled into: orgasm – the reflexes of the orgasm – you can't be healthy without normal sex love and orgasm – I won't go into Reich's theory since it is available in his own book – but at the same time Mardou kept saying 'O don't pull that Reich on me in bed, I read his damn book, I don't want our relationship all pointed out and f. . . . d up with what HE said,' (and I'd noticed that all the subterraneans and practically all intellectuals I have known have really in the strangest way always put down Reich if not at first, after awhile) – besides which, Mardou did not gain orgasm from normal copulation and only after awhile from stimulation as applied by myself (an old trick that I had learned with a previous frigid wife) so it wasn't so great of me to make her come but as she finally only yesterday said 'You're doing this just to give me the pleasure of coming, you're so kind,' which was a statement suddenly hard for either one of us to believe and came on the heels of her 'I think we ought to break up, we never do anything together, and I want to be indep – ' and so doubts I had of Mardou, that I the great Finn Macpossipy should take her for my long love wife here there or anywhere and with all the objections my family, especially my really but sweetly but nevertheless really tyrannical (because of my subjective view of her and her influence) mother's sway over me – sway or whatever. – 'Leo, I don't think it's good for you to live with your mother always,' Mardou, a statement that in my early confidence only made me think, 'Well naturally she, she's just jealous, and has no folks herself, and is one of those modern psychoanalyzed people who hate mothers anyway' – out loud saying, 'I really do really love her and love you too and don't you see how hard I try to spend my time, divide my time between the two of you – over there it's my writing work, my well-being

41

and when she comes home from work at night, tired, from the store, mind you, I feel very good making her supper, having the supper and a martini ready when she walks in so by 8 o'clock the dishes are all cleared, see, and she has more time to look at her television – which I worked on the railroad six months to buy her, see.' – 'Well you've done a lot of things for her,' and Adam Moorad (whom my mother considered mad and evil) too had once said 'You've really done a lot for her, Leo, forget her for a while, you've got your own life to live,' which is exactly what my mother always was telling me in the dark of the South San Francisco night when we relaxed with Tom Collinses under the moon and neighbours would join us, 'You have your own life to live, I won't interfere, Ti Leo, with anything you want to do, you decide, of course it will be all right with me,' me sitting there goopy realizing it's all myself, a big subjective phantasy that my mother really needs me and would die if I weren't around, and nevertheless having a bellyful of other rationalizations allowing me to rush off two or three times a year on gigantic voyages to Mexico or New York or Panama Canal on ships – A million doubts of Mardou, now dispelled, now (and even without the help of Reich who shows how life is simply the man entering the woman and the rubbing of the two in soft – that essence, that dingdong essence – something making me now almost so mad as to shout, I GOT MY OWN LITTLE BANGTAIL ESSENCE AND THAT ESSENCE IS MIND RECOGNITION –) now no more doubts. Even, a thousand times, I without even remembering later asked her if she'd really stolen the pornographic picture from Bernard and the last time finally she fired 'But I've told you and told you, about eight times in all, I did not take that picture and I told you too a thousand times I don't even didn't even have any pockets whatever in that particular suit I was wearing that night – no pockets at all,' yet it never making an impression (in feverish folly brain me) that it was Bernard now who was really crazy, Bernard had gotten older and developed some personal sad foible, accusing others of stealing, solemnly – 'Leo don't you see and you keep asking it' – this being the last deepest final doubt I wanted about Mardou that she was really a thief of some sort and therefore was out to steal my heart, my white man heart, a Negress sneaking in the world sneaking the holy white men for sacrificial rituals later when they'll be roasted and roiled (remembering the Tennessee Williams story about the

42

Negro Turkish bath attendant and the little white fag) because, not only Ross Wallenstein had called me to my face a fag – 'Man what are you, a fag? you talk you just like a fag,' saying this after I'd said to him in what I hoped were cultured tones, 'You're on goofballs tonight? you ought to try three sometimes, they'll really knock you out and have a few beers too, but don't take four, just three,' it insulting him completely since he is the veteran hipster of the Beach and for anyone especially a brash newcomer stealing Mardou from his group and at the same time hoodlum-looking with a reputation as a great writer, which he didn't see, from only published book – the whole mess of it, Mardou becoming the big buck nigger Turkish bath attendant, and I the little fag who's broken to bits in the love affair and carried to the bay in burlap bag, there to be distributed piece by piece and broken bone by bone to the fish (if there are still fish in that sad water) – so she'd thieve my soul and eat it – so told me a thousand times, 'I did not steal that picture and I'm sure Aylward whatshisname didn't and you didn't it's just Bernard, he's got some kind of fetish there' – But it never impressed and stayed till the last, only the other night, time – that deepest doubt about her arising too from the time, (which she'd told me about) she was living in Jack Steen's pad in a crazy loft down on Commercial Street near the seamen's union halls, in the glooms, had sat in front of his suitcase an hour thinking whether she ought to look in it to see what he had there, then Jack came home and rummaged in it and thought or saw something was missing and said, sinister, sullen, 'Have you been going thru my bag?' and she almost leaped up and cried YES because she HAD – 'Man I had, in Mind, been going thru that bag all day and suddenly he was looking at me, with that look – I almost flipped' – that story also not impressing into my rigid paranoia-ridden brain, so for two months I went around thinking she'd told me, 'Yes, I did go thru his bag but of course took nothing,' but so I saw she'd lied to Jack Steen in reality – but in reality now, the facts, she had only thought to do so, and so on – my doubts all of them hastily ably assisted by a driving paranoia, which is really my confession – doubts, then, all gone.

For now I want Mardou – she just told me that six months ago a disease took root deeply in her soul, and forever now – doesn't this make her more beautiful? – But I want Mardou – because I see her standing, with her black velvet slacks, handsa-pockets,

43

thin, slouched, cig hanging from lips, the smoke itself curling up, her little black back hairs of short haircut combed down fine and sleek, her lipstick, pale brown skin, dark eyes, the way shadows play on her high cheekbones, the nose, the little soft shape of chin to neck, the little Adam's apple, so hip, so cool, so beautiful, so modern, so new, so unattainable to sad bagpants me in my shack in the middle of the woods – I want her because of the way she imitated Jack Steen that time on the street and it amazed me so much but Adam Moorad was solemn watching the imitation as if perhaps engrossed in the thing itself, or just sceptical, but she disengaged herself from the two men she was walking with and went ahead of them showing the walk (among crowds) the soft swing of arms, the long cool strides, the stop on the corner to hang and softly face up to birds with like as I say Viennese philosopher – but to see her do it, and to a T, (as I'd seen his walk indeed across the park), the fact of her – I love her but this song is . . . broken – but in French now . . . in French I can sing her on and on . . .

Our little pleasures at home at night, she eats an orange, she makes a lot of noise sucking it –

When I laugh she looks at me with little round black eyes that hide themselves in her lids because she laughs hard (contorting all her face, showing the little teeth, making lights everywhere) 'the first time I saw her, at Larry O'Hara's, in the corner, I remember, I'd put my face close to hers to talk about books, she'd turned her face to me close, it was an ocean of melting things and drowning, I could have swimmed in it, I was afraid of all that richness and looked away) –

With her rose bandana she always puts on for the pleasures of the bed, like a gipsy, rose, and then later the purple one, and the little hairs falling black from the phosphorescent purple in her brow as brown as wood –

Her little eyes moving like cats –

We play Gerry Mulligan loud when he arrives in the night, she listens and chews her fingernails, her head moves slowly side to side like a nun in profound prayer –

When she smokes she raises the cigarette to her mouth and slits her eyes –

She reads till grey dawn, head on one arm, *Don Quixote*, Proust, anything –

We lie down, look at each other seriously, saying nothing, head to head on the pillow –

Sometimes when she speaks and I have my head under hers on the pillow and I see her jaw the dimple the woman in her neck, I see her deeply, richly, the neck, the deep chin, I know she's one of the most *enwomaned* women I've seen, a brunette of eternity incomprehensibly beautiful and for always sad, profound, calm –

When I catch her in the house, small, squeeze her, she yells out, tickles me furiously, I laugh, she laughs, her eyes shine, she punches me, she wants to beat me with a switch, she says she likes me –

I'm hiding with her in the secret house of the night –

Dawn finds us mystical in our shrouds, heart to heart –

'My sister!' I thought suddenly the first time I saw her –

The light is out.

Day dreams of she and I bowing at big fellaheen cocktail parties somehow with glittering Parises in the horizon and in the forefront – she's crossing the long planks of my coor with a smile.

Always putting her to a test, which goes with 'doubts' – doubts indeed – and I would like to accuse myself of bastardliness – such tests – briefly I can name two, the night Arial Lavalina the famous young writer suddenly was standing in the Mask and I was sitting with Carmody also now famous writer in a way who'd just arrived from North Africa, Mardou around the corner in Dante's cutting back and forth as was our wont all around, from bar to bar, and sometimes she'd cut unescorted there to see the Juliens and others – I saw Lavalina and called his name and he came over. – When Mardou came to get me to go home I wouldn't go, I kept insisting it was an important literary moment, the meeting of those two (Carmody having plotted with me a year earlier in dark Mexico when we'd lived poor and beat and he's a junkey, 'Write a letter to Ralph Lowry find out how I can get to meet this here good-looking Arial Lavalina, man, look at that picture on the back of *Recognition of Rome*, ain't that something?' my sympathies with him in the matter being personal and again like Bernard also queer he was connected with the legend of the bigbrain of myself which was my WORK, that all consuming work, so wrote the letter and all that) but now suddenly (after of course no reply from the Ischia and

45

otherwise grapevines and certainly just as well for me at least) he was standing there and I recognized him from the night I'd met him at the Met ballet when in New York in tux I'd cut out with tuxed editor to see glitter nightworld New York of letters and wit, and Leon Danillian, so I yelled 'Arial Lavalina! come here!' which he did. – When Mardou came I said whispering gleefully 'This is Arial Lavalina ain't that mad!' – 'Yeah man but I want to go home.' – And in those days her love meaning no more to me than that I had a nice convenient dog chasing after me (much like in my real secretive Mexican vision of her following me down dark dobe streets of slums of Mexico City not walking with me but following, like Indian woman) I just goofed and said 'But wait, you go home and wait for me, I want to dig Arial and then I'll be home.' – 'But baby you said that the other night and you were two hours late and you don't know what pain it caused me to wait.' (Pain!) – 'I know but look,' and so I took her around the block to persuade her, and drunk as usual at one point to prove something I stood on my head in the pavement of Montgomery or Clay Street and some hoodlums passed by, saw this, saying 'That's right' – finally (she laughing) depositing her in a cab, to get home, wait for me – going back to Lavalina and Carmody whom gleefully and now alone back in my big world might adolescent literary vision of the world, with nose pressed to window glass, 'Will you look at that, Carmody and Lavalina, the great Arial Lavalina tho not a great great writer like me nevertheless so famous and glamorous etc. together in the Mask and I arranged it and everything ties together, the myth of the rainy night, Master Mad, Raw Road, going back to 1949 and 1950 and all things grand great the Mask of old history crusts' – (this my feeling and I go in) and sit with them and drink further – repairing the three of us to 13 Pater a lesbian joint down Columbus, Carmody, high, leaving us to go enjoy it, and we sitting in there, further beers, the horror the unspeakable horror of myself suddenly finding in myself a kind of perhaps William Blake or Crazy Jane or really Christopher Smart alcoholic humility grabbing and kissing Arial's hand and exclaiming 'Oh Arial you dear – you are going to be – you are so famous – you wrote so well – I remember you – what – ' whatever and now unrememberable and drunkenness, and there he is a well-known and perfectly obvious homosexual of the first water, my roaring brain – we go to his suite in some hotel – I wake up in the morning on the couch, filled with the first horrible recognition, 'I didn't go back to Mardou's at all' so in the cab he gives me – I ask for fifty cents but he gives me a dollar saying 'You owe me a dollar' and I rush out and walk fast in the hot sun face all broken from drinking and chagrin to her place down in Heavenly Lane arriving just as she's dressing up to go to the therapist. – Ah sad Mardou with little dark eyes looking with pain and had waited all night in a dark bed and the drunken man leering in and I rushed down in fact at once to get two cans of beer to straighten up ('To curb the fearful hounds of hair' Old Bull Balloon would say), so as she abluted to go out I yelled and cavorted – went to sleep, to wait for her return, which was in the late afternoon, waking to hear the cry of pure children in the alleyways down there – the horror the horror, and deciding, 'I'll write a letter at once to Lavalina,' enclosing a dollar and apologizing for getting so drunk and acting in such a way to mislead him – Mardou returning, no complaints, only a few a little later, and the days rolling and passing and still she forgives me enough or is humble enough in the wake of my crashing star in fact to write me, a few nights later, this letter:

DEAR BABY,
   Isn't it good to know winter
   is coming –

as we'd been complaining so much about heat and now the heat was ended, a coolness came into the air, you could feel it in the draining grey airshaft of Heavenly Lane and in the look of the sky and nights with a greater wavy glitter in streetlights

   – and that life will be a little more quiet – and you will be home writing and eating well and we will be spending pleasant nights wrapped round one another – and you are home now, rested and eating well because, you should not become too sad –

written after, one night, in the Mask with her and newly arrived and future enemy Yuri erstwhile close lil brother I'd suddenly said 'I feel impossibly sad and like I'll die, what can we do?' and Yuri suggested 'Call Sam,' which, in my sadness, I did, and so earnestly, as otherwise he'd pay no attention being a newspaper man and new father and no time to goof, but so earnestly he

47

accepted us, the three, to come at once, from the Mask, to his apartment on Russian Hill, where we went, I getting drunker than ever, Sam as ever punching me and saying 'The trouble with you, Percepied,' and, 'You've got rotten bags in the bottom of your store,' and, 'You Canucks are really all alike and I don't even believe you'll admit it when you die' – Mardou watching amused, drinking a little, Sam finally, as always falling over drunk, but not really, drunk-desiring, over a little lowtable covered a foot high with ashtrays piled three inches high and drinks and doodads, crash, his wife, with baby just from crib, sighing eyed – Yuri, who didn't drink but only watched bead-eyed, after having said to me the first day of his arrival, 'You know Percepied I really like you now, I really feel like communicating with you now,' which I should have suspected, in him, as constituting a new kind of sinister interest in the innocence of my activities, that being by the name of, Mardou –

  – because you should not become too sad

was only sweet comment heartbreakable Mardou made about that disastrous awful night – similar to example 2, one following the one with Lavalina, the night of the beautiful faun boy who'd been in bed with Micky two years before at a great depraved wildparty I'd myself arranged in days when living with Micky the great doll of the roaring legend night, seeing him in the Mask, and being with Frank Carmody and everybody, tugging at his shirt, insisting he follow us to other bars, follow us around, Mardou finally in the blur and roar of the night yelling at me 'It's him or me goddamit,' because a subterranean but in her affair with Percepied but not really serious (herself usually not a drinker a big drinker now) – she left, I heard her say 'We're through' but never for a moment believed it and it was not so, she came back later, I saw her again, we swayed together, once more I'd been a bad boy and again ludicrously like a fag, this distressing me again in waking in grey Heavenly Lane in the morning beer roared. – This is the confession of a man who can't drink. – And so her letter saying:

  because you should not become too sad – and I feel better when you are well –

48

forgiving, forgetting all this sad folly when all she wants to do, 'I don't want to go out drinking and getting drunk with all your friends and keep going to Dante's and see all those Juliens and everybody again, I want us to stay quiet at home, listen to KPFA and read or something, or go to a show, baby I like shows, movies on Market Street, I really do.' – 'But I hate movies, life's more interesting!' (another putdown) – her sweet letter continuing:

I am full of strange feelings, reliving and refashioning many old things

– when she was 14 or 13 maybe she'd play hookey from school in Oakland and take the ferry to Market Street and spend all day in one movie, wandering around having hallucinated phantasies, looking at all the eyes, a little Negro girl roaming the shuffle restless street of winos, hoodlums, sams, cops, paper pedlars, the mad mixup there the crowd eyeing looking everywhere the sexfiend crowd and all of it in the grey rain of hookey days – poor Mardou – 'I'd get sexual phantasies the strangest kind, not with like sex acts with people but strange situations that I'd spend all day working out as I walked, and my orgasms the few I had only came, because I never masturbated or even knew how, when I dreamed that my father or somebody was leaving me, running away from me, I'd wake up with a funny convulsion and wetness in myself, in my thighs, and on Market Street the same way but different and anxiety dreams woven out of the movies I saw.' – Me thinking *O greyscreen gangster cocktail rainyday roaring gunshot spectral immortality B movie tire pile black-in-the-mist Wildamerica but it's a crazy world!* 'Honey' (out loud) 'wished I could have seen you walking around Market like that – I bet I DID see you – I bet Ifi did – you were thirteen and I was twenty-two – 1944, yeah I bet I saw you, I was a seaman, I was always there, I knew the gangs around the bars – ' So in her letter saying:

reliving and refashioning many old things

probably reliving those days and phantasies, and earlier cruder horrors of home in Oakland where her aunt hysterically beat her or hysterically tried and her sisters (tho occasional little-sister tenderness like dutiful kisses before bed and writing on one another's backs) giving her a bad time, and she roaming the street late, deep in broodthoughts and men trying to make her, the dark men of dark coloured-district doors – so going on,

and feeling the cold and the quietude even in the midst of my forebodings and fears – which clear nights soothe and make more sharp and real – tangible and easier to cope with

– said indeed with a nice rhythm, too, so I remember admiring her intelligence even then – but at the same time darkening at home there at my desk of well-being and thinking, 'But cope that old psychoanalytic cope, she talks like all of em, the city decadent intellectual dead-dended in cause-and-effect analysis and solution of so-called problems instead of the great JOY of being and will and fearlessness – rupture's their rapture that's her trouble, she's just like Adam, like Julien, the lot, afraid of madness, the fear of madness haunts her – not Me Not Me by God' –

But why am I writing to say these things to you. But all feelings are real and you probably discern or feel too what I am saying and why I need to write it –

– a sentiment of mystery and charm – but, as I told her often, not enough detail, the details are the life of it, I insist, say everything on your mind, don't hold it back, don't analyze or anything as you go along, say it out, 'That's' (I now say in reading letter) 'a typical example – but no mind, she's just a girl – humph' –

My image of you now is strange

– I see the bough of that statement, it waves on the tree –

I feel a distance from you which you might feel too which gives me a picture of you that is warm and friendly
and then inserts, in smaller writing,

(and loving)

to obviate my feeling depressed probably over seeing in a letter from lover and only word 'friendly' – but that whole complicated phrase further complicated by the fact it is presented in originally written form under the marks and additions of a rewrite, which is not as interesting to me, naturally – the rewrite being

50

I feel a distance from you which you might feel too with pictures of you that are warm and friendly (and loving) – and because of the anxieties we are experiencing but never speak of really, and are similar too –

a piece of communication making me suddenly by some majesty of her pen feel sorry for myself, seeing myself like her lost in the suffering ignorant sea of human life feeling distant from she who should be closest and not knowing (no not under the sun) why the distance instead is the feeling, the both of us entwined and lost in that, as under the sea –

I am going to sleep to dream, to wake

– hints of our business of writing down dreams or telling dreams on waking, all the strange dreams indeed and (later will show) the further brain communicating we did, telepathizing images together with eyes closed, where it will be shown, all thoughts meet in the crystal chandelier of eternity – Jim – yet I also like the rhythm of *to dream, to wake*, and flatter myself I have a rhythmic girl in any case, at my metaphysical home-desk –

You have a very beautiful face and I like to see it as I do now –

– echoes of that New York girl's statement and now coming from humble meek Mardou not so unbelievable and I actually begin to preen and believe in this (O humble paper of letters, O the time I sat on a log near Idlewild airport in New York and watched the helicopter flying in with the mail and as I looked I saw the smile of all the angels of earth who'd written the letters which were packed in its hold, the smiles of them, specifically of my mother, bending over sweet paper and pen to communicate by mail with her daughter, the angelical smile like the smiles of working-women in factories, the world-wide bliss of it and the courage and beauty of it, recognition of which facts I shouldn't even deserve, treating Mardou as I have done) (O forgive me angels of the heaven and of the earth – even Ross Wallenstein will go to heaven) –

Forgive the conjunctions and double infinitives and the not said

– again I'm impressed and I think, she too there, for the first time self-conscious of writing to an author –

*I don't know really what I wanted to say but want you to have a few words
from me this Wednesday morning*

and the mail only carried it in much later, after I saw her, the
letter losing therefore its hopeful impactedness

*We are like two animals escaping to dark warm holes and live our
pains alone*

– at this time my dumb phantasy of the two of us (after all the
drunks making me drunksick city sick) was, a shack in the middle
of the Mississippi woods, Mardou with me, damn the lynchers,
the not-likings, so I wrote back: 'I hope you meant by that line
(*animals to dark warm holes*) you'll turn out to be the woman who
can really live with me in profound solitude of woods finally
and at the same time make the glittering Parises (there it is)
and grow old with me in my cottage of peace' (suddenly seeing
myself as William Blake with the meek wife in the middle of
London early dewy morning, Crabbe Robinson is coming with
some more etching work but Blake is lost in the vision of the Lamb
at breakfast leavings table). – Ah regrettable Mardou, and never
a thought of that thing beats in your brow, that I should kiss, the
pain of your own pride, enough 19th-century romantic general
talk – the details are the life of it – (a man may act stupid and
top tippity and bigtime 19th-century boss type dominant with a
woman but it won't help him when the chips are down – the loss
lass'l make it back, it's hidden in her eyes, her future triumph and
strength – on his lips we hear nothing but 'of course love'). – Her
closing words a beautiful pastichepattisee, or pie, of –

Write to me anything Please Stay Well Your Freind [misspelled] *And my
love And Oh* [over some kind of hiddenforever erasures] [and many
X's for of course kisses] *And Love for You* MARDOU
[underlined]

and weirdest, most strange, central of all – ringed by itself, the
word, PLEASE – her lastplea neither one of us knowing – Answering
this letter myself with a dull boloney bullshit rising out of my anger
with the incident of the pushcart.

(And tonight this letter is my last hope.)

*   *   *

The incident of the pushcart began, again as usual, in the Mask and Dante's, drinking, I'd come in to see Mardou from my work, we were in a drinking mood, for some reason suddenly I wanted to drink red Burgundy wine which I'd tasted with Frank and Adam and Yuri the Sunday before – another, and first, worthy of mention incident, being – but that's the crux of it all – THE DREAM. Oh the bloody dream! In which there was a pushcart, and everything else prophesied. This too after a night of severe drinking, the night of the red shirt faun boy – where everybody afterwards of course said 'You made a fool of yourself, Leo, you're making yourself a reputation on the Beach as a big fag tugging at the shirts of well-known punks.' – 'But I only wanted him for you to dig.' – 'Nevertheless' (Adam) 'really.' – And Frank: 'You really makin a horrible reputation.' – Me: 'I don't care, you remember 1948 when Sylvester Strauss that fag composer got sore at me because I wouldn't go to bed with him because he'd read my novel and submitted it, yelled at me "I know all about you and your awful reputation." – "What?" – "You and that there Sam Vedder go around the Beach picking up sailors and giving them dope and he makes them only so he can bite, I've heard about you." – "Where did you hear this fantastic tale?" – you know that story, Frank.' – 'I should imagine' (Frank laughing) 'what with all the things you do right there in the Mask, drunk, in front of everybody, if I didn't know you I'd swear you were the craziest piece of rough trade that ever walked' (a typical Carmodian pithy statement) and Adam 'Really that's true' – After the night of the redshirt boy, drunk, I'd slept with Mardou and had the worst nightmare of all, which was, everybody, the whole world was around our bed, we lay there and everything was happening. Dead Jane was there, had a big bottle of Tokay wine hidden in Mardou's dresser for me and got it out and poured me a big slug and spilled a lot out of the waterglass on the bed (a symbol of even further drinking, more wine, to come) – and Frank with her – and Adam, who went out the door to the dark tragic Italian pushcart Telegraph Hill street, going down the rickety wooden Shatov stairs where the subterraneans were 'digging an old Jewish patriarch just arrived from Russia' who is holding some ritual by the barrels of the fish head cats (the fish heads, in the height of the hot days Mardou had a fish head for our crazy little visiting cat who was almost human in his insistence to be loved his scrolling of neck and purring to be against you,

53

for him she had a fish head which smelled so horrible in the almost airless night I threw part of it out in the barrel downstairs after first throwing a piece of slimy gut unbeknownst I'd put my hands against in the dark icebox where was a small piece of ice I wanted to chill my sauterne with, smack against a great soft mass, the guts or mouth of a fish, this being left in the icebox after disposal of fish I threw it out, the piece draped over fire escape and was there all hot-night and so in the morning when waking I was being bitten by gigantic big blue flies that had been attracted by the fish, I was naked and they were biting like mad, which annoyed me, as the pieces of pillow had annoyed me and somehow I tied it up with Mardou's Indianness, the fish heads the awful sloppy way to dispose of fish, she sensing my annoyance but laughing, ah bird) – that alley, out there, in the dream, Adam, and in the house, the actual room and bed of Mardou and I the whole world roaring around us, back ass flat – Yuri also there, and when I turn my head (after nameless events of the millionfold mothswarms) suddenly he's got Mardou on the bed laid out and wiggling and is necking furiously with her – at first I say nothing – when I look again, again they're at it, I get mad – I'm beginning to wake up, just as I give Mardou a rabbit punch in the back of her neck, which causes Yuri to reach a hand for me – I wake up I'm swinging Yuri by the heels against the brick fireplace wall. – On waking from this dream I told all to Mardou except the part where I hit her or Yuri – and she too (in tying in with our telepathies already experienced that sad summer season now autumn mooned to death, we'd communicated many feelings of empathy and I'd come running to see her on nights when she sensed it) had been dreaming like me of the whole world around our bed, of Frank, Adam, others, her recurrent dream of her father rushing off, in a train, the spasm of almost orgasm. – 'Ah honey I want to stop all this drinking these nightmares'll kill me – you don't know how jealous I was in that dream' (a feeling I'd not yet had about Mardou) – the energy behind this anxious dream had obtained from her reaction to my foolishness with the redshirt boy ('Absolutely insufferable type anyway' Carmody had commented 'tho obviously good-looking, really Leo you were funny' and Mardou: 'Acting like a little boy but I like it.') – Her reaction had of course been violent, on arriving home, after she'd tugged me in the Mask in front of everyone including her Berkeley friends who saw her and probably even heard 'It's me or him!' and the madness humour futility of that – arriving in Heavenly Lane she'd found a balloon in the hall, nice young writer John Golz who lived downstairs had been playing balloons with the kids of the Lane all day and some were in the hall, with the balloon Mardou had (drunk) danced around the floor, puffing and poooshing and flupping it up with dance interpretive gestures and said something that not only made me fear her madness, her hospital type insanity, but cut my heart deeply, and so deeply that she could not therefore have been insane, in communicating something so exactly, with precise – whatever – 'You can go now I have this balloon.' – 'What do you mean?' (I, drunk, on floor blearing). – 'I have this balloon now – I don't need you any more – goodbye – go away leave me alone' – a statement that even in my drunkenness made me heavy as lead and I lay there, on the floor, where I slept an hour while she played with the balloon and finally went to bed, waking me up at dawn to undress and get in – both of us dreaming the nightmare of the world around our bed – and that GUILT-Jealousy entering into my mind for the first time – the crux of this entire tale being: I want Mardou because she has begun to reject me – BECAUSE – 'But baby that was a mad dream.' – 'I was so jealous – I was sick.' – I harkened suddenly now to what Mardou'd said the first week of our relationship, when, I thought secretly, in my mind I had privately superseded her importance with the importance of my writing work, as, in every romance, the first week is so intense all previous worlds are eligible for throwover, but when the energy (of mystery, pride) begins to wane, elder worlds of sanity, well-being, common sense, etc., return, so I had secretly told myself: 'My work's more important than Mardou.' Nevertheless she'd sensed it, that first week, and now said, 'Leo there's something different now – in you – I feel it in me – I don't know what it is.' I knew very well what it was and pretended not to be able to articulate with myself and least of all with her anyway – I remembered now, in the waking from the jealousy nightmare, where she necks with Yuri, something had changed, I could sense it, something in me was cracked, there was a new loss, a new Mardou even – and, again, the difference was not isolated in myself who had dreamed the cuckold dream, but in she, the subject, who'd not dreamed it, but participated somehow in the general

55

rueful mixed up dream of all this life with me – so I felt she could now this morning look at me and tell that something had died – not due to the balloon and 'You can go now' – but the dream – and so the dream, the dream, I kept harping on it, desperately I kept chewing and telling about it, over coffee, to her, finally when Carmody and Adam and Yuri came (in themselves lonely and looking to come get juices from that great current between Mardou and me running, a current everybody I found out later wanted to get in on, the act) I began telling *them* about the dream, stressing, stressing, stressing the Yuri part, where Yuri 'every time I turn my back' is kissing her – naturally the others wanting to know their parts, which I told with less vigour – a sad Sunday afternoon, Yuri going out to get beer, a spread, bread – eating a little – and in fact a few wrestling matches that broke my heart. For when I saw Mardou for fun wrestling with Adam (who was not the villain of the dream tho now I figured I must have switched persons) I was pierced with that pain that's now all over me, that firstpain, how cute she looked in her jeans wrestling and struggling (I'd said 'She's strong as hell, d'jever hear of her fight with Jack Steen? try her Adam') – Adam having already started to wrestle with Frank on some impetus from some talk about holds, now Adam had her pinned in the coitus position on the floor (which in itself didn't hurt me) – it was her beautifulness, her game guts wrestling, I felt proud, I wanted to know how Carmody felt NOW (feeling he must have been at the outset critical of her for being a Negro, he being a Texan and a Texas gentleman-type at that) to see her be so great, buddy like, joining in, humble and meek too and a real woman. Even somehow the presence of Yuri, whose personality was energized already in my mind from the energy of the dream, added to my love of Mardou – I suddenly loved her. – They wanted me to go with them, sit in the park – as agreed in solemn sober conclaves Mardou said 'But I'll stay here and read and do things, Leo, you go with them like we said' – as they left and trooped down the stairs I stayed behind to tell her I loved her now – she was not as surprised, or pleased, as I wished – she had looked at Yuri now already with the point of view eyes not only of my dream but had seen him in a new light as a possible successor to me because of my continual betrayal and getting drunk.

Yuri Gligoric: a young poet, 22, had just come down from apple-picking Oregon, before that a waiter in a big dude ranch dininghall – tall thin blond Yugoslavian, good-looking, very brash and above all trying to cut Adam and myself and Carmody, all the time knowing us as an old revered trinity, wanting, naturally, as a young unpublished unknown but very genius poet to destroy the big established gods and raise himself – wanting therefore their women too, being uninhibited, or unsaddened, yet, at least. – I liked him, considered him another new 'young brother' (as Leroy and Adam before, whom I'd 'shown' writing tricks) and now I would show Yuri and he would be a buddy with me and walk around with me and Mardou – his own lover, June, had left him, he'd treated her badly, he wanted her back, she was with another life in Compton, I sympathized with him and asked about the progress of his letters and phone calls to Compton, and, most important, as I say, he was now for the first time suddenly looking at me and saying 'Percepied I want to talk to you – suddenly I want to really know you.' – In a joke at the Sunday wine in Dante's I'd said 'Frank's leching after Adam, Adam's leching after Yuri' and Yuri'd thrown in 'And I'm leching after you.'

Indeed he was indeed. On this mournful Sunday of my first pained love of Mardou after sitting in the park with the boys as agreed, I dragged myself again home, to work, to Sunday dinner, guiltily, arriving late, finding my mother glum and all-weekend-alone in a chair with her shawl . . . and my thoughts rich on Mardou now – not thinking it of any importance whatever that I had told young Yuri not only 'I dreamed you were necking with Mardou' but also, at a soda fountain en route to the park when Adam wanted to call Sam and we all sat at counter waiting, with limeades, 'Since I saw you last I've fallen in love with that girl,' information which he received without comment and which I hope he still remembers, and of course does.

And so now brooding over her, valuing the precious good moments we'd had that heretofore I'd avoided thinking of, came the fact, ballooning in importance, the amazing fact she is the only girl I've ever known who could really understand bop and sing it, she'd said that first cuddly day of the redbulb at Adam's 'While I was flipping I heard bop, on juke boxes and in the Red Drum and wherever I was happening to hear it, with an entirely new and different sense, which tho, I really can't describe.' – 'But what was it like?' – 'But I can't describe it, it not only sent waves – went through me – I can't like, *make* it, in telling it in words, you know?

OO dee bee dee dee' singing a few notes, so cutely. – The night we walked swiftly down Larkin past the Blackhawk with Adam actually but he was following and listening, close head to head, singing wild choruses of jazz and bop, at times I'd phrase and she did perfect in fact interesting modern and advanced chords (like I'd never heard anywhere and which bore resemblance to Bartok modern chords but were hep wise to bop) and at other times she just did her chords as I did the bass fiddle, in the old great legend (again of the roaring high davenport amazing smash-afternoon which I expect no one to understand) before, I'd with Ossip Popper sung bop, made records, always taking the part of the bass fiddle thum thum to his phrasing (so much I see now like Billy Eckstine's bop phrasing) – the two of us arm in arm rushing longstrides down Market the hip old apple of the California Apple singing bop and well too – the glee of it, and coming after an awful party at Roger Walker's where (Adam's arrangement and my acquiescence) instead of a regular party were just boys and all queer including one Mexican younghustler and Mardou far from being nonplussed enjoyed herself and talked – nevertheless of it all, rushing home to the Third Street bus singing gleeful –

The time we read Faulkner together, I read her *Spotted Horses*, out loud – when Mike Murphy came in she told him to sit and listen as I'd go on but then I was different and I couldn't read the same and stopped – but next day in her gloomy solitude Mardou sat down and read the entire Faulkner portable.

The time we went to a French movie on Larkin, the Vogue, saw *The Lower Depths*, held hands, smoked felt close – tho out on Market Street she would not have me hold her arm for fear people of the street there would think her a hustler, which it would look like but I felt mad but let it go and we walked along, I wanted to go into a bar for a wine, she was afraid of all the behatted men ranged at the bar, now I saw her Negro fear of American society she was always talking about but palpably in the streets which never gave me any concern – tried to console her, show her she could do anything with me, 'In fact baby I'll be a famous man and you'll be the dignified wife of a famous man so don't worry' but she said 'You don't understand' but her little-girl like fear so cute, so edible, I let it go, we went home, to tender love scenes together in our own and secret dark –

Fact, the time, one of those fine times when we, or that is, I didn't drink and we spent the whole night together in bed, this time telling ghost stories, the tales of Poe I could remember, then we made some up, and finally we were making madhouse eyes at each other and trying to frighten with round stares, she showed me how one of her Market Street reveries had been that she was a catatonic ('Tho then I didn't know what the word meant, but like, I walked stiffly hang arming arms hanging and man not a soul dared to speak to me and some were afraid to look, there I was walking along zombie-like and just thirteen.') (Oh gleeful shnuff-fleeflue in fluffle in her little lips, I see the out-thrust teeth, I say sternly, 'Mardou you must get your teeth cleaned at once, at that hospital there, the therapist, get a dentist too – it's all free so do it – ' because I see beginnings of bad congestion at the corners of her pearlies which would lead to decay) – and she makes the madwoman face at me, the face rigid, the eyes shining shining shining like the stars of heaven and far from being frightened I am utterly amazed at the beauty of her and I say 'And I also see the earth in your eyes that's what I think of you, you have a certain kind of beauty, not that I'm hung-up on the earth and Indians and all that and wanta harp all the time about you and us, but I see in your eyes such warm – but when you make the madwoman I don't see madness but glee glee – it's like the ragamuffin dusts in the little kid's corner and he's asleep in his crib now and I love you, rain'll fall on our eaves some day sweetheart' – and we have just candlelight so the mad acts are funnier and the ghost stories more chilling – the one about the – but a lack, a lark, I go larking in the good things and don't and do forget my pain –

Extending the eye business, the time we closed our eyes (again not drinking because of broke, poverty would have saved this romance) and I sent her messages, 'Are you ready,' and I see the first thing in my black eye world and ask her to describe it, amazing how we came to the same thing, it was some rapport, I saw crystal chandeliers and she saw white petals in a black bog just after some melding of images as amazing as the accurate images I'd exchange with Carmody in Mexico – Mardou and I both seeing the same thing, some madness shape, some fountain, now by me forgotten and really not important yet, come together in mutual descriptions of it and joy and glee in this telepathic triumph of ours, ending where our thoughts meet at the crystal white and petals, the mystery – I see the gleeful hunger of her face devouring the sight of mine, I could die, don't break my heart radio with beautiful music, O world – the candlelight again, flickering, I'd bought a slue of candles in the store, the corners of our room in darkness, her shadow naked brown as she hurries to the sink – our use of the sink – my fear of communicating WHITE images to her in our telepathies for fear she'll be (in her fun) reminded of our racial difference, at that time making me feel guilty, now I realize it was one love's gentility on my part – Lord.

The good ones – going up on the top of Nob Hill at night with a fifth of Royal Chalice Tokay, sweet, rich, potent, the lights of the city and of the bay beneath us, the sad mystery – sitting on a bench there, lovers, loners pass, we pass the bottle, talk – she tells all her little girlhood in Oakland. – It's like Paris – it's soft, the breeze blows, the city may swelter but the hillers do fly – and over the bay is Oakland (ah me Hart Crane Melville and all ye assorted brother poets of the American night that once I thought would be my sacrificial altar and now it is but who's to care, know, and I lost love because of it – drunkard, dullard, poet) – returning via Van Ness to Aquatic Park beach, sitting in the sand, as I pass Mexicans I feel that great hepness I'd been having all summer on the street with Mardou my old dream of wanting to be vital, alive like a Negro or an Indian or a Denver Jap or a New York Puerto Rican come true, with her by my side so young, sexy, slender, strange, hip, myself in jeans and casual and both of us as if young (I say as if, to my 31) – the cops telling us to leave the beach, a lonely Negro passing us twice and staring – we walk along the waterslap, she laughs to see the crazy figures of reflected light of the moon dancing so bug-like in the ululating cool smooth water of the night – we smell harbour, we dance –

The time I walked her in broad sweet dry Mexico plateau-like or Arizona-like morning to her appointment with therapist at the hospital, along the Embarcadero, denying the bus, hand in hand – I proud, thinking, 'In Mexico she'll look just like this and not a soul'll know I'm not an Indian by God and we'll go along' – and I point out the purity and clarity of the clouds, 'Just like Mexico honey, O you'll love it' and we go up the busy street to the big grimbrick hospital and I'm supposed to be going home from there but she lingers, sad smile, love smile, when I give in and agree to wait for her 20-minute interview and her coming out she radiantly breaks out glad and rushes to the gate which we've already passed in her almost therapy-giving-up strolling-with-me meandering, men – love – not for sale – my prize – possession – nobody gets it but gets a Sicilian line down his middle – a German boot in the kisser, an axe Canuck – I'll pin them wriggling poets to some London wall right here, explained. – And as I wait for her to come out, I sit on side of water, in Mexico-like gravel and grass and concrete blocks and take our sketchbooks and draw big word pictures of the skyline and of the bay, putting in a little mention of the great fact of the huge all-world with its infinite levels, from Standard Oil top down to waterslap at barges where old bargemen dream, the difference between men, the difference so vast between concerns of executives in skyscrapers and seadogs on harbour and psycho-analysts in stuffy offices in great grim buildings full of dead bodies in the morgue below and madwomen at windows, hoping thereby to instill in Mardou recognition of fact it's a big world and psychoanalysis is a small way to explain it since it only scratches the surface, which is, analysis, cause and effect, why instead of what – when she comes out I read it to her, not impressing her too much but she loves me, holds my hand as we cut down along Embarcadero towards her place and when I leave her at Third and Townsend train in warm clear afternoon she says 'O I hate to see you go, I really miss you now' – 'But I gotta be home in time to make the supper – and write – so honey I'll be back tomorrow remember promptly at ten. – And tomorrow I arrive at midnight instead.

The time we had a shuddering come together and she said 'I was lost suddenly' and she was lost with me tho not coming herself but frantic in my franticness (Reich's beclouding of the senses) and how she loved it – all our teachings in bed, I explain me to her, she explains her to me, we work, we wail, we bop – we throw clothes off and jump at each other (after always her little trip to the diaphragm sink and I have to wait holding softer and making goofy remarks and she laughs and trickles water) then here she comes padding to me across the Garden of Eden, and I reach up and help her down to my side on the soft bed, I pull her little body to me and it is warm, her warm spot is hot, I kiss her brown breasts both of them, I kiss her love-shoulders – she keeps with her lips going 'ps ps ps' little kiss sounds where actually no contact is made with my face except when haphazardly while doing something else

61

I do move it against her and her little ps ps kisses connect and are as sad and soft as when they don't – it's her little litany of night – and when she's sick and we're worried, then she takes me on her, on her arm, on mine – she services the mad unthinking beast – I spend long nights and many hours making her, finally I have her, I pray for it to come, I can hear her breathing harder, I hope against hope it's time, a noise in the hall (or whoop of drunkards next door) takes her mind off and she can't make it and laughs – but when she does make it I hear her crying, whimpering, the shuddering electrical female orgasm makes her sound like a little girl crying, moaning in the night, it lasts a good twenty seconds and when it's over she moans, 'O why can't it last longer,' and 'O when will I when you do?' – 'Soon now I bet,' I say, 'you're getting closer and closer' – sweating against her in the warm sad Frisco with its damn old scows mooing on the tide out there, voom, voooom, and stars flickering on the water even where it waves beneath the pierhead where you expect gangsters dropping encemented bodies, or rats, or The Shadow – my little Mardou whom I love, who'd never read my unpublished works but only the first novel, which has guts but has a dreary prose to it when all's said and done and so now holding her and spent with sex I dream of the day she'll read great works by me and admire me, remembering the time Adam had said in sudden strangeness in his kitchen, 'Mardou, what do you really think of Leo and myself as writers, our positions in the world, the rack of time,' asking her that, knowing that her thinking is in accord in some ways more or less with the subterraneans whom he admires and fears, whose opinions he values with wonder – Mardou not really replying but evading the issue, but old man me plots greatbooks for her amaze – all those good things, good times we had, others I am now in the heat of my frenzy forgetting but I must tell all, but angels know all and record it in books –

But think of all the bad times – I have a list of bad times to make the good times, the times I was good to her and like I should be, to make it sick – when early in our love I was three hours late which is a lot of hours of lateness for younglovers, and so she wigged, got frightened, walked around the church handsapockets brooding looking for me in the mist of dawn and I ran out (seeing her note saying 'I am gone out to look for you') (in all Frisco yet! that east and west, north and south of soulless

62

loveless bleak she'd seen from the fence, all the countless men in hats going buses and not caring about the naked girl on the fence, why) – when I saw her, I myself running out to find her, I opened my arms a halfmile away –

The worst almost worst time of all when a red flame crossed my brain, I was sitting with her and Larry O'Hara in his pad, we'd been drinking French Bordeaux and blasting, a subject was up, I had a hand on Larry's knee shouting 'But listen to me, but listen to me!' wanting to make my point so bad there was a big crazy plead in the tone and Larry deeply engrossed in what Mardou is saying simultaneously and feeding a few words to her dialogue, in the emptiness after the red flame I suddenly leap up and rush to the door and tug at it, ugh, locked, the indoor chain lock, I slide and undo it and with another try I lunge out in the hall and down the stairs as fast as my thieves' quick crepesole shoes'll take me, putt pitterpit, floor after floor reeling around me as I round the stairwell, leaving them agape up there – calling back in half hour, meeting her on the street three blocks away – there is no hope –

The time even when we'd agreed she needed money for food, that I'd go home and get it and just bring it back and stay a short while, but I'm at this time far from in love, but bugged, not only her pitiful demands for money but that doubt, that old Mardou-doubt, and so rush into her pad, Alice her friend is there, I use that as an excuse (because Alice dike-like silent unpleasant and strange and likes no one) to lay the two bills on Mardou's dishes at sink, kiss a quick peck in the malt of her ear, say 'I'll be back tomorrow' and run right out again without even asking her opinion – as if the whore'd made me for two bucks and I was sore.

How clear the realization one is going mad – the mind has a silence, nothing happens in the physique, urine gathers in your loins your ribs contract.

Bad time she asked me, 'What does Adam really think of me, you never told me, I know he resents us together but – 'and I told her substantially what Adam had told me, of which none should have been divulged to her for the sake of her peace of mind, 'He said it was just a social question of his not now wanting to get hung-up with you lovewise because you're Negro' – feeling again her telepathic little shock cross the room to me, it sunk deep, I question my motives for telling her this.

The time her cheerful little neighbour young writer John Golz came up (he dutifully eight hours a day types working on magazine stories, admirer of Hemingway, often feeds Mardou and is a nice Indiana boy and means no harm and certainly not a slinky snaky interesting subterranean but openfaced, jovial, plays with children in the court for God's sake) – came up to see Mardou, I was there alone (for some reason, Mardou at a bar with our accord arrangement, the night she went out with a Negro boy she didn't like too much but just for fun and told Adam she was doing it because she wanted to make it with a Negro boy again, which made me jealous, but Adam said 'If I should if she should hear that you went out with a white girl to see if you could make it again she'd sure be flattered, Leo') – that night, I was at her place waiting, reading, young John Golz came in to borrow cigarettes and seeing I was alone wanted to talk literature – 'Well I believe that the most important thing is selectivity,' and I blew up and said 'Ah don't give me all that high school stuff I've heard it and heard it long before you were born almost for krissakes and really now, say something interesting and new about writing' – putting him down, sullen, for reasons mainly of irritation and because he seemed harmless and therefore could be counted on to be safe to yell at, which he was – putting him down, her friend, was not nice – no, the world's no fit place for this kind of activity, and what we gonna do, and where? when? wha wha wha, the baby bawls in the midnight boom.

Nor could it have been charming and helpful to her fears and anxieties to have me start out, at the outset of our romance, 'kissing her down between the stems' – starting and then suddenly quitting so later in an unguarded drinking moment she said, 'You suddenly stopped as tho I was –' and the reason I stopped being in itself not as significant as the reason I did it at all, to secure her greater sexual interest, which once tied on with a bow knot, I could dally out of – the warm lovemouth of the woman, the womb, being the place for men who love, not . . . this immature drunkard and egomaniacal . . . this . . . knowing as I do from past experience and interior sense, you've got to fall down on your knees and beg the woman's permission, beg the woman's forgiveness for all your sins, protect her, support her, doing everything for her, die for her but for God's sake love her and love her all the way in and every way you can

64

– yes psychoanalysis, I hear (fearing secretly the few times I had come into contact with the rough stubble-like quality of the pubic, which was Negroid and therefore a little rougher, tho not enough to make any difference, and the insides itself I should say the best, the richest, most fecund moist warm and full of hidden soft slidy mountains, also the pull and force of the muscles being so powerful she unknowing often vice-like closes over and makes a dam-up and hurt, tho this I only realized the other night, too late –). And so the final lingering physiological doubt I have that this contraction and great-strength of womb, responsible I think now in retrospect for the time when Adam in his first encounter with her experienced piercing unsupportable screaming sudden pain, so he had to go to the doctor and have himself bandaged and all (and even later when Carmody arrived and made a local orgone accumulator out of a big old watercan and burlap and vegetative materials placing the nozzle of himself into the nozzle of the can to heal), I now wonder and suspect if our little chick didn't really intend to bust us in half, if Adam isn't thinking it's his own fault and doesn't know, but she contracted mightily there (the lesbian!) (always knew it) and busted him and fixed him and couldn't do it to me but tried enough till she threw me over a dead hulk that now I am – psychoanalyst, I'm serious!

It's too much. Beginning, as I say with the pushcart incident – the night we drank red wine at Dante's and were in a drinking mood now both of us so disgusted – Yuri came with us, Ross Wallenstein was in there and maybe to show off to Mardou Yuri acted like a kid all night and kept hitting Wallenstein on the back of his head with little finger taps like goofing in a bar but Wallenstein (who's always being beaten up by hoodlums because of this) turned around a stiff death's-head gaze with big eyes glaring behind glasses, his Christlike blue unshaven cheeks, staring rigidly as tho the stare itself will floor Yuri, not speaking for a long time, finally saying, 'Man, don't bug me,' and turning back to his conversation with friends and Yuri does it again and Ross turns again the same pitiless awful subterranean sort of non-violent Indian Mahatma Gandhi defence of some kind (which I'd suspected that first time he talked to me saying, 'Are you a fag you talk like a fag' a remark coming from him so absurd because so inflammable and me 170 pounds to his 130 or 120 for

65

God's sake so I thought secretly No you can't fight this man he will only scream and yell and call cops and let you hit him again and haunt all your dreams, there is no way to put a subterranean down on the floor or for that matter put em down at all, they are the most unputdownable in this world and new culture) – finally Wallenstein going to the head for a leak and Yuri says to me, Mardou being at the bar gathering three more wines, 'Come on let's go in the john and bust him up,' and I get up to go with Yuri but not to bust up Ross rather to stop anything might happen there – Yuri having been in his own in fact realer way than mine almost a hoodlum, imprisoned in Soledad for defending himself in some vicious fight in reform school – Mardou stopping us both as we head to the head, saying, 'My God if I hadn't stopped you' (laughing embarrassed little Mardou smile and shniffle) 'you'd actually have gone in there' – a former love of Ross's and now the bottomless toilet of Ross's position in her affections I think probably equal to mine now, O damblast the thorny flaps of the pap time page –

Going thence to the Mask as usual, beers, get worse drunk, then out to walk home, Yuri having just arrived from Oregon having no place to sleep is asking if it's all right to sleep at our place, I let Mardou speak for her own house, tho feebly say some 'okay' in the middle of the confusion, and Yuri comes heading homeward with us – en route finds a pushcart, says 'Get in, I'll be a taxicab and push you both home up the hill.' – Okay we get in, and lie on our backs drunk as only you can get drunk on red wine, and he pushes us from the Beach at that fateful park (where we'd sat that first sad Sunday afternoon of my dream and premonitions) and we ride along in the pushcart of eternity, Angel Yuri pushing it, I can only see stars and occasional rooftops of blocks – no thought in any mind (except briefly in mine, possibly in others) of the sin, the loss entailed for the poor Italian beggar losing his cart there – on down Broadway clear to Mardou's, in the pushcart, at one point I push and they ride, Mardou and I singing bop and also bop to the tune *Are the Stars out Tonight* and just drunk – parking it foolishly in front of Adam's and rushing up, making noise. – Next day, after sleeping on floor with Yuri snoring on the couch, waiting up for Adam as if beaming to hear told about our exploit, Adam comes home blackfaced mad from work and says 'Really you have no idea the pain you're causin' some poor old Armenian pedlar you never think that – but jeopardizing my pad with that thing in front, supposing the cops find it, and what's the matter with you.' And Carmody saying to me 'Leo I think you perpetrated this masterpiece' or 'You master-minded this brilliant move' or such which I really didn't – and all day we've been cutting up and down stairs looking at pushcart which far from being cop-discovered still sits there but with Adam's landlord teetering in front of it, waiting to see who's going to claim it, sensing something fishy, and of all things Mardou's poor purse still in it where drunkenly we'd left it and the landlord finally confiscating IT and waiting for further development (she lost a few dollars and her only purse). – 'Only thing that can happen, Adam, is the cops'll find the pushcart, they can very well see the purse, the address, and take it to Mardou's but all she has to say is "O I found my purse," and that's that, and nothing'll happen.' But Adam cries, 'O you even if nothing'll happen to screw up the security of my pad, come in making noise, leave a licensed vehicle out front, and tell me nothing'll happen.' – And I had sensed he'd be mad and am prepared and say, 'To hell with that, you can give hell to these but you won't give hell to me, I won't take it from you – that was just a drunken prank,' I add, and Adam says, 'This is my house and I can get mad when it's – 'so I up and throw his keys (the keys he'd had made for me to walk in and out any time) at him but they're entwined with the chain of my mother's keys and for a moment we fumble seriously at the mixed keys on the floor disengaging them and he gets his and I say 'No that, that's mine, there,' and he puts it in his pocket and there we are. – I want to rush up and leave like at Larry's. – Mardou is there seeing me flip again – far from helping her from flips. (Once she'd asked me 'If I ever flip what will you do, will you help me? – Supposing I think you're trying to harm me?' – 'Honey,' I said, 'I'll try in fact I'll reassure you I'm not harming you and you'd come to your senses, I'll protect you,' the confidence of the old man – but in reality himself flipping more often.) – I feel great waves of dark hostility, I mean hate, malice, destructiveness flowing out of Adam in his corner chair, I can hardly sit under the withering telepathic blast and there's all that *yage* of Carmody's around the pad, in suitcases, it's too much – (it's a comedy tho, we agree it will be a comedy later) – we talk of other things – Adam suddenly flips the key back at me, it lands in my thighs, and instead of dangling it in my finger (as if considering, as if a wily Canuck calculating advantages) I boy-like jump up and throw the key back in my pocket with a little giggle, to make Adam feel better, also to impress Mardou with my 'fairness' – but she never noticed, was watching something else – so now that peace is restored I say 'And in any case it was Yuri's fault it isn't at all as Frank says my unqualified masterminding' – (this pushcart, this darkness, the same as when Adam in the prophetic dream descended the wood steps to see the 'Russian Patriarch', there were pushcarts there) – So in the letter that I write to Mardou answering her beauty which I have paraphrased, I make stupid angry but 'pretending to be fair,' 'to be calm, deep, poetic' statements, like, 'Yes, I got mad and threw Adam's keys back at him, because "friendship, admiration, poetry sleep in the respectful mystery" and the invisible world is too beautific to have to be dragged before the court of social realities,' or some such twaddle that Mardou must have glanced at with one eye – the letter, which was supposed to match the warmth of hers, her cuddly-in-October masterpiece, beginning with the inane-if-at-all confession: 'The last time I wrote a love note it turned out to be boloney' (referring to an earlier in the year half-romance with Arlene Wohlstetter) 'and I am glad you are honest,' or 'have honest eyes,' the next sentence said – the letter intended to arrive Saturday morning to make her feel my warm presence while I was out taking my hardworking and deserving mother to her bi-six-monthlial show and shopping on Market Street (old Canuck workingwoman completely ignorant of arrangement of mingled streets of San Francisco) but arriving long after I saw her and read while I was there, and dull – this not a literary complaint, but something that must have pained Mardou, the lack of reciprocity and the stupidity regarding my attack at Adam – 'Man, you had no right to yell at him, really, it's his pad, his right' – but the letter a big defence of this 'right to yell at Adam' and not at all response to her love notes –

The pushcart incident not important in itself, but what I saw, what my quick eye and hungry paranoia ate – a gesture of Mardou's that made my heart sink even as I doubted maybe I wasn't seeing, interpreting right, as so oft I do. – We'd come in and run upstairs and jumped on the big double bed waking Adam up and yelling and tousling and Carmody too sitting on the edge as if to say 'Now children now children,' just a lot of drunken lushes – at one time in the play back and forth between the rooms Mardou and Yuri ended on the couch together in front, where I think all three of us had flopped – but I ran to the bedroom for further business, talking, coming back I saw Yuri who knew I was coming flop off the couch onto the floor and as he did so Mardou (who probably didn't know I was coming) shot out her hand at him as if to say OH YOU RASCAL as if almost he'd before rolling off the couch goosed her or done something playful – I saw for the first time their youthful playfulness which I in my scowlingness and writer-ness had not participated in and my old man-ness about which I kept telling myself 'You're old you old sonofabitch you're lucky to have such a young sweet thing' (while nevertheless at the same time plotting, as I'd been doing for about three weeks now, to get rid of Mardou, without her being hurt, even if possible 'without her noticing' so as to get back to more comfortable modes of life, like say, stay at home all week and write and work on the three novels to make a lot of money and come in to town only for good times if not to see Mardou then any other chick will do, this was my three week thought and really the energy behind or the surface one behind the creation of the Jealousy Phantasy in the Grey Guilt dream of the World Around Our Bed) – now I saw Mardou pushing Yuri with a OH YOU and I shuddered to think something maybe was going on behind my back – felt warned too by the quick and immediate manner Yuri heard me coming and rolled off but as if guiltily as I say after some kind of goose or feel up some illegal touch of Mardou which made her purse little love loff lips at him and push at him and like kids. – Mardou was just like a kid I remember the first night I met her when Julien, rolling joints on the floor, she behind him hunched, I'd explained to them why that week I wasn't drinking at all (true at the time, and due to events on the ship in New York, scaring me, saying to myself 'If you keep on drinking like that you'll die you can't even hold a simple job any more,' so returning to Frisco and not drinking at all and everybody exclaiming 'O you look wonderful'), telling that first night almost heads together with Mardou and Julien, they so kidlike in their naïve WHY when I told them I wasn't drinking any more, so kidlike listening to my explanation about the one can of beer leading to the second, the sudden gut explosions and glitters, the third can, the fourth, 'And then I go off and drink for days and I'm gone man, like, I'm afraid I'm an alcoholic' and they kidlike and othergenerationey making no comment, but awed, curious – in the same rapport with young Yuri here (her age) pushing at him, Oh You, which in drunkenness I paid not too much attention to, and we slept, Mardou and I on the floor, Yuri on the couch (so kidlike, indulgent, funny of him, all that) – this first exposure of the realization of the mysteries of the guilt jealousy dream leading, from the pushcart time, to the night we went to Bromberg's, most awful of all.

Beginning as usual in the Mask.

Nights that begin so glitter clear with hope, let's go see our friends, things, phones ring, people come and go, coats, hats, statements, bright reports, metropolitan excitements, a round of beers, another round of beers, the talk gets more beautiful, more excited, flushed, another round, the midnight hour, later, the flushed happy faces are now wild and soon there's the swaying buddy da day oobab bab smash smoke drunken latenight goof leading finally to the bartender, like a seer in Eliot, TIME TO CLOSE UP – in this manner more or less arriving at the Mask where a kid called Harold Sand came in, a chance acquaintance of Mardou's from a year ago, a young novelist looking like Leslie Howard who'd just had a manuscript accepted and so acquired a strange grace in my eyes I wanted to devour – interested in him for same reasons as Lavalina, literary avidity, envy – as usual paying less attention therefore to Mardou (at table) than Yuri whose continual presence with us now did not raise my suspicions, whose complaints 'I don't have a place to stay – do you realize Percepied what it is not to even have a place to write? I have not girls, nothing, Carmody and Moorad won't let me stay up there any more, they're a couple of old sisters,' not sinking in, and already the only comment I'd made to Mardou about Yuri had been, after his leaving, 'He's just like that Mexican stud comes up here and grabs up your last cigarettes,' both of us laughing because whenever she was at her lowest financial ebb, bang, somebody who needed a 'mooch' was there – not that I would call Yuri a mooch in the least (I'll tread lightly on him on this point, for obvious reasons). – (Yuri and I'd had a long talk that week in a bar, over port wines, he claimed everything was poetry, I tried to make the common old distinction between verse and prose, he said, 'Lissen Percepied do you believe in freedom? – then say what you want, it's poetry, poetry, all of it is poetry,

great prose is poetry, great verse is poetry.' – 'Yes' I said 'but
verse is verse and prose is prose.' – 'No no' he yelled 'it's all
poetry.' – 'Okay,' I said, 'I believe in you believing in freedom
and maybe you're right, have another wine.' And he read me his
'best line' which was something to do with 'seldom nocturne' that
I said sounded like small magazine poetry and wasn't his best –
as already I'd seen some much better poetry by him concerning
his tough boyhood, about cats, mothers in gutters, Jesus striding
in the ashcan, appearing incarnate shining on the blowers of slum
tenements or that is making great steps across the light – the sum
of it something he could do, and did, well – 'No, seldom nocturne
isn't your meat' but he claimed it was great, 'I would say rather it
was great if you'd written it suddenly on the spur of the moment.'
– 'But I did – right out of my mind it flowed and I threw it down,
it sounds like it's been planned but it wasn't, it was bang! just
like you say, spontaneous vision!' – Which I now doubt tho his
saying 'seldom nocturne' came to him spontaneously made me
suddenly respect it more, some falsehood hiding beneath our
wine yells in a saloon on Kearney.) Yuri hanging out with
Mardou and me every night almost – like a shadow – and
knowing Sand himself from before, so he, Sand, walking into
the Mask, flushed successful young author but 'ironic' looking
and with a big parkingticket sticking out of his coat lapel, was
set upon by the three of us with avidity, made to sit at our table –
made to talk. – Around the corner from Mask to 13 Pater thence
the lot of us going, and en route (reminiscent now more strongly
and now with hints of pain of the pushcart night and Mardou's OH
YOU) Yuri and Mardou start racing, pushing, shoving, wrestling
on the sidewalk and finally she lofts a big empty cardboard box
and throws it at him and he throws it back, they're like kids again
– I walk on ahead in serious tone conversation with Sand tho
– he too has eyes for Mardou – somehow I'm not able (at least
haven't tried) to communicate to him that she is my love and
I would prefer if he didn't have eyes for her so obviously, just
as Jimmy Lowell, a coloured seaman who'd suddenly phoned
in the midst of an Adam party, and came, with a Scandinavian
shipmate, looking at Mardou and me wondering, asking me 'Do
you make it with her sex?' and I saying yes and the night after
the Red Drum session where Art Blakey was whaling like mad
and Thelonious Monk sweating leading the generation with his

71

elbow chords, eyeing the band madly to lead them on, *the monk and saint bop* I kept telling Yuri, smooth sharp hep Jimmy Lowell leans to me and says 'I would like to make it with your chick,' (like in the old days Leroy and I always swopping so I'm not shocked), 'would it be okay if I asked her?' and I saying 'She's not that kind of girl, I'm sure she believes in one at a time, if you ask her that's what she'll tell you man' (at that time still feeling no pain or jealousy, this incidentally the night before the Jealousy Dream) – not able to communicate to Lowell that's – that I wanted her – to stay – to be stammer stammer be mine – not being able to come right out and say, 'Lissen this is my girl, what are you talking about, if you want to try to make her you'll have to tangle with me, you understand that pops as well as I do.' – In that way with a stud, in another way with polite dignified Sand a very interesting young fellow like, 'Sand, Mardou is my girl and I would prefer, etc.' – but he has eyes for her and the reason he stays with us and goes around the corner to 13 Pater, but it's Yuri starts wrestling with her and goofing in the streets – so when we leave 13 Pater later on (a dike bar slummish now and nothing to it, where a year ago there were angels in red shirts straight out of Genet and Djuna Barnes) I get in the front seat of Sand's old car, he's going at least to drive us home, I sit next to him at the clutch in front for purposes of talking better and in drunkenness again avoiding Mardou's womanness, leaving room for her to sit beside me at front window – instead of which, no sooner plops her ass behind me, jumps over seat and dives into backseat with Yuri who is alone back there, to wrestle again and goof with him and now with such intensity I'm afraid to look back and see with my own eyes what's happening and how the dream (the dream I announced to everyone and made a big issue of and told even Yuri about) is coming true.

We pull up at Mardou's door at Heavenly Lane and drunkenly now she says (Sand and I having decided drunkenly to drive down to Los Altos the lot of us and crash in on old Austin Brómberg and have big further parties) 'If you're going down to Bromberg's in Los Altos you two go out, Yuri and I'll stay here' – my heart sank deep – it sank so I gloated to hear it for the first time and the confirmation of it crowned me and blessed me.

And I thought, 'Well boy here's your chance to get rid of her' (which I'd plotted for three weeks now) but the sound of this in

72

my own ears sounded awfully false, I didn't believe it, myself, any more.

But on the sidewalk going in flushed Yuri takes my arm as Mardou and Sand go on ahead up the fish head stairs, 'Lissen, Leo I don't want to make Mardou at all, she's all over me, I want you to know that I don't want to make her, all I want to do if you're going out there is go to sleep in your bed because I have an appointment tomorrow.' – But now I myself feel reluctant to stay in Heavenly Lane for the night because Yuri will be there, in fact now is already on the bed tacitly as if, one would have to say, 'Get off the bed so we can get in, go to that uncomfortable chair for the night.' – So this more than anything else (in my tiredness and growing wisdom and patience) makes me agree with Sand (also reluctant) that we might as well drive down to Los Altos and wake up good old Bromberg, and I turn to Mardou with eyes saying or suggesting, 'You can stay with Yuri you bitch' but she's already got her little travelling basket or weekend bag and is putting my toothbrush hairbrush and her things in and the idea is we three drive out – which we do, leaving Yuri in the bed. – En route, at near Bayshore in the great highway roadlamp night, which is now nothing but a bleakness for me and the prospect of the 'weekend' at Bromberg's a horror of shame, I can't stand it any more and look at Mardou as soon as Sand gets out to buy hamburgs in the diner, 'You jumped in the backseat with Yuri why'd you do that? and why'd you say you wanted to stay with him?' – 'It was silly of me, I was just high baby.' But I don't darkly any more now want to believe her – art is short, life is long – now I've got in full dragon bloom the monster of jealousy as green as in any cliché cartoon rising in my being. 'You and Yuri play together all the time, it's just like the dream I told you about, that's what's horrible – O I'll never believe in dreams come true again.' – 'But baby it isn't anything like that' but I don't believe her – I can tell by looking at her she's got eyes for the youth – you can't fool an old hand who at the age of sixteen before even the juice was wiped off his heart by the Great Imperial World Wiper with Sadcloth fell in love with an impossible flirt and cheater, this is a boast – I feel so sick I can't stand it, curl up in the back seat, alone – they drive on, and Sand having anticipated a gay talkative weekend now finds himself with a couple of grim lover worriers, hears in fact the fragment 'But I didn't mean you to think that baby' so

73

obviously harkening to his mind the Yuri incident – finds himself with this pair of bores and has to drive all the way down to Los Altos, and so with the same grit that made him write the half million words of his novel bends to it and pushes the car through the Peninsula night and on into the dawn.

Arriving at Bromberg's house in Los Altos at grey dawn, parking, and ringing the doorbell the three of us sheepishly I most sheepish of all – and Bromberg comes right down, at once, with great roars of approval cries 'Leo I didn't know you knew each other' (meaning Sand, whom Bromberg admired very much) and in we go to rum and coffee in the crazy famous Bromberg kitchen. – You might say, Bromberg the most amazing guy in the world with small dark curly hair like the hip girl Roxanne making little garter snakes over his brow and his great really angelic eyes shining, rolling, a big burbling baby, a great genius of talk, really wrote research and essays and has (and is famous for) the greatest possible private library in the world, right there in that house, library due to his erudition and this no reflection also on his big income – the house inherited from father – was also the sudden new bosom friend of Carmody and about to go to Peru with him, they'd go dig Indian boys and talk about it and discuss art and visit literaries and things of that nature, all matters so much had been dinning in Mardou's ear (queer, cultured matters) in her love affair with me that by now she was quite tired of cultured tones and fancy explicity, emphatic daintiness of expression, of which roll-eyed ecstatic almost spastic big Bromberg almost the pastmaster, 'O my dear it's such a charming thing and I think much MUCH better than the Gascoyne translation tho I do believe –' and Sand imitating him to a T, from some recent great meeting and mutual admiration – so the two of them there in the once-to-me adventurous grey dawn of the Metropolitan Great-Rome Frisco talking of literary and musical and artistic matters, the kitchen littered, Bromberg rushing up (in pyjamas) to fetch three-inch thick French editions of Genet or old editions of Chaucer or whatever he and Sand'd come to, Mardou darklashed and still thinking of Yuri (as I'm thinking to myself) sitting at the corner of the kitchen table, with her getting-cold rum and coffee – O I on a stool, hurt, broken, injured, about to get worse, drinking cup after cup and loading up on the great heavy brew – the birds beginning to sing finally at about eight and Bromberg's great voice, one of the mightiest you can hear, making the walls of the kitchen throw back great shudders of deep ecstatic sound – turning on the phonograph, an expensive well-furnished completely appointed house, with French wine, refrigerators, three-speed machines with speakers, cellar, etc. – I want to look at Mardou I don't know with what expression – I am afraid in fact to look only to find there the supplication in her eyes saying 'Don't worry baby, I told you, I confessed to you I was silly, I'm sorry sorry sorry – ' that 'I'm-sorry' look hurting me the most as I glance side eyes to see it . . .

It won't do when the very bluebirds are bleak, which I mention to Bromberg, he asking 'Whatsamatter with you this morning Leo?' (with burbling peek under eyebrows to see me better and make me laugh). – 'Nothing, Austin, just that when I look out the window this morning the birds are bleak.' – (And earlier when Mardou went upstairs to toilet I did mention, bearded, gaunt, foolish, drunkard, to these erudite gentlemen, something about 'inconstancy', which must have surprised them tho – O inconstancy!

So they try anyway to make the best of it in spite of my palpable unhappy brooding all over the place, while listening to Verdi and Puccini opera recordings in the great upstairs library (four walls from rug to ceiling with things like *The Explanation of the Apocalypse* in three volumes, the complete works and poems of Chris Smart, the complete this and that, the apology of so-and-so written obscurely to you-know-who in 1839, in 1638 –). I jump at the chance to say, 'I'm going to sleep,' it's now eleven, I have a right to be tired, been sitting on the floor and Mardou with dame-like majesty all this time in the easy chair in the corner of the library (where once I'd seen the famous one-armed Nick Spain sit when Bromberg on a happier early time in the year played for us the original recording of *The Rake's Progress*) and looking so, herself, tragic, lost – hurt so much by my hurt – by my sorriness from her sorriness borrowing – I think sensitive – that at one point in a burst of forgiveness, need, I run and sit at her feet and lean head on her knee in front of the others who by now don't care any more, that is Sand does not care about these things now deeply engrossed in the music, the books, the brilliant conversation (the likes of which cannot be surpassed anywhere in the world, incidentally, and this too, tho now tiredly, crosses by my epic-wanting brain and I see the scheme of all my life, all acquaintances, loves, worries, travels rising again in a big symphonic mass but now I'm beginning not to care so much any more because of this 105 pounds of woman and brown at that whose little toenails, red in the thonged sandals, make my throat gulp) – 'O dear Leo, you do seem to be bored.' – 'Not bored! how could I be bored here!' – I wish I had some sympathetic way to tell Bromberg, 'Every time I come here there's something wrong with me, it must seem like some awful comment on your house and hospitality and it isn't at all, can't you understand that this morning my heart is broken and out the window is bleak' (and how explain to him the other time I was a guest at his place, again uninvited but breaking in at grey dawn with Charley Krasner and the kids were there, and Mary, and the others came, gin and Schweppes, I became so drunk, disorderly, lost, I then too brooded and slept in fact on the floor in the middle of the room in front of everybody in the height of day – and for reasons so far removed from now, tho still as tho an adverse comment on the quality of Bromberg's weekend) – 'No Austin I'm just sick –.' No doubt, too, Sand must have hipped him quietly in a whisper somewhere what was happening with the lovers, Mardou also being silent – one of the strangest guests ever to hit Bromberg's, a poor subterranean beat Negro girl with no clothes on her back worth a two penny (I saw to that generously), and yet so strange faced, solemn, serious, like a funny solemn unwanted probably angel in the house – feeling, as she told me, later, really unwanted because of the circumstances. – So I cop out, from the lot, from life, all of it, go to sleep in the bedroom (where Charley and I that earlier time had danced the mambo naked with Mary) and fall exhausted into new nightmares waking up about three hours later, in the heartbreakingly pure, clear, sane, happy afternoon, birds still singing, now kids singing, as if I was a spider waking up in a dusty bin and the world wasn't for me but for the other airier creatures and more constant themselves and also less liable to the stains of inconstancy too –

While sleeping they three get in Sand's car and (properly) drive out to the beach, twenty miles, the boys jump in, swim, Mardou wanders on the shores of eternity her toes and feet that I love pressing down in the pale sand against the little shells and anemones and paupered dry seaweed long washed up and the wind blowing back her short haircut, as if Eternity'd

76

met Heavenly Lane (as I thought of it in my bed) (seeing her also wandering around pouting, not knowing what to do next, abandoned by Suffering Leo and really alone and incapable of chatting about every tom dick and harry in art with Bromberg and Sand, what to do?) – So when they return she comes to the bed (after Bromberg's preliminary wild bound up the stairs and bursting in of door and 'WAKE up Leo you don't want to sleep all day we've been to the beach, really it's not fair!') – 'Leo,' says Mardou, 'I didn't want to sleep with you because I didn't want to wake up in Bromberg's bed at seven o'clock in the evening, it would be too much to cope with, I can't – ' meaning her therapy (which she hadn't been going to any more out of sheer paralysis with me and my gang and cups), her inadequacy, the great now-crushing weight and fear of madness increasing in this disorderly awful life and unloved affair with me, to wake up horrified from hangover in a stranger's (a kind but nevertheless not altogether wholeheartedwelcoming stranger's) bed, with poor incapable Leo. – I suddenly looked at her, listening not to these real poor pleas so much as digging in her eyes that light that had shined on Yuri and it wasn't her fault it could shine on all the world all the time, my light o love –

'Are you sincere?' – ('God you frighten me,' she said later, 'you make me think suddenly I've been two people and betrayed you in one way, with one person, and this other person – it really frightened me – ') but as I ask that, 'Are you sincere?' the pain I feel is so great, it has just risen fresh from that disordered roaring dream ('God is so disposed as to make our lives less cruel than our dreams,' is a quote I saw the other day God knows where) – feeling all that and harkening to other horrified hangover awakenings in Bromberg's and all the hangover awakenings in my life, feeling now, 'Boy, this is the real real beginning of the end, you can't go on much further, how much more vagueness can your positive flesh take and how long will it stay positive if your psyche keeps blamming on it – boy, you are going to die, when birds get bleak – that's the sign –.' But thinking more roars than that, visions of my work neglected, my well-being (so-called old well-being again) smashed, brain permanently injured now – ideas for working on the railroad – O God the whole host and foolish illusion and entire rigmarole and madness that we erect in the place of onelove, in our sadness – but now with Mardou leaning over me, tired, solemn, sombre, capable as she played with the little unshaven uglies of my chin of seeing right through my flesh into my horror and capable of feeling every vibration of pain and futility I could send, as, too, attested by her recognition of 'Are you sincere?' as the deep-well sounded call from the bottom – 'Baby, let's go home.'

'We'll have to wait till Bromberg goes, take the train with him – I guess –.' So I get up, go into the bathroom (where I'd been earlier while they were at the beach and sex-phantasized in remembrance of the time, on another even wilder and further back Bromberg weekend, poor Annie with her hair done up in curlers and her face no makeup and Leroy poor Leroy in the other room wondering what his wife's doing in there, and Leroy later driving off desperately into the night realizing we were up to something in the bathroom and so remembering myself now the pain I had caused Leroy that morning just for the sake of a little bit of sate for that worm and snake called sex) – I go into the bathroom and wash up and come down, trying to be cheerful.

Still I can't look at Mardou straight in the eye – in my heart, 'O why did you do it?' – sensing, in my desperation, the prophecy of what's to come.

As if not enough this was the day of the night of the great Jones party, which was the night I jumped out of Mardou's cab and abandoned her to the dogs of war – the war man Yuri wages gainst man Leo, each one. – Beginning, Bromberg making phone calls and gathering birthday gifts and getting ready to take the bus to make old 151 at 4.47 for the city, Sand driving us (a sorry lot indeed) to bus stop, where we have quick one in bar across street while Mardou by now ashamed not only of herself but me too stays in back seat of car (tho exhausted) but in broad daylight, trying to catch a wink – really trying to think her way out of trap only I could help her out of if I'm given one more chance – in the bar, parenthetically amazed I am to hear Bromberg going right on with big booming burbling comments on art and literature and even in fact by God queer anecdotes as sullen as Santa Clara Valley farmers guzzle at rail, Bromberg doesn't even have consciousness of his fantastic impact on the ordinary – and Sand enjoying, himself in fact also weird – but minor details. – I come out to tell Mardou we have decided to take later train in order to go back to house to pick up forgotten package which is just another ringaroundtherosy of futility for her, she receives this news with solemn lips – ah my love and lost darling (out of date word) – if then I'd known what I know now, instead of returning to bar, for further talks, and looking at her with hurt eyes, etc., and let her lay there in the bleak sea of time untended and unsolaced and unforgiven for the sin of the sea or time I'd have gone in and sat down with her, taken her hand, promised her my life and protection – 'Because I love you and there's no reason' – but then far from having completely successfully realized this love, I was still in the act of thinking I was climbing out of my doubt about her – but the train came, finally, 153 at 5.31 after all our delays, we got in, and rode to the city – through South San Francisco and past my house, facing one another in coach seats, riding by the big yards in Bayshore and I gleefully (trying to be gleeful) point out a kicked boxcar ramming a hopper and you see the tinscrap shuddering far off, wow – but most of the time sitting bleakly under either stare and saying, finally, 'I really do feel I must be getting a rummy nose' – anything I could think of saying to ease the pressure of what I really wanted to weep about – but in the main the three of us really sad, riding together on a train to gaiety, horror, the eventual H bomb.

– Bidding Austin adieu finally at some teeming corner on Market where Mardou and I wandered among great sad sullen crowds in a confusion mass, as if we were suddenly lost in the actual physical manifestation of the mental condition we'd been in now together for two months, not even holding hands but I anxiously leading the way through crowds (so's to get out fast, hated it) but really because I was too 'hurt' to hold her hand and remembering (now with greater pain) her usual insistence that I not hold her in the street or people'll think she's a hustler – ending up, in bright lost sad afternoon down Price Street (O fated Price Street) towards Heavenly Lane, among the children, the young good-looking Mex chicks each one making me say to myself with contempt 'Ah they're almost all of 'em better than Mardou, all I gotta do is get one of the m . . . but O, but O' – neither one of us speaking much, and such chagrin in her eyes that in the original place where I had seen that Indian warmth which had originally prompted me to say to her, on some happy candlelit night, 'Honey what I see in your eyes is a lifetime of affection not only from the Indian in you but because as part Negro somehow you are the

79

first, the essential woman, and therefore the most, most originally most fully affectionate and maternal' – there now is the chagrin too, some lost American addition and mood with it – 'Eden's in Africa,' I'd added one time – but now in my hurt hate turning the other way and so walking down Price with her every time I see a Mexican gal or Negress I say to myself, 'hustlers,' they're all the same, always trying to cheat and rob you – harking back to all relations in the past with them – Mardou sensing these waves of hostility from me and silent.

And who's in our bed in Heavenly Lane but Yuri – cheerful – 'Hey I been workin' all day, so tired I had to come back and get some more rest.' – I decide to tell him everything, try to form the words in my mouth, Yuri sees my eyes, senses the tenseness, Mardou senses the tenseness, a knock on the door brings in John Golz (always romantically interested in Mardou in a naïver way), he senses the tenseness, 'I've come to borrow a book' – grim expression on his face and remembering how I'd put him down about selectivity – so leaves at once, with book, and Yuri in getting up from bed (while Mardou hides behind screen to change from party dress to home jeans) – 'Leo hand me my pants.' – 'Get up and get 'em yourself, they're right there on the chair, she can't see you' – a funny statement, and my mind feels funny and I look at Mardou who is silent and inward.

The moment she goes to the bathroom I say to Yuri 'I'm very jealous about you and Mardou in the backseat last night man, I really am.' – 'It's not my fault, it was her started it.' – 'Lissen, you're such – like don't let her, keep away – you're such a lady-killer they all fall for you' – saying this just as Mardou returns, looking up sharply not hearing the words but seeing them in the air, and Yuri at once grabs the still open door and says 'Well anyway I'm going to Adam's I'll see you there later.'

'What did you tell Yuri –?' – I tell her word for word – 'God the tenseness in here was unbearable' – (sheepishly I review the fact that instead of being stern and Moses-like in my jealousy and position I'd instead chatted with nervous 'poet' talk with Yuri, as always, giving him the tension but not the positiveness of my feelings in words – sheepishly I review my sheepishness – I get sad to see old Carmody somehow –

'Baby I'm gonna – you think they got chickens on Columbus? – I've seen some – And cook it, see, we'll have a nice chicken supper.' – 'And,' I say to myself, 'what good is a nice domestic chicken supper when you love Yuri so much he has to leave the moment you walk in because of the pressure of my jealousy and your possibility as prophesied in a dream?' 'I want' (out loud) 'to see Carmody, I'm sad – you stay here, cook the chicken, eat – alone – I'll come back later and get you.' – 'But it always starts off like this, we always go away, we never stay alone.' – 'I know but tonight I'm sad I gotta see Carmody, for some reason don't ask me I have a tremendous sad desire and reason just to – after all I drew his picture the other day' (I had drawn my first pencil sketches of human figures reclining and they were greeted with amazement by Carmody and Adam and so I was proud) 'and after all in drawing those shots of Frank the other day I saw such great sadness in the lines under his eyes that I know he – ' (to myself: I know he'll understand how sad I am now, I know he has suffered on four continents this way). – Pondering Mardou does not know which way to turn but suddenly I tell her of my quick talk with Yuri the part I'd forgotten in the first report (and here too) 'He said to me "Leo I don't want to make your girl Mardou, after all I have no eyes –".' 'Oh, so he has no eyes! A hell of a thing to say!' (the same teeth of glee now the portals where pass angry winds, and her eyes glitter) and I hear that junkey-like emphasis on the *ings* where she presses down on her *ings* like many junkies I know, from some inside heavy somnolent reason which in Mardou I'd attributed to her amazing modernness culled (as I once asked her) 'From where? where did you learn all you know and that amazing way you speak?' but now to hear that interesting *ing* only makes me mad as it's coming in a transparent speech about Yuri where she shows she's not really against seeing Yuri again at party or otherwise, 'if he's gonna talk like that about no eyes,' she's gonna tell him. – 'O,' I say, 'now you WANT to come to the party at Adam's, because there you can get even with Yuri and tell him off – you're so transparent.'

'Jesus,' as we're walking along the benches of the church park sad park of the whole summer season, 'now you're calling me names, transparent.'

'Well that's what it is, you think I can't see through that, at first you didn't want to go to Adam's at all and now that you hear – well the hell with that if it ain't transparent I don't know what is.' – 'Calling me names, Jesus' (shnuffling to laugh) and both of us actually hysterically smiling and as tho nothing had happened at all and in fact like happy unconcerned people you see in newsreels busy going down the street to their chores and where-go's and we're in the same rainy newsreel mystery sad but inside of us (as must then be so inside the puppet filmdolls of screen) the great tumescent turbulent turmoil alliterative as a hammer on the brain bone bag and balls, bang I'm sorry I was ever born . . .

To cap everything, as if it wasn't enough, the whole world opens up as Adam opens the door bowing solemnly but with a glint and secret in his eye and some kind of unwelcomeness I bristle at the sight of – 'What's the matter?' Then I sense the presence of more people in there than Frank and Adam and Yuri. – 'We have visitors.' – 'Oh,' I say, 'distinguished visitors?' – 'I think so.' – 'Who?' – 'MacJones and Phyllis.' – 'What?' – the great moment has come when I'm to come face to face, or leave, with my arch literary enemy Balliol MacJones erstwhile so close to me we used to slop beer on each other's knees in leaning-over talk excitement, we'd talked and exchanged and borrowed and read books and literarized so much the poor innocent had actually come under some kind of influence from me, that is, in the sense, only, that he learned the talk and style, mainly the history of the hip or beat generation or subterranean generation and I'd told him 'Mac, write a great book about everything that happened when Leroy came to New York in 1949 and don't leave a word out and blow, go!' which he did, and I read it, critically Adam and I in visits to his place both critical of the manuscript but when it came out they guarantee him 20,000 dollars an unheard of sum and all of us beat types wandering the Beach and Market Street and Times Square when in New York, tho Adam and I had solemnly admitted, quote, 'Jones is not of us – but from another world – the midtown sillies world' (an Adamism). And so his great success coming at the moment when I was poorest and most neglected by publishers and worse than that hung-up on paranoiac drug habits I became incensed but I didn't get too mad, but stayed black about it, changing my mind after father time's few local scythes and various misfortunes and trips around, writing him apologetic letters on ships which I tore up, he too writing them meanwhile, and then, Adam acting a year later as some kind of saint and mediator reported favourable inclinations on both our parts, to both parties – the great moment when I would have to face old Mac and shake with him and call it quits, let go all the rancour – making as little impression on Mardou, who is so independent and unavailable in that new heartbreaking way. Anyway MacJones was there, immediately I said out loud 'Good, great, I been waiting to see him,' and I rushed into the livingroom and over someone's head who was getting up (Yuri it was) I shook hands firmly with Balliol, sat brooding awhile, didn't even notice how poor Mardou had managed to position herself (here as at Bromberg's as everywhere poor dark angel) – finally going to the bedroom unable to bear the polite conversation under which not only Yuri but Jones (and also Phyllis his woman who kept staring at me to see if it was still crazy) rumbled, I ran to the bedroom and lay in the dark and at the first opportunity tried to get Mardou to lie down with me but she said 'Leo I don't want to lay around in here in the dark.' – Yuri then coming over, putting on one of Adam's ties, saying, 'I'm going out and find me a girl,' and we have a kind of whispering rapport now away from them in the parlour – all's forgiven. – But I feel that because Jones does not move from his couch he really doesn't want to talk to me and probably wishes secretly I'd leave. When Mardou roams back again to my bed of shame and sorrow and hidingplace, I say, 'What are you talking about in there, bop? Don't tell *him* anything about music.' – (Let him find out for himself! I say to myself pettishly) – *I'm* the bop writer! – But as I'm commissioned to get the beer downstairs, when I come in again with beer in arms they're all in the kitchen, Mac foremost, smiling and saying, 'Leo! let me see those drawings they told me you did, I want to see them.' – So we become friends again bending over drawings and Yuri has to be showing his too (he draws) and Mardou is in the other room, again forgotten – but it is a historic moment and as we also, with Carmody, study Carmody's South American bleak pictures of high jungle villages and Andean towns where you can see the clouds pass, I notice Mac's expensive goodlooking clothes, wrist watch, I feel proud of him and now he has an attractive little moustache that makes his maturity – which I announce to everyone – the beer by now warming us all up, and then his wife Phyllis begins a supper and the conviviality flows back and forth –

In the red bulblight parlour in fact I see Jones alone with

Mardou questioning, as if interviewing her, I see that he's grinning and saying to himself 'Old Percepied's got himself another amazing doll' and I inside yearn to myself, 'Yeah, for how long' – and he's listening to Mardou, who, impressed, forewarned, understanding everything, makes solemn statements about bop, like, 'I don't like bop, I really don't, it's like junk to me, too many junkies are bop men and I hear the junk in it.' – 'Well,' Mac adjusting glasses, 'that's interesting.' – And I go up and say, 'But you never like what you come from' (looking at Mardou). – 'What do you mean?' – 'You're the child of Bop,' or the children of bop, some such statement, which Mac and I agree on – so that later when we all the whole gang troop out to further festivities of the night, and Mardou wearing Adam's long black velvet jacket (for her long) and a mad long scarf too, looking like a little Polish underground girl or boy in a sewer of the same old dreary mystery of personality in KaJa the great – disgusted she seemed indeed, and looking into space.

So later when in my drunkenness I managed to get Paddy Cordavan over to our table and he invited us all to his place for further drinking (the usually unattainable social Paddy Cordavan due to his woman who always wanted to go home alone with him, Paddy Cordavan of whom Buddy Pond had said, 'He's too beautiful I can't look,' tall, blond, big-jawed sombre Montana cowboy slowmoving, slow talking, slow shouldered) Mardou wasn't impressed, as she wanted to get away from Paddy and all the other subterraneans of Dante's anyway, whom I had just freshly annoyed by yelling again at Julien, 'Come here, we're all going to Paddy's party and Julien's coming,' at which Julien immediately leaped up and rushed back to Ross Wallenstein and the others at their own booth, thinking, 'God that awful Percepied is screaming at me and trying to drag me to his silly places again, I wish someone would do something about him.' And Mardou wasn't any further impressed when, at Yuri's insistence, I went to the phone and spoke to Sam (calling from work) and agreed to meet him later at the bar across from the office – 'We'll all go! we'll all go!' I'm screaming by now and even Adam and Frank are yawning ready to go home and Jones is long gone – rushing around up and down Paddy's stairs for further calls with Sam and at one point here I am rushing into Paddy's kitchen to get Mardou to come meet Sam with me and Ross Wallenstein having arrived while I was in the bar calling says, looking up, 'Who let this guy in, hey, who is this? how'd you get in here! Hey Paddy!' in serious continuation of his original dislike and 'are-you-a-fag' come-on, which I ignored, saying, 'Brother I'll take the fuzz off your peach if you don't shut up', or some such putdown, can't remember, strong enough to make him swivel like a soldier, the way he does, stiff necked, and retire – I dragging Mardou down to a cab to rush to Sam's and all this wild world swirling night and she in her little voice I hear protesting from far away, 'But Leo, dear Leo, I want to go home and sleep.' – 'Ah hell!' and I give Sam's address to the taxidriver, she says NO, insists, gives Heavenly Lane, 'Take me there first and then go to Sam's' but I'm really seriously hung-up on the undeniable fact that if I take her to Heavenly Lane first the cab will never make it to Sam's waiting bar before closing time, so I argue, we harangue hurling different addresses at the cab driver who like in a movie waits, but suddenly, with that red flame that same red flame (for want of a better image) I leap out of the cab and rush out and there's another one, I jump in, give Sam's address and off he guns her – Mardou left in the night, in a cab, sick, and tired, and me intending to pay the second cab with the buck she'd entrusted to Adam to get her a sandwich but which in the turmoil had been forgotten but he gave it to me for her – poor Mardou going home alone, again, and drunken maniac was gone.

Well, I thought, this is the end – I finally made the step and by God I paid her back for what she done to me – it had to come and this is it – ploop.

> Isn't it good to know winter is coming –
> and that life will be a little
> more quiet – and you will be home
> Write to me Anything.
> be spending pleasant nights wrapped
> round one another – and you are home
> now, rested and eating well because you
> should not become too sad – and I feel
> better when I know you are well.

and

> Write to me Anything.
> Please stay well
> Your friend
> and my love

and Oh
And love for you
MARDOU
Please

BUT THE DEEPEST premonition and prophecy of all had always been, that when I walked into Heavenly Lane, cutting in sharply from sidewalk, I'd look up, and if Mardou's light was on Mardou's light was on – 'But some day, dear Leo, that light will not shine for you' – this a prophecy irrespective of all your Yuris and attenuations in the snake of time. – 'Someday she won't be there when you want her to be there, the light'll be out and you'll be looking up and it will be dark in Heavenly Lane and Mardou'll be gone, and it'll be when you least expect it and want it.' – Always I knew this – it crossed my mind that night I ran up, met Sam in the bar, he was with two newspapermen, we bought drinks, I spilled money on the floor, I hurried to get drunk (through with my baby!), rushed up to Adam and Frank's, woke them up again, wrestled on the floor, made noise, Sam tore my T-shirt off, bashed the lamp in, drank a fifth of bourbon as of old in our tremendous days together, it was just another big downcrashing in the night and all for nothing . . . waking up, I, in the morning with the final hangover that said to me, 'Too late' – and got up and staggered to the door through the debris, and opened it, and went home, Adam saying to me as he heard me fiddle with the groaning faucet, 'Leo go home and recuperate well,' sensing how sick I was tho not knowing about Mardou and me – and at home I wandered around, couldn't stay in the house, couldn't stop, had to walk, as if someone was going to die soon, as if I could smell the flowers of death in the air, and I went in the South San Francisco railyard and cried.

Cried in the railyard sitting on an old piece of iron under the new moon and on the side of the old Southern Pacific tracks, cried because not only I had cast off Mardou whom now I was not so sure I wanted to cast off but the die'd been thrown, feeling too her empathetic tears across the night and the final horror both of us round-eyed realizing we part – but seeing suddenly not in the face of the moon but somewhere in the sky as I looked up and hoped to figure, the face of my mother – remembering it in fact from a haunted nap just after supper that same restless unable-to-stay-in-a-chair or on-earth day – just as

86

I woke to some Arthur Godfrey programme on the TV, I saw
bending over me the visage of my mother, with impenetrable
eyes and moveless lips and round cheekbones and glasses that
glinted and hid the major part of her expression which at first
I thought was a vision of horror that I might shudder at, but it
didn't make me shudder – wondering about it on the walk and
suddenly now in the railyards weeping for my lost Mardou and
so stupidly because I'd decided to throw her away myself, it had
been a vision of my mother's love for me – that expressionless
and expressionless-because-so-profound face bending over me in
the vision of my sleep, and with lips not so pressed together as
enduring and as if to say, *'Pauvre Ti Leo, pauvre Ti Leo, tu souffri, les
hommes souffri tant, y'ainque toi dans le monde j'va't prendre soin, j'aim'ra
beaucoup t'prendre soin tous tes jours mon ange.'* – 'Poor Little Leo, poor
little Leo, you suffer, men suffer so, you're all alone in the world
I'll take care of you, I would very much like to take care of you all
your days my angel.' – My mother an angel too – the tears welled
up in my eyes, something broke, I cracked – I had been sitting
for an hour, in front of me was Butler Road and the gigantic
rose neon ten blocks long BETHLEHEM WEST COAST STEEL with stars
above and the smashby Zipper and the fragrance of locomotive
coalsmoke as I sit there and let them pass and far down the line
in the night around that South San Francisco airport you can see
that sonofabitch red light waving Mars signal light swimming in
the dark big red markers blowing up and down and sending fires
in the keenpure lostpurity lovelyskies of old California in the late
sad night of autumn spring comefall winter's summertime tall, like
trees – the only man in South City who ever walked from the neat
suburban homes and went and hid by boxcars to think – broke.
– Something fell loose in me – O blood of my soul I thought and
the Good Lord or whatever's put me here to suffer and groan and
on top of that be guilty and gives me the flesh and blood that is so
painful the – women all mean well – this I knew – women love,
bend over you – you'd as soon betray a woman's love as spit on
your own feet, clay –

That sudden short crying in the railyard and for a reason I
really didn't fathom, and couldn't – saying to myself in the bottom,
'You see a vision of the face of the woman who is your mother who
loves you so much she has supported you and protected you for
years, you a bum, a drunkard – never complained a jot – because

she knows that in your present state you can't go out in the world and make a living and take care of yourself and even find and hold the love of another protecting woman – and all because you are poor stupid Ti Leo – deep in the dark pit of night under the stars of the world you are lost, poor, no one cares, and now you threw away a little woman's love because you wanted another drink with a rowdy fiend from the other side of your insanity.'

And as always.

Ending with the great sorrow of Price Street when Mardou and I, reunited on Sunday night according to my schedule (I'd made up the schedule that week thinking in a yard tea-reverie, 'This is the cleverest arrangement I ever made, why with this thing I can live a full love-life,' conscious of Mardou's Reichian worth, and at the same time write those three novels and be a big – etc.) (schedule all written out, and delivered to Mardou for her perusal, it said, 'Go to Mardou at 9 in the evening, sleep, return following noon for afternoon of writing and evening supper and aftersupper rest and then return at 9 p.m. again,' with holes in the schedule left open on weekends for 'possible going out') (getting plastered) – with this schedule still in mind and after spending the weekend at home steeped in that awful – I rushed anyway to Mardou's on Sunday night at 9 p.m., as scheduled, there was no light in her window ('Just as I knew it would happen someday') – but on the door a note, and for me, which I read after quick leak in the hall john – 'Dear Leo, I'll be back at 10.30,' and the door (as always) unlocked and I go in to wait and read Reich – carrying again my big forward-looking healthybook Reich and ready at least to 'throw a good one in her' in case it's all bound to end this very night and sitting there eyes shifting around and plotting – 11.30 and she hasn't come yet – fearing me – missing – ('Leo,' later, she told me, 'I really thought we were through, that you wouldn't come back at all') – nevertheless she'd left that Bird of Paradise note for me, always and still hoping and not aiming to hurt me and keep me waiting in dark – but because she does not return at 11.30 I cut out, to Adam's, leaving message for her to call, with ramifications that I erase after a while – all a host of minor details leading to the great sorrow of Price Street taking place after we spend a night of 'successful' sex (when I tell her, 'Mardou you've become much more precious to me since everything that happened,' and because, of that, as we

agree, I am able to make her fulfill better, which she does –
twice, in fact, and for the first time – spending a whole sweet
afternoon as if reunited but at intervals poor Mardou looking
up and saying, 'But we should really break up, we've never done
anything together, we were going to Mexico, and then you were
going to get a job and we'd live together, then remember the loft
idea, all big phantasm that like haven't worked out because you
haven't pushed them from your mind out into the open world,
haven't acted on them, and like, me, I don't – I've missed my
therapist for weeks.' (She'd written a fine letter that very day to
the therapist begging forgiveness and permission to come back
in a few weeks and advice for her lostness and I'd approved of
it.) – All of this unreal from the moment I walked into Heavenly
Lane after my crying-in-the-railyard lonely dark sojourn at home
to see her light was out at last (as deeply promised), but the note
saving us awhile, my finding her a little later that night as she did
finally call me at Adam's and told me to come to Rita's, where I
brought beer, then Mike Murphy came and he brought beer too
– ending with another silly yelling conversation drunk night. –
Mardou saying in the morning, 'Do you remember anything you
said last night to Mike and Rita?' and me, 'Of course not.' – The
whole day, borrowed from the sky day, sweet – we make love and
try to make promises of little kinds – no go, as in the evening
she says 'Let's go to a show' (with her pitiful cheque money). –
'Jesus, we'll spend all your money.' – 'Well goddamit I don't care,
I'm going to spend that money and that's all there is to it,' with
great emphasis – so she puts on her black velvet slacks and some
perfume and I go up and smell her neck and God, how sweet
can you smell – and I want her more than ever, in my arms she's
gone – in my hand she's as slippy as dust – something's wrong.
– 'Did I cut you when I jumped out of the cab?' – 'Leo it was
baby, it was the most maniacal thing I ever saw.' – 'I'm sorry.'
– 'I know you're sorry but it was the most maniacal thing I ever
saw and it keeps happening and getting worse and like, now, oh
hell – let's go to a show.' – So we go out, and she has on this
little heartbreaking never-seen-by-me before red raincoat over
the black velvet slacks and cuts along, with black short hair
making her look so strange, like a – like someone in Paris – I
have on just my old ex-brakeman railroad Cant Bust Ems and a
workshirt without undershirt and suddenly it's cold October out

there, and with gusts of rain, so I shiver at her side as we hurry up Price Street – towards Market, shows – I remember that afternoon returning from the Bromberg weekend – something is caught in both our throats, I don't know what, she does.

'Baby I'm going to tell you something and if I tell it to you I want you to promise nevertheless you'll come to the movie with me.' – 'Okay.' – And naturally I add, after a pause, 'What is it?' – I think it has something to do with 'Let's break up really and truly, I don't want to make it, not because I don't like you but it's by now or should be obvious to both of us by now – ' that kind of argument that I can, as of yore and again, break, by saying, 'But let's, look, I have, wait – ' for always the man can make the little woman bend, she was made to bend, the little woman was – so I wait confidently for this kind of talk, tho feel bleak, tragic, grim, and the air cold. – 'You know the other night' (she spends some time trying to order confused nights of recent – and I help her straighten them out, and have my arm around her waist, as we cut along we come closer to the brittle jewel lights of Price and Columbus that old North Beach corner so weird and ever weirder now that I have my private thoughts about it as from older scenes in my San Francisco life, in brief, almost smug and snug in the rug of myself – in any case we agree that the night she means to tell me about is Saturday night, which was the night I cried in the railyards – that short sudden, as I say, crying, that vision – I'm trying in fact to interpose and tell her about it, trying also to figure out if she means now that on Saturday night something awful happened that I should know –).

'Well I went to Dante's and didn't want to stay, and tried to leave – and Yuri was trying to hang around – and he called somebody – and I was at the phone – and told Yuri he was wanted' (as incoherent as that) 'and while he is in the booth I cut on home, because I was tired – baby at two o'clock in the morning he came and knocked on the door – '

'Why?' – 'For a place to sleep, he was drunk, he rushed in – and – well –.'

'Huh?'

'Well baby we made it together,' – that hip word – at the sound of which even as I walked and my legs propelled under me and my feet felt firm, the lower part of my stomach sagged into my pants or loins and the body experienced a sensation of deep melting downgoing into some soft somewhere, nowhere – suddenly the streets were so bleak, the people passing so beastly, the lights so unnecessary just to illumine this . . . this cutting world – it was going across the cobbles when she said it, 'made it together,' I had (locomotive wise) to concentrate on getting up on the kerb again and I didn't look at her – I looked down Columbus and thought of walking away, rapidly, as I'd done at Larry's – I didn't – I said 'I don't want to live in this beastly world' – but so low she barely if at all heard me and if so never commented, but after a pause she added a few things, like, 'There are other details, like what – but I won't go into them – like,' stammering, and slow – yet both of us swinging along in the street to the show – the show being *Brave Bulls* (I cried to see the grief in the matador when he heard his best friend and girl had gone off the mountain in his own car, I cried to see even the bull that I knew would die and I knew the big deaths bulls do die in their trap called bullring) – I wanted to run away from Mardou. ('Look man,' she'd said only a week before when I'd suddenly started talking about Adam and Eve and referred to her as Eve, the woman who by her beauty is able to make the man do anything, 'don't call me Eve.') – But now no matter – walking along, at one point so irritable to my senses she stopped short on the rainy sidewalk and coolly said 'I need a neckerchief' and turned to go into the store and I turned and followed her from reluctant ten feet back realizing I hadn't known what was going on in my mind really ever since Price and Columbus and here we were on Market – while she's in the store I keep haggling with myself, shall I just go now, I have my fare, just cut down the street swiftly and go home and when she comes out she'll see you're gone, she'll know you broke the promise to go to the movies just like you broke a lot of promises but this time she'll know you have a big male right to – but none of this is enough – I feel stabbed by Yuri – by Mardou I feel forsaken and shamed – I turn to look in the store blindly at anything and there she comes at just that moment wearing a phosphorescent purple bandana (because big raindrops had just started flying and she didn't want the rain to string out her carefully combed for the movies hair and here she was spending her small monies on kerchiefs.) – In the movie I hold her hand, after a fifteen-minute wait, not thinking to at all not because I was mad but I felt she would feel it was too subservient at this time to take her hand in the movie-show, like

91

lovers – but I took her hand, she was warm, lost – ask not the sea why the eyes of the dark-eyed woman are strange and lost – came out of the movie, I glum, she businesslike to get through the cold to the bus, where, at the bus stop, she walked away from me to lead me to a warmer waiting place and (as I said) I'd mentally accused her of wanderingfoot.

Arriving home, where we sat, she on my lap, after a long warm talk with John Golz, who came in to see her, but found me too, and I might have left, but in my new spirit I wanted at once to show him that I respected and liked him, and talked with him, and he stayed two hours – in fact I saw how he annoyed Mardou by talking literature with her beyond the point where she was interested and also about things she'd long known about – poor Mardou.

So he left, and I curled her on my lap, and she talked about the war between men – 'They have a war, to them a woman is a prize, to Yuri it's just that your prize has less value now.'

'Yeah,' I say, sad, 'but I should have paid more attention to the old junkey nevertheless, who said there's a lover on every corner – they're all the same boy, don't get hung-up on one.'

'It isn't true, it isn't true, that's just what Yuri wants is for you to go down to Dante's now and the two of you'll laugh and talk me over and agree that women are good lays and there are lots of them. – I think you're like me you want one love – like, men have the essence in the woman, there's an essence' ('Yes,' I thought, 'there's an essence, and that is your womb') 'and the man has it in his hand, but rushes off to build big constructions.' (I'd just read her the first few pages of *Finnegans Wake* and explained them and where Finnegan is always putting up 'buildung supra buildung supra buildung' on the banks of the Liffey – dung!)

'I will say nothing,' I thought – 'Will you think I am not a man if I don't get mad?'

'Just like that war I told you about.'

'Women have wars too – '

Oh what'll we do? I think – now I go home, and it's all over for sure, not only now is she bored and has had enough but has pierced me with an adultery of a kind, has been inconstant, as prophesied in a dream, the dream the bloody dream – I see myself grabbing Yuri by the shirt and throwing him on the floor, he pulls out a Yugoslavian knife, I pick up a chair to bash him with, everybody's watching ... but I continue the day dream and I look into his eyes and I see suddenly the glare of a jester angel who made his presence on earth all a joke and I realize that this too with Mardou was a joke and I think, 'Funny Angel, elevated amongst the subterraneans.'

'Baby it's up to you,' is what she's actually saying, 'about how many times you wanta see me and all that – but I want to be independent like I say.'

And I go home having lost her love.

And write this book.

Pic

CHAPTER 1

Me and Grandpa

Ain't never nobody loved me like I love myself, cept my mother and she's dead. (My grandpa, he's so old he can remember a hunnerd years back but what happened last week and the day before, he don't know.) My pa gone away so long ago ain't nobody remember what his face like. My brother, ever' Sunday afternoon in his new suit in front of the house, out on that old road, and grandpa and me just set on the porch rockin and talkin, but my brother paid it no mind and one day he was gone and ain't never been back.

Grandpa, when he was alone, said he'd ten' the pigs and I go mend the fence yonder, and said, 'I seed the Lawd come thu that fence a hunnerd years ago and He shall come again.' My Aunt Gastonia come by buttin and puffin said that it was all right, she believed it too, she'd seen the Lord more times than they could ever count, and hallelujahed and hallelujahed, said, 'While's all this the Gospel word and true, little Pictorial Review Jackson' (that's me) 'must go to school to learn and read and write,' and grandpa looked at her plum in the eye like if'n to spit tobacco juice in it, and answered, 'Thass awright wif me,' jess like that, 'but that ain't the Lawd's school he's goin' to and he shall never mend his fences.'

So I went to school, and came on home from school the afternoon after it and seed nobody would ever know where I come from, if what they called it was North Carolina. It didn't feel like no North Carolina to me. They said I was the darkest, blackest boy ever come to that school. I always knowed *that*, cause I seen white boys come by my house, and I seed pink boys, and I seed blue boys, and I seed green boys, and I seed orange boys, then black, but never seed one so black as me.

Well, I gave this no never mind, and 'joyed myself and made some purty pies when I was awful little till I seed it rully did smell awful bad; and all that, and grandpa a-grinnin from the porch, and smokin his old green pipe. One day two white boys came by seed me and said I was verily black as nigger chiles go. Well, I said that I knowed *that* indeedy. They said they seed I was too small for what they was about, which I now forget, and I said it was a mighty fine frog peekin from his hand. He said it was no frog, but a TOAD, and said TOAD like to make me jump a hunnerd miles high, he said it so plain and loud, and they skedaddled over the hill back of my grandpa's property. So I knew they was a North Carolina, and they was a *toad*, and I dreamed of it 'at night.

On the crossroads Mr Dunaston let me and old hound dog sit on the steps of his store ever' blessed evenin and I heard the purty singin on the radio just as *plain*, and just as *good*, and learned me two, th'ee, seben songs and sing them. Here come Mr Otis one time in his big old au-to, bought me two bottles Dr Pepper, en I took one home to grandpa: *he* said Mr Otis was a mighty fine man and he knowed his pappy and his pappy's pappy clear back a hunnerd years, and they was good folks. Well, I knowed *that*: and we 'greed, and 'greed Dr Pepper allus did make a spankin' good fizzle for folkses' moufs. Y'all can tell how I 'joyed myself then.

Well here's all where it was laid out. My grandpa's house, it was all lean-down and 'bout to break, made of sawed planks sawed when they was new from the woods and here they was all wore out like poor dead stumplewood and heavin out in the middle. The roof was like to slip offen its hinges and fall on my grandpa's head. He make it no mind and set there, rockin. The inside of the house was clean like a ear of old dry corn, and jess as crinkly and dead and good for me barefoot as y'all seed if you tried it. Grandpa and me sleep in the big old tinkle-bed and gots room all over, it's so big. Hound dog sleep in the door. Never did close that door till winter come. I cut the wood, grandpa light it into stove. Set there eatin peas and greens and sassmeat and here's a BIG spoon and eat a lot till my belly's all out – when they was a lot. Well, Aunt Gastonia, she brings us food, here, there, last week, next month. Bring us sassmeat, storebread, streak-a-lean. Grandpa grow the peas in the field, and grow the corn field by the fence, and then we fetched the pigs what we grind outen our moufs cause we cain't chaw it. Hound dog eat too. House set in the middle of the field. Yonder's the road, sand road all wore hard and pebbly, and the mules comin' up and every now'n then a big au-to thrown up a fine cloud a mile high and me smellin it ever'where and sayin to myself, 'Now what fo the Lawd don't make hisself mo clean?' Then I snups out me nose, Shah! Well, over yonder is Mr Dunaston's store at the crossroads, and then the piney woods wif old crow settin ever' mornin on the branch jess cra-a-cra-a-kin, to beat hisself, and me say cra-cra-cra-cra jess like he do, and I gotsa laugh, ever' morning, hee hee hee, it tickle me so. Then yonder th' other way is Mr Dunaston's brother's tobacco, n'a big, big house Mr Otis live in, and Miz Bell's house in the middler the field and Miz Bell she like to be as old as grandpa and smoke the pipe jess like he do. Well, she like me. Ever' night ever'body sleep in this house and that house and ever' house, and the only thing you can hear is a old owl – hooo! hooo! – out in the woods, and yek! yek! yek! all the bats, and the yowlin hound dogs, 'n the cricket-bugs a-creakin' in the dark. Then there's the choo-choo out by TOWN, y'know. Only thing you can't hear is a old spider spinnin his cobweb. I go on in the shanty and break a cobweb – after I wipe myself that old spider, he make 'nother cobweb for me. Up yonder in the sky, they's a hunnerd motion stars and here on the ground hit's as *wet*, as like to'd rain. I gets me in the bed and grandpa say, 'Boy, keep your big wet feet from me!' but in a little bitty while my feets is dry and I'se tucked in good. Then I see the stars thu the window n' I sleep good.

Y'all can tell how I 'joyed myself then?

CHAPTER 2

What Happened

Po grandpa, he never get up one mornin, and ever'body come over from Aunt Gastonia's and said he was 'bout to die of misery. On grandpa's pillow I laid my head down and HE tell me it ain't so. And he yell to the Lord to git ever'body outen the house except the good hound dog. Hound dog set a-whinin' under the bed and lick grandpa in the hand. Aunt Gastonia shoo him out. 'Hound dog, shoo!' Aunt Gastonia wash my face at the pump. Aunt Gastonia, she put the rag in my ear and stop up the ear and take her finger and turn and turn till I'se 'bout to die. Well, I cry. Grandpa cry too. Aunt Gastonia's son, he run and he run down that road and pooty soon, here come Aunt Gastonia's son run and run back up the road and zip-zip I never seed nobody run s'fast. Then here come Mr Otis in his big old au-to and pull right in front of the house. Well, he was a pow'ful tall man with yaller hair, you know, and *he* 'membered me, and says, 'Well there, what's to become of you, li'l boy?'

Then he take grandpa by the hand, and roll up his eyeballs, and fish in the black satchel fo a thing he listens with, and listen, and ever'body else lean close and listen, and Aunt Gastonia slap her son away, and Mr Otis 'bout to tap grandpa with one hand under th'other on grandpa's chest, when him and grandpa gits they eyes fixed on theirselves all sow'ful and Mr Otis stop what he doing. 'Ah, old man,' Mr Otis say to grandpa, 'and how have you been?' And grandpa show his yaller teeth in a grin and he say, and he cackle, 'Yonder's the pipe, hit's a pow'ful smokin-pipe,' and wink at Mr Otis. Nobody know what he talk like that fo, but Mr Otis *he* know and grandpa he laugh so much he jess shake like the tree when the possum climb up in it. Mr Otis says 'Where?' and grandpa point to the shelf, still a'cacklin and 'joyin Mr Otis so. Well, he sho liked Mr Otis ever so much. Up yonder on the shelf so high I never seed it, Mr Otis fetched a pipe they was

100

talkin about. It was made outen corncob and it was the biggenest best pipe grandpa made. Mr Otis, he looks at it so sow'ful I never seed that man so. He say, 'Five years,' and that's all he say, 'case that was the last time he seed grandpa, and grandpa knowed it.

After a bit, grandpa fell asleep, and ever'body stand around talkin till I cain't see how anybody can sleep, and here's what they said. They said grandpa was mighty sick and would die for sho, and me, li'l Pic, well what was they t'do with me? Oh, it was a tar'ble lot of cryin they was doing. Aunt Gastonia and her friend Miz Jones, 'case they loved grandpa like I do, the son *he* cry too, and all the little bitty chiles that come in the door from the road t'see. Hound dog, he whined outdoor t'come in. Mr Otis, he told ever'body t'stop worryin' their minds so, mebbe grandpa be all right soon, but he'd no fo-sure about it, so he's gwine see about sendin grandpa to the *hospital*, and there he be all right. Ever'body 'gree this is what to do and's grateful to Mr Otis, 'case he pay with all his money t'see grandpa try to get good again. 'The boy,' he say, t' Aunt Gastonia, 'you sure your husband and your father see eye to eye with you 'bout keepin that boy?' And she say, 'The Lord shall bring mercy unto them.' And Mr Otis say, 'Well, I don't reckon it will be so but you take good care of him, hear, and let me know if ever'thing's all right.' Lordy, I cry when I heard ever'thing and ever'body talkin so. Oh Lordy, I cry when they takes poor grandpa and carry him to the car like some old sick run-over hound dog and lay him in the back seat, and carry him off to the *hospital*. I cry, Aunt Gastonia she close grandpa's door, and *he* never close it, never did once close it for a hunnerd years. The tar'ble fear make me sick and like to drop on the ground and dig me a hole and cry in it, n'hide, 'case I never seen anything but this house and grandpa all my born days, and here they come draggin me away from th'empty house and my grandpa's done died on me and can't help hisself dyin. Oh Lord, and I remember what he say 'bout the fence and the Lord, and 'bout Mr Otis and 'bout my big wet feet, and remember him so awful recent and him s'far gone, I cry, and shame ever'body.

CHAPTER 3

Aunt Gastonia's House

Well,they takes me down the road to Aunt Gastonia's house, and it's a big old busted house 'case they's eleben, twell folks livin there, from down the littlest baby-chile up to old Grandpa Jelkey 'at sits inside the house all old and blind. It ain't like grandpa's house no way. Is all them windows roundabout and a big brick chimbley, and the porch, it go clean around the house and chairs on it, and watermelon rinds and sand on the boards so's a body can't roll hisself without. My, I never seed such many flies in all born days like I seed in that house. No, I don't wantsa stay here. Trees in the barnyard, and cherry tree, and the good swing, but they's six, seben chiles all squealin and squawkin and the pigs is not so good as grandpa's pigs never nohow. I never seed nothin so tedious. No, I don't wantsa stay here. Gots no place to sleep at night exceptin in one bed with th'ee, fo boys, and I can't sleep with they elbows in my face.

Grandpa Jelkey, that man scare me 'case he say, 'Bring that boy here,' and they brings me, and he take a holt of me by th' arms and look at me with one great big yaller eye but don't aim it right, poor thing, and look clear over my head and can't see nothing. Th' other eye, it ain't there no more, th' eyeball sunk inside his head. He got no eyes, that old man. He holt me tight and hurt me, and he say, 'This here is the boy. Well I ain't gots to touch the boy more'n one time a day.' Aunt Gastonia, she run up and pull me off. 'Why you wantsa curse that boy when y'already cursed ever'body seven times? It ain't his fault what his father done to your eyes, he's jess a chile.' And Grandpa Jelkey, he shout up, 'I'se gwine touch him seben times afore he dies, ain't nobody stop me.' 'You ain't neither,' Aunt Gastonia shout up, and Uncle Sim, that's Aunt Gastonia's husband, he gotsa take Aunt Gastonia outdoor, and me, I gotsa run and hide in the barnyard, 'case I'se sho scared Grandpa

102

Jelkey reach out and catch me again. Nos'r, I don't like Aunt Gastonia's house, no.

Serpentine, Grandpa Jelkey sit in the corner and eat offen his knee and ever'body else eat 'round the table-top, and Grandpa Jelkey, hear ever'body talkin, and say, 'Is that you, boy?' and mean me. I hide b'hind Aunt Gastonia. 'Come on stand by me, boy, so's I can touch you twicet. T'won't leave me none but four, and then you pays the curse.' 'Never pay no mind what he say,' Aunt Gastonia say to me. Uncle Sim he don't say nothin, and he never *look* at me neither, and I'se so scared and so sickly, well, I don't expect I'd a-lived in Aunt Gastonia's house long but t'go die in the woods and being so lowly and blue. Aunt Gastonia say I gits sick and lose eleben pounds, I'se so awful and feeble and lain in the dust all day. 'What for you wantsa cry in the dirt, chile,' she says to me, 'and git all that mud on your face like that?' She gotsa wipe the mud. Aunt Gastonia, it wasn't ever her, it was Grandpa Jelkey, and Uncle Simeon, and all the chiles th'ow sand at me. And ain't *nobody* take me see grandpa in the hospital. 'Oh Lord, I gotsa stop cryin so.'

Grandpa Jelkey, he reach out the window and cotch me and hurt me so I'se fall down dead, and he yell, and he whoop, and he says, 'Now I'se cotch the boy and now I done touch him twicet!' – Then he say, then he say, 'Th'ee! – fo! – ' and Aunt Gastonia she yank me away s'ard I fall in the ground. 'I done seed the sign, when I reach out to cotch him,' Grandpa Jelkey yell, 'and ain't but th'ee left now.' Aunt Gastonia bust out cryin and fall on the bed and thrash hesself and don't know what and all the chiles run down the road t'git Uncle Sim what's in the field with the mule, and he come runnin to the road. Lordy, then that old Grandpa Jelkey come out on the porch lookin f'me and spread his arms f'me, and he come right straight t'where I is standin like he was not blind nohow, but then he stumble over the chair and yowl out, fall down and hurt hisself. Ever'body say Oh! Uncle Sim pick up th' old man and carry him in the house and put him on the bed, and th' old man gaspin. Uncle Simeon, he told cousin take me outdoor, so me and cousin go stand outdoor, and hear Uncle Sim and Aunt Gastonia a-yellin at each other.

'What for you wantsa keep that boy in this house what has the curse laid on him, fool woman?' Uncle Sim yell. And Aunt Gastonia, she pray and she pray, 'Oh Lord, he jess a chile, he ain't

103

done a thing t'nobody, what for the Lord bring shame and destruction on the head of a innocent lamb, and a leastest chile.' 'I ain't got nothin to do with what the Lord decide,' yell Uncle Sim. Aunt Gastonia say, 'Lord God, his blood is my blood, and my sister's blood is my blood, Oh Lord, dear Jesus, save us from sin, save my husband from sin, save my father-'n-law from sin, save my chillun from sin, and Lord, dear Lord, save *me*, Gastonia Jelkey, from sin.' Uncle Sim, he come out on the poch and give the blackenest look, and walk away, 'case Aunt Gastonia she pray all night now, and *he* don't got nothing to say. Grandpa Jelkey, he fall asleep.

Well, cousin older'n me take me down the road and show me TOWN out yonder, 'case he knowed I'se so forlorn. He say, 'Tonight Satty night, ever'body git drunk and go to TOWN yonder and they *rocks*, thass what they do, yas'r.' I say, 'What you mean *rocks*?' He say, 'Boy, they gots jumpin-music and jamboree-singin and dancin, all that truck. Yas'r, I seed it Satty night, had some barbecue pig and daddy he drink the bottle down like 'is' – and he throw his big head back, cousin, and he have the biggenest head, y'know, and show me and say – 'Whooee!' Then he jump around a-holtin hissel by the arms t'show me, and he say, 'This here dancin. B'you cain't go to no jamboree 'case you gotsa curse on you.' So me'n cousin go down the road a bit, and they's all the lights of TOWN I ain't never seed before, and we sits up in the apple tree and sees all that. But I is so lowdown it don't make no neither much to me. Lordy, what's I care about all that old town?

Well, cousin go thisaway and I go thataway, and I traipse back up the woods and down the hill to Mr Dunaston's store, and hear me some radio singin again. Then, you bet, I go way down that road t'grandpa's house. It's all so.still, s'empty, well, ain't nobody know it but I is 'bout to die and go to my death in the ground. Old hound dog yowlin at grandpa's door, but *he* ain't livin there, and I ain't livin there neither, ain't nobody livin 'bout it, and he yowl his soul.

Well, grandpa seed the Lord come thu the fence a hunnerd years ago, and now he gotsa die in the hospital and never get t'see no fence nor nothin no more. I ask to th' Lord, 'What for the Lord do it to po grandpa?'

I cain't remember no more 'bout Aunt Gastonia's house and ever'thing done happened there.

CHAPTER 4

Brother Come To Fetch Me

A boy like me ain't go no place to sleep lessen he stay where he's at, and I sho didn't wantsa stay at Aunt Gastonia's no more, but jess ain't was nowhere for me to sleep but that po woman's house, so I traipse back thu the black woods, yes'r and there she is, Aunt Gastonia, waitin up f'me with the oil lamp in the kitchen. 'Sleep, my chile,' she say to me, and so kindly I'se like to fall and sleep on her knee, like I done on my mother's knee when I'se a little bitty chile, before she got dic. 'Aunt Gastonia take care of you no matter what,' she say, and stroke m'head, and I fall asleep.

Well, I'se sick in the bed for two, th'ee, seben days and it rain and rain all the time and Aunt Gastonia feed me grits and sugar and heat up collard greens for me. Grandpa Jelkey, he sit on the other side of the house and say, 'Bring that boy to me,' but ain't nobody brings me to him nor tell him where I is, and Aunt Gastonia tell ever'body to shush. Grandpa Jelkey cotch cousin thu the window like he done me, and he say, 'Nope, I reckon this ain't the boy.' And cousin he howl like I did.

I sleep two days, and don't wake up none but for to sleep again, and Aunt Gastonia she send cousin to fetch Mr Otis, but Mr Otis he gone up NORTH. 'Where he gone up NORTH?' she say to cousin, and cousin say, 'Why he jess gone up NORTH'. 'What part the NORTH he gone up there?' and cousin say, 'Why, he's gone up to NORTH VIRGINIA.' Aunt Gastonia she bow her po head down and don't know whatsa do.

So Mr Otis is gone, and Aunt Gastonia pray for me, and bring Miz Jones to pray for me too.

Uncle Sim, he look at me once, and he say to Aunt Gastonia, 'That boy's 'bout to folly his grandaddy I reckon,' and she look up to the roof and say, 'Amen, the world ain't fit for no such a lamb, Jesus save his soul.' 'Well,' say Uncle Sim, 'I don't guess it's but one less mouf t'feed,' and she shriek, 'Oh Jehovah guide my man from sinful ways.'

'Shush your mouf, woman, this man ain't got no time for sinful ways and he ain't a-gonna get no new stove this winter neither, 'case that tobacco patch been cursed, hear, the bugs done started eatin leaves since that boy been here.' And he stomp out the door.

Well, thass the longest talk I ever hear that man make.

I lay in the bed one Satty mornin, and WHOOP! they's ever'body yellin and talkin outdoor, and carryin on so loud I try to see and stretch my head way out but cain't see nothin. They all comes traipsin up the porch. Well I pull my head back 'case I'se sick. Well, who do you guess come in that door, and all the chillun grinnin behind?

If it ain't my brother, dog my cats, and he change so much since he go away from me and grandpa, I cain't for sure say *who* that man is standin in the door, 'case he gots a bitty round hat on his head with a little bitty button on top of it, and hairs a-hangin from his chin p'culiar, and he all thin, and lean, and all drew-out tall, and sorry-lookin too. He laugh and laugh when he see me and come over to the bed for t'catch me, and look at me in th'eye. 'Here he is,' he say, and it ain't nobody he talk it to, 'case he say it to hisself and smile, and me, I'se so s'prised I don't say nothin. Well, y'know, I'se so s'prised it make me sit up in the bed.

All the chillun is grinnin, but Aunt Gastonia she trouble and fuss hesself, poor soul, and she keep lookin over her shoulder for fear Uncle Sim come up the road, 'case he don't like my brother neither, I don't reckon. 'Looky here John, where you been and what's you come here for?' she say to my brother, and he say, 'Hey now' and jump up and do the most comical shufflin 'bout the house I ever seed and I laugh, and all the chillun laugh with me, and Grandpa Jelkey, he rare up and say, 'What fo ever'body laugh?'

'I come here to fetch Mister Pic, ma'm, and bring him on my *magic carpet* up NORTH to NEW YORK CITY, your grace,' he say, and do the most comical bow-down and fetch off his comical hat and show ever'body his head. The chiles and me, we gotsa laugh again and you ain't never seed such 'joyin and laughin. 'Who that talkin?' Grandpa Jelkey say, and he say, 'Why-all's them chillun laugh so?' But ain't nobody tell him.

106

'How come you here?' Aunt Gastonia ask my brother, and he tuck his hat under his arm and say, 'Why, for to get my brother, that's how come,' and he don't traipse about no more, and the chillun teeter on th' edge of their feets, 'case they wantsa laugh some more, but now the big folkses solemn actin.

Me, well great day in the mornin, I get up and trample on the bed with m'feet, hear, I cotch m' breath so hard and feel so good. Whoo!

'You dassn't,' Aunt Gastonia say to him, and he say, 'Yes I do, and why do you say I dassn't?' 'Why?' Aunt Gastonia say, 'and ain't you some no-account man come in here and say you's gwine take this sick chile away from the roof over his head?'

'No roof of his own, Aunt Gastonia,' he say, and that woman rare up and yell, 'Don't Aunt Gastonia with *me* none, folks around know you's no-account and never did anything b'drink and traipse around the highway ever' blessed night and then jess up and leave when you most was needed by your po old folks. Go away, go away.'

'Who that in the house?' Grandpa Jelkey yell, and fuss and pull at th'arms of his chair and look around. Well, you know, me and the chillun don't laugh no more now.

'Lady,' say my brother, 'how you talk,' and Aunt Gastonia she yell, 'Don't lady *me*, and don't come here fetchin no chile from outen my roof and learn him the ways of evil like you done learned from your pappy. YES,' she yell, 'you no better'n your pappy ever was and no better'n no *Jackson* ever was.'

Well, I seed all about my life right then. 'Who that man in the house?' yell Grandpa Jelkey, and he was so pow'ful mad I ain't never seed that old blind man so mad. He fetch up his cane and holt it tight. Well, right then here come Uncle Sim on the porch, and when that man see my brother standin in the middle of the house his eyes git big they's like chicken eggs, and white, and round, and hard. And he say soft, and p'culiar, 'You ain't got no call bein in this house, man, and you knowed that.' He don't turn away none but reach behind the door and pull out that old shovel what's leaning there. 'Git out of here.' Aunt Gastonia cotch her neck quick, and open her mouth to scream, but ain't scarce ready yet, and ever'body wait.

CHAPTER 5

Some Argufyin

Well, you know, my brother he ain't so scared of Mr Sim with his big old shovel, and say, 'I ain't pickin up this here chair to hit nobody with, nor kill nobody 'cause I come here peaceable and quiet, but I'm sure holdin on to this chair so long as you hold that shovel, Mr Jelkey,' and he holt up that chair like the man with lion. His eyeballs get red and he don't like so much none of this. Uncle Sim, he look at him, then he look at Aunt Gastonia, and he say, 'What's that boy doin here, tell me, hear?'

And she tell him. And he say, 'Well then, hush up, woman,' and he turn to my brother and say, 'Well go *on*, and go on mighty quick,' and he point out the door.

'Get him, Sim,' Grandpa Jelkey yell, and he get up from his chair again and holt out his cane, and yell, 'Hit him over the head with the stick, boy.'

'Sit that old man down,' say Uncle Sim, but Aunt Gastonia she start wailin and carryin on for me, 'case she don't wants me to leave with my brother, and she say, 'No, Sim, no, that boy's sick and go hungry and cotch cold and ever' single thing in the world will happen to him and he'll turn bad, sinful bad, with that man, and the Lord shall drop it on my soul like the hot irons of hell and perdition, on your soul too, and on this house,' and she say this rarin up most tearful and pitiful, for me to see, and come over to hold me and hide me from ever'body and kiss me all over. Whoo!

'Put on your clothes, Pic,' my brother say to me, and Uncle Sim put down the shovel, and my brother put down the chair, and Aunt Gastonia cry and cry, and holt me, poor woman, and I jess can't move an inch I'se so sorry t'see ever'thing come so mean and bad. Well, Uncle Sim, he come over and cotch Aunt Gastonia and pull her 'way from me, and my brother find my shirt and put it on me, and Aunt Gastonia shriek. Lordy, I find my shoes and

I find my hole-hat and I'se ready to go, and brother fetch me up piggy-back, and here we go for the door.

Well then, what you supposed happened? Here come Mr Otis' au-to licketysplit to the door, and out he come and knock on the house, and look in, and say, 'Well what's this?' and look at ever'body and push his hat back.

Well, here go ever'body talkin at the same time. Aunt Gastonia, she argufy so hard, and explain so loud, and pray so shriekly, ain't nobody else can hear what's goin on, and Mr Otis listen to her and look at ever'body else most quiet, and don't say nothin. Well, brother put me down 'case he can't scarce stand there with me on his back whilst ever'body yell, and Mr Otis take my wrist, and listen, then he roll up m'eyeball like he done poor grandpa and look in there, then he back up and look me all over, and say, 'Well, 'pears Pic's in good enough health anyway. Now will you explain ever'thing once around again for me?' and, after Aunt Gastonia done that, and he shooked his head yes, uh-huh, yes, uh-huh, he say, 'Well, I don't want to interfere with you folks but I don't guess I was wrong when I said it wouldn't ever do to bring the boy here, ma'm, and likewise don't guess he can stay here.' He look at Uncle Sim when he say that, and Uncle Sim say, 'Yes'r, I don't 'spect, Mr Otis, ain't been but trouble since he come here.' Then Mr Otis go over and say hello to Grandpa Jelkey, and Grandpa Jelkey say, 'I'se shore pleased to hear your voice again, Mr Otis' and he jess sit there grinning from ear to ear 'case Mr Otis visitin.

Then Mr Otis say, 'I feel I owe it to this child's grandaddy to see he's taken care of proper,' and he turn to my brother, and I don't reckon he like my brother no more'n ever'body else, 'case he say, and shake his head, 'It don't 'pear to me like you can take care of this child, neither. You got a *job* up north?'

'Yes'r, I got a job,' my brother say, and he make a plain face and tuck his hat under his arm again, but Mr Otis don't 'pear to 'gree with him, and say, 'Well, is that the only clothes you got to wear when you travel?' and ever'body look at my brother's clothes, which ain't much of a much, and Mr Otis say, 'All you got there is a army jacket, and there's holes in the side of your pants, and they don't fit right much anyhow because they're all swole up at the legs and come down to your ankles so's I can't see how you can take 'em off, and you've got a red shirt that ain't been washed, and GI boots pretty well scraggly by now, and that there *beret* on your head, so how do you ever expect me to believe you've got a job when you come travellin on home like that?'

'Well sir,' my brother say, 'it's the *style* nowadays in NEW YORK,' but that don't satisfy Mr Otis none, and he say, 'Goatee and all? Well, I just got back from New York City myself and I ain't 'shamed to say it was my first time up there, and I don't think it's a fit place for folks to live whether they be white or colored. I don't see any harm takin care of your brother if you stay home, for after all your grandaddy's house *is* still standin and you can get a job *home* as well as ever'where else.'

'Well sir,' my brother say, 'I got a wife in New York,' and Mr Otis say quick, 'Does she work?' and my brother teeter a little bit on that, and say, 'Yes, she works,' and Mr Otis say, 'Well then who's goin to take care of this child durin the day?' and my brother get red in the eyeball again 'case he can't conjure up no more to say. Well, you know, I has my fingers crossed, 'case I be so pleased when my brother and me was headin for that door, and here I'se stopped dead in that old house again.

'He'll go to *school* in the daytime,' my brother say, and give Mr Otis a look all tuckered-out and s'prised from such some talk, and Mr Otis, he smile, and he say, 'Well, I don't cast any doubt on your intentions, but who's goin to watch that child when he comes *home* from school in that NEW YORK *traffic*? Who's goin to help him cross the street in that coldhearted city, see he don't get run over by a truck and such-like? Yes, and where's that boy likely to get some *fresh air* to breathe? And proper friends that don't go about with knives and guns at fourteen? I ain't seen anything like it in all *my* born days. I don't aim to wish such a life on that boy, and don't guess his grandaddy would neither in these last days of his, and I'm only doin this because I owe it at least to a very old friend of mine who taught me how to fish when I was no higher 'n his knee. Well,' and he turn to Aunt Gastonia, and heave a sigh all under him, 'the only proper thing to do is put him in a good home till he's old enough t' decide for himself.' And he pull out a fine book from his coat, and uncork a fine pen, and write most handsome inside it. 'First thing in the morning I'll call up and make whatever arrangements are necessary, and meanwhile the boy can stay here,' and he turn to Aunt Gastonia, 'because I'm sure, ma'm, you'll see that ever'thing is maintained proper.' Yes, and Mr Otis speak jess as fine and jess as pleasin as that.

But it ain't so pleasin to me none, 'case I don't like to stay in Aunt Gastonia's house 'nother minute, 'nother night, 'nother no time, nor go to no GOOD HOME like Mr Otis said, nor see m'brother traipse off so lone and blue down the road like he done. Well, he look back over his shoulder, poor brother, ever' now and then, and dust up the sand slow with his ARMY BOOTS, and Aunt Gastonia's chillun they folly him a piece down the road 'case they like him so and wantsa see him shuffle and bow-down some more like he done in the house, but he don't. Mr Otis stay on the porch talkin to Uncle Sim till my brother gone in the woods, then Mr Otis get in his big au-to and go.

Well O well, they I was.

CHAPTER 6

I Go Thu the Window

Come nightfall ever'body go to bed, and I'se in the bed with my th'ee little bitty cousins and can't sleep none, and say to myself, 'Oh me, what happen to me next?' and I'se wearisome for ever'thing and can't neither cry nor nothing no more. Ever'thing I fixed on done run out on me and wasn't nothin I could do. Lord, it was a bad long night.

Well, next thing I know I'se sleepin 'case I wake up and hear the hound dogs yelpin outdoor, and Uncle Sim open the window from where he sleep and sing out, 'Shet up that snappin and squallin out there,' and Aunt Gastonia say, 'What for the hound dogs cry?'

And Uncle Sim look, and come back in and say, 'Y'ere's a black sat spittin in the tree up yonder', and he go back to sleep. Aunt Gastonia she say, 'Black cat go 'way from my do,' and she make the sign, and go back to sleep likewise.

Then I hear m' little bitty cousin Willis what sleep by the window say, 'Who dat?' and I hear, ever so soft, 'Shhh,' and I look. Whooee, it's my brother in the window, and me and Willis creep up over little bitty Henry, and puts our noses to the screen, and then Jonas, he come too, and put *his* nose to the screen. 'It the man done dance,' say little Willis, and he go, 'Hee hee hee,' but my brother put his finger on his mouth and say, 'Shhh!' Here ever'body listen close for Aunt Gastonia and Uncle Sim, and Grandpa Jelkey y'at sleep in the corner, but they jess sleepin and snorin, and the hound dogs whine so they don't hear nothin neither.

'What for you come here, Mister Dancin Man?' say little Willis, and Jonas say, 'Uh-huh?' and little Henry wake up and say, '*Git offen my laig!*' awful loud and ever'body jump back in the bed under the covers and m'brother duck down behind the window.

Well, woof, you know, I hold up my breath then. But ain't nobody wake up.

Ever'body rare back up the window, soft.

'Is you gwine shuffle again?' Jonas say, and little bitty Henry he woke up and seed what was in the window, and rub his eye, and say, 'Ish-yo-gin-shuff-gin?' 'case he always r'peats what Jonas say. My brother say, 'Shhh', and little bitty Henry put his finger to his mouth and turn around and nudge *me*, you know, like it was my foot, then ever'body look at my brother again.

'I'se come to get Pic,' my brother say thu his hands, 'but I come back tomorrow or next year and dance all over for ever'one of you and give yu each fifty cents, hear me now?'

'What fo you don't wantsa dance now?' little Willis say, and Jonas say, 'Jess a little bit?' and little bitty Henry say, 'Jiz-il-bit, hmm?' and my brother put his head on one side, and look at ever'body, and say, 'Well, I do really b'lieve they's a Heaven somewhere,' and he say, 'Pic, git in your clothes quiet whilst I dance for these folks,' and I do that quick and my brother he shuffle-up soft and dance in the yard in the moonlight and the chiles watch with a great big old s'prised grin on they faces. Well, you never seed such a dance like he done b'neath the moon like that, and no chiles like them seed one neither.

'*Shet up that snappin and squallin out there!*' yell Uncle Sim from t'other side of the house, and I tell *you*, ever'body duck down again s'fast nobody seed th' other do it. But Uncle Sim, he only mean the hounds, poor sleepin man.

Then ever'body raise up 'nother time again.

Brother undone the screen from the window and say 'Shh' and reach in, and Jonas say 'Shh' and little Henry say 'S' and I cotch brother's neck, and out I go with my head first and then the feet, and dog my cats, and cat my dogs, and looky-here, if I ain't out in that barnyard in the middle of the dark and ready to leave and go.

'Less go,' my brother say, and he haul me up on his back like he done in th' afternoon, and we turn around and look at the chiles in the window, and they's so sorry-lookin they's fixin to cry, you know, and my brother know this, and he say, 'Don't cry, chillun, 'case me and Pic come back tomorrow or next year

113

and we all have a big fine time t'gether and go down the crick and fish, and eat candy, and th'ow the baseball, and tell tales t'each other, and climb up the tree and *hant* the folks below, and *all* such fine things, you jess wait awhile, you jess see, y'hear me now?'

'Yas'r,' Jonas say, and little Henry say, 'Yass,' and little Willis say 'Uh-huh' and off me and m' brother go, 'cross the barnyard and over the fence and into the woods and don't make a sound. Whoo! We gone and done it.

CHAPTER 7

We Come to Town

Grandpa, it was the darkenest night 'case the moon got covered over by clouds jess as soon as brother and me reach the woods, and that moon was jess a scant banana moon and showed but scraggy and feeble betwixt the clouds when it look out. It got cold, too, and I shore was chill. I reckon they was a rainstorm comin to warm me, 'case I don't at all feel so good as I done when we begun. Seem like they was somethin I forgot to do, or somethin I forgot to bring from back at Aunt Gastonia's house, but I knowed they was nothin like that, exceptin I all dreamed it. Lordy why'd I go dass dream such a thing and fret myself there? Way across the woods and thu the black yonder, here come the *train*, but it's pow'ful far off 'case me and brother only getsa hear it when the wind blow, and hear it *wooo* – all long draw-out and goin away, sound like waitin for to get to the hills. Shoo! it was cold, and p'culiar, and black. But my brother, he don't mind.

He carry me thu the woods a space, then he put me down and say, 'Woof, boy, I ain't goin to carry you on my back all the way to New York,' and we tramp along till we get to the corn field, and then he say, 'Here, you sure you can walk all right after bein sick like you was?' and I say, 'Yas'r, I'se jess a little chill,' and walk along.

My brother say, 'I get you a coat first thing,' and then he say, 'Get up, little boy,' and he haul me up on his back again and look around at me out the corner of his eye. 'Listen t' me Pic,' he say, 'you're every bit sure you want to come along with me ain't you?' and I say, 'Yas'r.'

'Well what for you call me *sir* when you know I'm your brother?'

'Yas'r,' I say, and then I cotch myself and say 'Yas'r, brother,' and don't know what to say. Well, I reckon I was scared for I don't scarce know where we's goin and what happen to me when

115

we get there if we gets there, and it don't sit right to myself to *ask* brother 'at come get me so glad and so pleased like that.

'Listen to me, Pic,' he say, 'you jess go along with me till we get home and call me *Slim* like ever'body else, do, hear?'

'Yas'r, Slim,' I say, and then I cotch myself again, and say, 'Yass, Slim.'

'Well there you go,' he laugh. 'Now say, you seen that black cat back yonder in the Jelkeys' tree that had all them hound dogs barkin at it? I brung it there myself to make them dogs miss me, and didn't it spit, and fetch them up fine and bring us good luck that old black cat? Well, lookout!' Slim say to a tree, and dodge of it, and duck behind it, and bark at it, and go 'Fsst!' like a cat, and both of us laugh some. That's the way *he* was, grandpa.

'Po little boy,' he say, and give a sigh, and hitch me up higher on his back. 'I guess you're as much scared of ever'thing like a grown man is. It's like the man say in the Bible – A fugitive and a vagabond shalt thou be in the earth. You ain't scarce eleven years old and already knowed that, I don't guess you didn't. Well, I come and made a vagabond out of you proper,' and we walk along and come to see the lights of town up ahead, and he don't say nothin. Then here we go step on the road.

'Now, I'll tell you where we're goin,' my brother say like if he read my mind and see all the troubles in it, and he say, 'Then we'll unnerstand each other fine and be friends to go out to the world together. When I heard about grandpa I knowed all the trouble and shame that would come down on your head, Pic, and told Sheila, that's my wife, she'll be your new mother now, and she agreed with me and said – Go down get that poor chile. Well,' he said, 'Sheila's a mighty fine woman and you see pretty soon. So here I come down South for you 'case I'm the only kin you got left, and you're the only kin I got, baby. Now, you know why Mr Otis give Grandpa Jackson that shack and that piece of land you was born on? – and why Mr Otis wanted to help you today?'

'Nos'r, Slim,' I say, and I shore wantsa hear it.

'Because your grandpa was born a slave and Mr Otis' grandpa owned him once, you never knowed that, did you?'

'Nos'r, Slim, nobody never told me that,' I say, and seem to me I heard folks talk about *slave* one time, and it fetch up recollections, you know.

116

'Mr Otis,' my brother say, 'he's a good man and feels he owes some of the colored folks some help now and then, and he has a nice way by him though it ain't by *me*, and mean well. Ever'body mean well, in their own pitiful way, and Aunt Gastonia mostly, poor woman. Uncle Sim Jelkey ain't no bad man, he's jess poor and can't support no vagabond Pics like you none. He don't too much hate anybody in his inside heart. Old Grandpa Jelkey, he's jess a old crazy man and I don't guess I'd – be crazy too if the same thing happened to me that happened to him. I tell you about that a minute. Well, I don't aim to see you go to no *foster home* like Mr Otis was fixin to send you today. Now, you know why Aunt Gastonia take you in but the menfolk Jelkeys don't want you?'

Well, I wantsa hear this, and I say, 'Why that?'

'That's because your daddy, Alpha Jackson, my daddy as well as yours, done blinded old Grandpa Jelkey in a fearsome fight about ten years ago and ain't nothin but bad blood left betwixt the two families. Aunt Gastonia, she was your mother's sister and loved your mother very much all her life, and took care of her right down the end when daddy come out of five years' sentence in the work gang, three of 'em in the Dismal Swamp, and never did come back to her.'

'Where'd he go?' I ax my brother, and try to remember my father's face, but it wasn't no use.

'Nobody know,' my brother say, and he walk along glum, and he say, 'Little man, your father was a *wild man* and a *bad man* and that's all he was, or is, and whether he's alive or dead and where-*ever* he's at tonight. Your mother's long dead, poor soul, and nobody blamed *her* for becomin crazy and dyin like she done. Boy,' my brother say to me, and turn his head to look at me, 'you and me come from the *dark*.' He said that, and said it jess as glum.

Well, here we come off the sand road and step on the most level and pleasin road I ever seed, and it's got white posts on the side with little bitty jewels shinin where the road go across the creek, and's got a fine white line painted in the middle of it and all such things. Well! And yonder straight ahead's all the lights of town, and here come three, four au-tos followin each other and havin a fine fast time, zoom, zoom, zoom.

'Well,' my brother say, 'you still want to come along with me?'

'Yas'r, Slim, I shore do wantsa go with you.'

117

'Boy,' he say, 'you and me's hittin that old road for the WAY-yonder. Hey, look out everybody, here we come,' and ain't nobody 'round he say that to, but here we go jumpin down the road along two, th'ee white houses, both of us feelin so fine, and my brother say, 'Here we come to the outskirts of town,' and wave his arm and yell, 'Wheee,' and we hoop-de-doop along.

Here we go by a old white house as big as the woods in back of it, and the house got white poles and a porch mighty pleasin to see up front, and ever so many grand windows clear round back, and lights shinin from out the windows on the handsome grassy yard, and my brother say, 'Yonder's the ancestrial home of General Clay Tucker Jefferson Davis Calhoun retired hero of the Seventeenth Regimental Divisional Brigade of the Confederate Union 'at got hisself shot in the left side tibular tendon and got hisself stick-pinned with a Gold Star Purple Honour of Congress medal and is now a hunnerd years old in his libr'y up yonder writin the Immemoriam Memories of the Gettysburg Shiloh Battle of Smoky Appamatoxburg, whoo!' and he carry on like that with ever'thing, and he don't care.

And here we go jumpin 'longside a regular house, and another regular house, then they's a whole heap of regular houses, and then they get un-regular and all red-rock colour and lights pop up ever'where you see. Whoo! I never seed so many lights, and poles, and window-glass, nor so many people walkin on such even and fine roads. 'This is town,' my brother say, and well, you know, it seem to me jess 'bout then I seed this here TOWN a long time ago with my mother in a au-to, when we come to the movie show one time and I was little and small and couldn't guess to remember such things. And now here I was in town again, but I was growed-up and I was goin out to the *world* with my brother. Well, ever'thing began to be pow'ful fetchin to watch at.

Here we turn thu a black old place and my brother say, 'This here's the alley you're going to wait for me in whilst I get some sandwiches for the bus,' and he put me down 'case he's all tucker out, and he take my hand and we walk. Here we come to the end of the alley, right across from a road at's all lit-up and brightly, but the alley it's in a shadow for me to wait in. 'Yonder's the chicken shack,' he say. 'I'll go cross the street quick, and don't dass let nobody see you in case the Jelkeys done woke up and fix to send somebody find us, hear? Stand right here,' he say, and push me

118

agin the red-rock wall, and set me there, and then off he go toot across that *street*.

Well, grandpa, they I was with my back agin that wall, and look up at the sky betwixt it and th'other wall, and ever'where I turn my ear I hear au-tos, and folkses talkin, and all kinds of noises and music, and I tell you, it was the noise of ever'body *doin somethin* at the same time all over with they hands and feet and voices, jess as plain. I never heard it before in the country, exceptin it come to my ear, jess like the water in the crick way yonder in the nighttime, swash, swash, and come most jumble-up and jolly. I'se so still and listenin, seem like *ever'body* doin somethin 'cept me. Across the street is that chicken shack, and it ain't nothin but a little bitty old shack jess like it say, but's got a most pow'ful bright light inside and they's men sittin in front of a long table-top, and they's eatin somethin 'at smell so *good* to me my mouth start waterin right where I is. They's a heap of radio music in there, and I can hear it clear across the street loud, hear the man sing: *'Where you been hiding baby, been looking everywhere, how come you treat me mean, can't you see I care?'* Well, it was fine radio music, the best I ever did hear, and come out of a big box with red and yaller lights turnin round in it. Over the door they was a wheel spin in a screen, and go humm, humm, and behind it a body could hear still another humm-humm from far away and it sound like a biggener wheel than that. Well, I reckon that was the *world wheel* I heard then. Wasn't it, grandpa? Oh, I was jess pleased.

I say to myself, 'I jess take two step-ups this *alley*,' and I move up along the wall and come to see more of the street. Whoo! It shore was brightly and pleasin.

Then here come my brother out of the chicken shack with a paper bag in his hand, and here come a bunch of men along the street, and they see him and yell, 'Hey there Slim, what you doin down from NEW YORK?' And he yell, 'Hello there Harry, and hello there Mr Redtop Tenorman, and hello there Smoky Joe. Well, what you boys up to?' and they say, 'Oh, we jess draggin along, you know.' And he say, 'Ain't heard you boys jump in a *long* time,' and they say, 'Oh, we jump now and then. Say, how you make it with that mustache on your chin?' My brother say, 'Oh, jess goin along tryin to have a good time, you know,' and they say, 'Well hey now,' and go off down the street and ever'body say see you later.

119

Yes, I shore liked town and never knowed it was so lively.

Me and brother sneak on down the alley and back to the skirts of town, and skedaddle along feelin good 'case we gets to eat some of them sandwiches soon and 'case brother say we wait for the *bus* by the *junction*, and that bus it's about due any minute, and when we get on that bus I won't be cold no more, and he won't neither. 'Bus station ain't no place for us tonight, boy,' he says to me, and he say, 'Oh well, oh well, and who cares, I guess it's all the same when you believe in the Lord like I do, now say, You hear me Lord?'

And we sit on the white posts with the shiny buttons in em and wait 'bout half an hour for the bus, or two half hours, I don't recollect.

Here it come. It come big and brawly in the road, and said 'WASHINGTON' on it, and the man at the wheel jam down the speed to stop for us, and it go zoom-boom right by us like it NEVER stop, and spit sand and wind and a old hot smell in my face, but stop yonder jess for us, and we run for it. Well, when I seed that big machine I said to myself, 'Ain't nobody know where *I'm* goin in this thing but my brother watch over me from now on.'

I never see Aunt Gastonia no more now.

CHAPTER 8

The Bus Go Up North

Grandpa, ain't gonta tell too much about the bus 'case a heap of doins was croppin up in NEW YORK, and I didn't have no notion about em in that bus, and jess gawked, you know.

Well, brother and me paid the man some money, then we walked back thu the people in the seats and ever'body look at us and we look at them, then we sit down in the back sofa, only it ain't rightly a soft sofa, and there we sit lookin straight ahead over ever'body's head at the driver, and he turn off the light and zoom-up the bus, and faster and faster we go with two big old lights leadin us the way thu the land. Brother fall asleep right away, but I stayed awake. I reckon we left *North Carolina* after 'bout a half hour, or two half hours, 'case the road change from black to brown and on each side of it I didn't get to see no more houses but jess the wilderness. I guess it was jess great big old woods without no houses, and dark? and black? and jess as solemn? It was the *wilderness* Aunt Gastonia pray about when she pray agin it so loud.

And here come the rain pourin down on that wilderness, and the road run wet and lonesome right thu it.

It was a scarifying thing to see and make a body glad he's in a bus with a whole lot of people.

I watched ever'body all night long, but they was most sleepin in their chairs and it was too black to see, and I tried to see, but it wasn't no use. I shore didn't wantsa go to sleep that night.

I say to myself, 'Pic, you're going to *New York* now, and ain't it somethin, now ain't it?' and I prod myself, and feel good.

And I got all sleepy p'culiar in m'eyes 'case I sleep this time of the evenin back home here, and over to Aunt Gastonia's too, so next thing I know I jess has to sleep, and that's all I done that night.

Come 'bout mornin I look up and see where I am, in the *bus*, and

121

can't believe it, and say to myself, 'Now that's why I'se bouncin so dadblame much.' And I look over to brother, and he's still sleepin and's got the whole back sofa to hisself and's all stretched out loose and peaceful, and I'se pleased to see him sleep so 'case I know he must be tired. And I look out the window.

And you know, I never seed anything so pow'ful grand and big, and I seed pow'fuller and grander things since then, all the way to *Califomy*. What I seed then was jess like when the first time I seed the *world* I tell you. It was a great river with a tree shore on both sides, and poureds a whole power of water betwixt the land about a mile long, and then it spread out yonder all flat I guess for to pass off to the *sea*. Way yonder on a hill they was a big old white house with posts on the porch like I seed the night before, a *ancestrial* home of a General retired hero of Appamatoxburg like brother said, and on the other side of the river I seed a grand and fearsome housetop, all white and round and jess like a handsome cup upside down, with little bitty far away trees and tiny little roofs rounderneath it. The man in front said to his wife, 'Yonder's the Capitol dome darling,' and point to it, and that's what it was. And they was the finest, softenest wind blew in from the land to the river, and make ever'thing ripple and jump in the water all over, most peaceful. The sun shine on that grand fine Capitol dome and hit flush on a streamer 'at's tied to a gold pole way on top of it, and do it dazzly, too. All that land I told you we done roll over in the bus all night, here we was in the middle of it, 'case they *never* was a town so white and so laid out grand, and brother woke up and said, 'This here is the city of *Washington* the nation's capitol where the President of the United States of America and ever'body is,' and he rub his eyes, and I look close and can see they's a heap of things goin on yonder in Washington, 'case I hear it hum all over when the bus slow down at the river red light and I put my head out the window to watch. Well, and I never seed such a big sky, and so many fine, solemn clouds as passed over Washington of the United States' at mornin.

After that, grandpa, I didn't get to sleep much. It was mighty hot inside the city of Washington when we stopped there and had to change to another bus 'at said NEW YORK on it, and crowded? Ever'body in the world lined up for that New York bus, and sat inside sweatin. I couldn't sleep no more except on brother's arm, and had to sit up straight in that back sofa and drop my head over most uncomfortable, and his poor shoulder was so hot. Busdriver man say, 'Baltimore next stop,' but run off to do somethin else instead and don't come back f'the longest time. Well, I wished we was back on that NIGHT bus in the WILDERNESS. Babies was cryin all up and down the bus, and felt jess as bad as I did, I guess. I look out the window and all I see is the wall on one side, and the wall th'other side, and the sun beat down on the roof, and whew! it was so daggone hot I was sickish. I say to myself, 'Why don't nobody open a window in here?' and I look around and ever'body's sweatin but don't make a move for the window. I say to Slim, 'Less open a window or we's dead.' And Slim pull and tug and rassle at that window, but can't bulge it one bit. 'Phew!' he say. 'This must be one of them *modern airconditioned* buses. Phew!' Slim say, 'Less go, bus, and blow some air in here.' And a man up front turn around and give us a look, then *he* try to open *his* window, and can't bulge it, and sweat and cuss over it. Here come a big soldier man and he reach out and give that window one big pull up, and it don't bulge none. So ever'body look straight ahead and go on sweatin.

Well, you know that busdriver man come back and seed Slim pullin some more at that window, and he said, 'Please leave the windows alone, this happens to be an air-conditioned bus,' and he turn on a button up front when he start the bus, and I tell you the finest cool air began to blow all over that bus, only thing is, ever'body got *cold* in a minute and the sweat turns on me like ice water. So Slim, he tugged at that window again to get some *hot air* back in, but couldn't do it, and we look thu the window at them beautiful green fields, and Slim said they was MARYLAND, and wished he was settin in the sunny grass. I reckon ever'body felt the same way too.

Grandpa, travellin ain't the easiest and pleasingest thing in the world but you shore gets to see many inneresting things and don't go 'bout it backwards neither.

When we got to *Philadelphia* folks got out the bus and me and Slim got ourselves a new seat smackdab up front in the driver's window, and bought-up some ice-cold soda orange and ain't nothin better when you feel sickish. Slim said, 'We can sit up front now because we crossed the Mason Dixie line,' and I axed him what that was, and he said it was the line of the law of *Jim*

Crow, and when I axed him who Jim Crow was, he said, 'That's you, boy.'

'I ain't no Jim Crow anyhow,' I told him, ''case you know my name is Pictorial Jackson.'

'Oh,' says Slim, 'is that so? Well, I never knowed that, uh-huh. Looky-here Jim,' he said, 'don't you know about the law that says you can't sit in the front of the bus when the bus runs below the Mason Dixie line?'

'What for you call me Jim?'

'Now Jim!' he says, and cluck-cluck at me solemn. 'You mean to tell me you don't know about that line?'

'What line?' I say. 'I ain't seed no such a line.'

'What?' he say. 'Why, we just crossed it back there in Maryland. Didn't you see Mason and Dixie holdin that line across the road?'

'Well,' I says, 'did we run over it or underneath it?' and I'se tryin to recollect such a thing but jess cain't. 'Well,' I say, 'I guess I musta been sleepin then.'

And Slim laugh, and push my hair, and slap his knee. 'Jim, you kill me!'

'What did that line look like?' I axed him, 'case I wasn't old enough to know it was a joke yet, you see. Well, Slim said he didn't know what such a line looked like neither on account he never seed it any more than I did.

'But there *is* such a line, only thing is, it ain't on the *ground*, and it ain't in the air neither, it's jess in the head of Mason and Dixie, jess like all other lines, border lines, state lines, parallel thirty-eight lines and iron Europe curtain lines is all jess 'maginary lines in people's heads and don't have nothin to do with the ground.'

Grandpa, Slim said that jess as quiet, and didn't call me Jim no more and said to hisself, 'Yes sir, that's all it is.'

The busdriver man come back, and said, 'All aboard for NEW YORK,' and like I tell you 'bout *travellin* and not goin backwards, we jess went *forwards*. Whoo! Straight ahead was that New York road, and all the traffic of the cars cuttin in and out, zoom, zip, but that driver man jess sit at that wheel 'thout movin a muscle and look right ahead and push his big machine straight on thu as fast as he can go. Anybody come out of a side street and see us comin, why they jess freeze right up and let us come by. That bus man jess cleared the way for hisself, *he* don't care. The others don't care neither 'case they jess barely miss us and go zip thisaway and zip thataway after they miss. I reckon his bus couldn't *ever* stop if somebody got dead in the way, and then you couldn't find their pieces if he did, and couldn't look for the pieces except in the next county. Grandpa, you never seed such drivin and breezin along and ever'body so nonchalant about it, and so sure. I· tell you, I couldn't look.

Slim, he was asleep again and this time his head dropped on my arm jess like mine done on his arm in Washington, and slept like that with his eyes closed right in front of the window and here's that bus man carryin him on thu all that road jess as faithful as you please. Slim wasn't scairt none, nor flinched awake or asleep. Well, I shore did love him a whole lot jess then, and said to myself, 'Pic, you had no call bein scairt last night when he come and carried you thu the woods and told you not to worry. Now, Pic, you gotsa grow up this minute for Slim. You ain't no country boy now.'

So I look straight ahead thu the window, and there we go north to NEW YORK in that tremenjous bus.

CHAPTER 9

First Night in New York

Now I gotsa tell you 'bout ever'thing happened in New York and how it happened so fast I jess barely had time to see what New York was like. You see, we come in I believe May 29th to stay and three days later we was all balled up and got to go on the road again, so you see how quick people has to live up in New York and how we was.

When I seed New York was from that bus, and Slim poked me up from the seat and said, 'Here we are in New York,' and I looked and the sun was *red* all over, I looked again, and rubbed my eyes to wake up, for grandpa, we was goin over a long big bridge 'at run over a whole sight of rooftops and all I has to do is look down to see the chillun running betwixt the houses below, Slim said it wasn't New York yet, jess the HOBOKEN SKYWAY he said, and pointed up ahead to show me New York. Well I jess could barely see a whole heap of walls and lanky steeples way, way off yonder all cloudy inside the smoke. Then I looked all round, and grandpa, it was the most monstrous and tremenjous stretch of rooftops and streets, and bridges and railroads, and boats and water, and great big things Slim said was *gas tanks*, and walls, and junkyards, and power lines, and in the middle of it set this old swamp 'at's got tall green grass and yaller oil in the water, and rusty rafts long the shore. It was a sight like I never dreamed to see. And here come more of it where we turn the bridge, and ever'thing's so smoky and tremenjous, and so laid out far I can't watch at some least littlest point of it without I see some more heaped up yonder behind it in the fog and smoke. Well grandpa, and that ain't all – I told you the sun was red, and that was 'case jess then the sun was peekin thu a big hole in the clouds up in Heaven, and was sending down great long sun-fingers ever'-whichway from the hole, and it was all jess so rosy and purty like if'n God come down thu the smoke to see the world. Well jess before I woked up I guess ever'body in New York done put on they lights, and I guess it was dark then, on account now all them lights they put on was caught feeble and strange in the red sunlight and ever'where I look was them po lights burnin up 'lectricity for nothin, deep inside the streets and the alleys, up on the walls, up on top the bridges, thisaway in the awful fog and thataway on the soft rosy water, and they jess tremble and shake jess like ever'thing's a big old campfire folks done lit before sundown and didn't dass put it out yet, 'case they knowed it wasn't no real day for long. Well, next thing you know, the sun turn purple and blue and leave jess one peel of fire on the cloudbank, and it gets almost dark.

Slim say, 'Ah me it's May again. Wish't I could go someplace tonight,' and I say, 'Ain't we goin no place?'

And he say, 'I mean *someplace* where all the boys and girls have their fun. Ain't never seen nor found such a place all my born days. It's what them boys is think 'bout right now.'

'What boys is that?' I say, and he point to New York and say, 'The boys in the jailhouse tonight.' Grandpa, I axed him last time if he was in the jailhouse in New York and he said yes, he was *busted* one time but he didn't do nothin wrong, his friend did. He said his friend was in that jailhouse still, and wasn't no better than him.

Well, now I told you how fearsome and grand New York was when I first seed it, and that ain't all. The bus come down into a tunnel and whoosh! it and ever'body else go barrellin along the walls, and it warn't dark in there but *bright* as you like and all lit-up jolly. 'Now we's under the Hudson River,' brother say, 'and wouldn't it be somethin if that river bust thu and come down on our heads?' I didn't dass guess 'bout that till we come out the other side, and when we did I plum forgot to guess, and I reckon most folks is like that, ain't they grandpa, till the day such a thing happen to them? The bus come out that LINCOLN TUNNEL it was called, and a great yaller light shine up the front of it, and ain't nobody but one man walkin on the street, and I look at him and he look at me too. Well, I guess that man said to hisself, 'There's a little boy comin to New York for the first time and cain't do nothin but gawk at a man like me 'at's so busy in New York and got so many things to do.'

And here we was in New York, and it didn't look half grand

now we was inside it on account you couldn't see far with all them *walls* risin clear up on every side. Well you know, I look straight up oncet and I look again and don't see but the most p'culiar brown air in the sky above the tall walls, and I seed it was on account all the lights of New York paint-up the nighttime way high yonder, and do it so much it don't need no more'n a few feeble stars in it. 'Them's skyscrapers,' Slim said when he seed me look up. Well then the bus turn on a big street, Slim said it was Thirty Four street, then I seed plenty far and a whole great gang of folks and grandpa it was jess so many lights strung out one after 'nother, and up, and down, and trembly along the walls, and red, and blue, and all the folks and the car traffic acting jess like ants as far as your eye can see. Grandpa, all the folks you do see, and things they do, and all the streets you do see, and the places there is, and whilst you gotsa keep in mind all the folks and streets you don't see, 'at's round the corner and way yonder ever'whichaway, and *up* in the skyscrapers, and *down* in the subway – well, you can see how t'aint pos'ble to make a body unnerstand it lessen they done come and looked for theirselves.

The bus stop, and me and Slim got off and went down the street to the *subway*, which is a tunnel train there underneath New York 'at's ever'body takes to git where they's goin the fastenest best way. 'Bus is fast in the country but's too slowed-up in *this* town,' Slim say. We pay the man when we pay the gate-machine, and get on the train when the door-machine bring the door open, and get inside and set and let the train-machine run along the rail. Wasn't nobody around to run the doggone thing 'case I looked up front and wasn't nobody steerin it. And I *knowed* we went fast and I wasn't fooled by no dark.

Brother and me got off at Hundred Twenty Five street in *Harlem*.

'We's just around the corner from home, old-timer,' Slim say to me, 'so you see we made it after all.' Well then we come upstairs on the street and it's all as jolly and brightly as Thirty Four street, and grandpa, here we was a *hunnerd* streets up along the city, so you can see how New York never gets to be near the country as you go along it.

'Stand right still whilst I wash your face for Sheila,' Slim said, and he stopt me on the street in front of the water-bubbler and rub off my mouth with his handkerchief and great big

128

crowds of folks walks by and it's a nice warm night again and I shore feels glad we come to New York. 'Slim,' I say, 'I's shore glad I ain't at Aunt Gastonia's no more and won't be scairt neither no more.' And I look down the street where we come from and say to myself, 'No, North Carolina ain't round here no more.'

'Well thass the way to talk, soldier,' Slim say, 'and just because ever'thing's so fine I'm gonta buy Sheila a little thing in the store here so's well all have a fine time our first night home.'

And we go into a *record store* 'at's full of men fishin through the record racks and jumpin up and down while they do so like they jess can't wait. Ain't nothin but music and noise in there, and a whole bunch of men out front jumpin jess the same way. Whoo, what fun! Slim, he went fishin and jumpin like ever'body else, and come up with a record, and yelled, 'Whee! Look what I found!' and ran to the man and throwed him a dollar. Then we go round the corner to a street 'at wasn't so bright but jess as gay and full of folks in the dark, and run upstairs into a old crumbly hallway, and knock on the door and push it in.

Well, there was Sheila, and I liked her jess as quick as I laid my eyes on her. She was a slim purty gal 'at wore glasses with red horn rims, and a purty red sweater, and purty green skirt, and fine jigglets on her wrists, and when we come in she was standin at the stove makin coffee and readin the paper all at the same time, and looked at us s'prised.

'Baby!' Slim yelled out, and run up and hugged her, and spun her round, and kissed her smack upon the mouth, and said, 'Looky yonder your new son, mother dear, ain't he somethin fine?'

'Is that Pic?' she said, and come over and took both my hands, and lookt at me down in the eye. 'I can see you've been havin lots of trouble lately haven't you, little boy,' she said, and I don't know how she could tell that, but she did, and I tried to smile to show I liked for her to be so nice but I was jess a little too bashful. 'Well won't you smile sometime?' she said, and I had to go freeze there so foolish and said but jess, 'Uh-huh,' and look away. Doggone it!

Then she said, 'Wasn't that chile cold comin up here in that little sweater full of holes? And look at his socks, they're full of holes too. Even his poor pants in the back here.'

'My hat too,' I said, and showed her my hole-hat.

Well, I caught her then and it was her 'at didn't know whether to laugh or look awful, and she got red and laughed. I reckon, grandpa, it was because a boy like me ain't got no call talkin about himself when a lady's doin that for him, ain't it? Well, she was the finest soul, and I knowed it jess then by the way she got red and didn't mind.

Slim said, 'I'll buy him clothes first thing in the mornin,' and Sheila said, 'How you gonna do that without money?' but he jess started that new record on the record machine in the corner and you shoulda seen him clap his hands and walk up and down with his feet right where he was, and shake his head and say, 'Oh where's my horn tonight? Oh where's my horn tonight?' over and over, and look up and laugh, 'case he likes the music so much, and say, 'Play that thing *Slop*jaw!' Grandpa, that record was by Slopjaw Jones done with a saxophone horn and everybody yellin and bangin the piano behind him, and you never heard such reckless jumpin and crashin in your ears out there in the country. Seem like the folks up in the city wants to have fun and ain't got time for no worry exceptin when worry catches up with them, that's when they ain't busy about worryin.

'What do you mean no money?' Slim said, and Sheila said, 'I don't like to tell you and Slopjaw, and everybody, and Pic here, but I went and lost my job day before yesterday because they're tearin down the building where the restaurant was down on Madison avenue and puttin up a new office building.'

'Office building?' Slim yelled. 'Did you say *office* building? What's they going to do with a *office* building? Ain't nobody get to *eat* in no office building.'

'You talk silly,' Sheila said, and look at him sad. 'Why shoo, all they've got to do is go round the corner to eat in a restaurant.'

'Then they put up another office building *there* and then where do you go?' said Slim, and then heaved a sigh. 'Doggone it, what are we goin to do now?' He turned off the record, and looked round the kitchen, and began walkin up and down in it, and worried himself to death. I seed then how Slim had worried before about a lot of things. His face dragged down awesome and his eyes jess went starin straight ahead and his bones of his face stuck out from his cheeks and made him look old. Poor Slim, I never forget *that* look on his face when I think about him now. 'Dog-*gone*,' he jess say, over and over, 'dog-*gone*.' Then he look at Sheila and she didn't know it but his face flinch a little bit like if they was pain way down deep in his heart, and he come back to say 'Dog-*gone!*' and he starin straight ahead after that, and for a long awesome time. Lord, Lord, Slim always tried so hard to explain to me and ever'body else the things on his mind, like he done then. 'Dog-gone it, are we goin to be beat all the time or *ever* make a livin around here? When will our troubles end? I'm tired of bein poor. My wife is tired of bein poor. I guess the *world* is tired of bein poor, because *I'm* tired of bein poor. Lord a mercy who's got some money? I know *I* ain't got some money and that's for sure, now look' and show his empty pocket.

'You shouldn't of bought that record,' Sheila said.

'Well,' he said, 'I didn't know then. Now so where'd this money go that folks is supposed to live on? I'd jess be satisfied if I had a field of my own I could jess grow things in and wouldn't need no money, and wouldn't worry *what* folks had it, not records neither. But I ain't got a field and I need money to eat. Well where am I goin to get this money? I gotsa get a job. Yes, a job, gotsa get, I-got-a-git-a-job. Sheila,' he call out, 'first thing in the mornin I am going out and find me a job. You know how I'm sure I can get one? Because I need one. You know why I need a job? Because I ain't got no money.' And he went on like that, and got hisself all 'volved in talk, and come round again to worry some more. 'Sheila, I shore hope I get a job tomorrow.'

'Well,' Sheila said, 'I'll have to look for one too.'

'It's so hard to get a job that you can't stick to all your life,' Slim said. 'I wish I could get a job playin tenor in a club and make my livin that way, and express myself with that horn. Show ever'body how I feel by the way I play, and make them see how happy I can be and ever'body can be. Make them learn how to enjoy life and do good in life and unnerstand the world. A whole lot of things. Play sometimes about God, by the way I can make my horn pray in the blues and get down on my knees to signify. Play in such a way as to show ever'body how hard a man tries all the time, and make somebody learn *that*. I want to be like a schoolteacher with that horn, or like a preacher, but

131

show ever'body that jess a musician can do so simple a thing as take a horn in his hand, and blow in it, and finger the stops, yet be a preacher and a schoolteacher in the *result* of what he's doin. I tear my heart out wherever I go. All over this country I've been, and ain't been liked because I was colored, by people who don't mind their own personal business, and don't want me to do good, but I've tore my heart out with that horn. That horn is the only way people come to listen to me. They won't talk on the street, but they'll clap and yell hooray when I'm on the bandstand, and smile at me. Well I smile back, I ain't cool about people, nor cool about nothin. I like to respond and listen and be with people. I feel good most of the time, and do it. Lord a mercy, I sure wantsa live and have my place in the world like they call it and I'm ready to work if I can only work with my horn, because that's the way I like to work and I don't know how to run a machine. Well, I ain't learned yet anyway, and like my horn better, I do. Ar-tist, I'm a ar-tist, jess like Mehoodi Lewin and the columnist in the paper and whoozit. I got a million ideas and can shore pour them out of that horn, and I ain't doin so bad pourin them without the horn. Sheila,' he said to her, 'less eat some supper and worry about ever'thing tomorrow. I'm hungry and want my strength back. Throw some beans in there, and after supper make a lunch for tomorrow noontime.'

'I'll have to make one for myself,' Sheila said, and then they wondered what was to happen to me tomorrow, and Slim decided for me to go with him to look for work and we could eat the lunch together. 'Make it a big one. You got *bread*? Throw somethin between that bread and that'll be fine. Wished we had a coffee mug. You got a coffee mug? Thermidor you say? Well, *thermidor* it shall be, with the coffee hot. Pic,' he said to me, 'you and me ain't even started travellin together is we? We just come four and fifty miles and here we go again. Eat, then we go to sleep and get up early. Got a nice old sweater of mine for you tomorrow, and clean socks. Well, we'll make it again. Here we go. Ladies and gentlemen, look out. *Look out for your boy!*' he shouted, and closed his eyes a minute, and stood like that.

Well, that was the first night in New York, and shore 'joyed the supper, and us sittin round the table till ten at night, talkin and recollectin and Sheila told about when she was my age in *Brooklyn*, and all such fine things went on of gabbin together in the night-time, and me lookin forward to what happen next ever'time I look out the window at New York. I say to myself, 'Pic, you left home and come into *New York*!'

I had me a fine cot-bed to sleep on all night.

But that next day wasn't so pleasin as this first night.

CHAPTER 10

How Slim Lost Two Jobs in One Day

I'll never forget that day because so many things happened all at oncet. Started off, me and Slim got up jess as the sun come back red, and he cooked up some eggs and breakfast so's Sheila could sleep some more. Grandpa, ain't nothin better in the world like eggs and breakfast in the mornin because your taster ain't worked all night and ever'thing comes so chawy and smells so fryin good it makes a body wish he could eat ever'body's breakfast all up and down the street seven times, ain't it the truth? When we come down on the street and I seed all them men eatin more eggs and breakfast in the corner store I wished I could eat all the breakfasts in *New York City*. It was a cool mornin and wasn't but six o'clock, I had my new socks, and Slim's black sweater, and Sheila done sewed up the holes in my pants, and I was all set. And you know the first thing happened? We was standin in the doorway and Slim was readin the newspaper *want ads*, and it was mighty chill, and keen, and ever'body come by to get to the work-bus coughin and spittin and shore looked mis'ble from work in New York City, and some of them was readin the papers with the most gloomy disappointed look like if'n the papers complained jess what they hankered to see, and here come a man out of that crowd who knew Slim. 'Well there *daddyo*,' he said and showed Slim the palm of his hand, and Slim showed him his, and they touched up like that. 'Don't tell me you're lookin for a job again,' the man said, and Slim told him he was shore enough.

'Well, I declare, I got a job for you. You know my brother *Henry*. He ain't got up yet this mornin. I jess talked to him. I say "*Henry*, ain't you supposed to go to work in that cookie factory down on whatzit street?" And he hid under the pillow and says, "Yes I guess so, uh-huh," but don't move a bone. I say, "*Henry*, ain't you gettin up? *Henry*! Well now *Henry*? Hey, yoo-hoo, *Henry*?" That man just made up his mind to sleep, that's all,' and Slim's friend walked off ten feet and come back again.

'Do you think he'll be fired?' Slim axed him curious, and the man said, '*Henry*? Will *he* be fired?' Dog my cats if he don't walk off again and come back. 'You mean *Henry*?' and he looked away, and shook his head, and felt too tired to do anything but hang his head, 'Shooee, he's got the *world record* for that. He's been fired more times than he's been hired.'

'What's the address of this place?' Slim said, and the man knew it and gave it to us, and made another couple of funny jokes and said, 'Lookout for the boogieman,' when me and Slim took off for the job factory. Well, he was all right.

We took the subway, then walked down a street to the river and there was the cookie factory. It was jess a great big old place with chimneys and lots of machines thunderin inside, and gave out a mighty sweet smell that made us smile. 'Why this will be a good job,' Slim said, ''cause it smells so good,' and we jumped up the steps and come in the office. The boss was there by the punchin clock and was wonderin where was *Henry*, I guess. We waited on a bench a half hour, then the boss said Slim had better start workin all right because nobody was never goin to show up. Slim had to spend some time writin papers, so he told me to wait in the park across the street till noon and then come in for lunch with him. And there he was straight into a job right off quick.

'Sheila'll be happy,' I said to myself, and knowed it.

I waited all mornin in that park. It was a tiny park with a iron rail and some bushes, and swings, and such, and jess sat most of the time watchin at a couple other children, and figurin life. I made friends with a little white boy who came into the park with his mother. He was all fine lookin in a blue suit with gold buttons, and knee high stockins, and a red huntin hat. He had a most admirable way of talkin and settin hisself on the bench. His mother read a book on the other bench and smiled at us kindly.

'And why are you waitin here?' he axed me, and I said, 'My brother works in that factory over yonder.'

He says, 'Why do you say *over yonder*, are you from Texas in the West?'

'*Texas in the West*?' I said. 'No, I don't come from up there, I'm from North Carolina.' 'Are there any cowboys there?' he axed, and I lied and said there was, and we talk. I liked that

135

boy a whole lot. We'd a talked more but he had to go home quick. We was fixin to have a race but he left. Why, he had the goldenest hair and the clearest blue eyes, and I never seed him again.

Well, at noon I went up to the factory, and seed Slim by the window with a shovel. All I had to do was sit on a barrel outside the window which was open, and watch Slim till it was time for us to eat.

Well, he was workin so fast he didn't even see me, and when he did, all he had time to do was yell. He bent over with the shovel, and dug into a truckload of fudge, and heaved it up on a belt that rolled around from wheels and carried the fudge clear down the other end of the factory. Before it hit a big roller Slim flatted out the fudge with his hands, then it rolled under and got to be like a sheet of fudge, and then got pieced full of holes by a knife machine 'at jabbed down and made cookies. Slim had to shovel up and then drop the shovel and hurry to use his hands, so's he never could stop one minute because the belt kept turnin. One time he blew his nose and the man down the way said, 'Send up some more of that chocolate,' thass how fast ever'body worked and the rollers rolled. The sweat jess fell from Slim's head and fell in the fudge, and he couldn't do nothin about it, had no time to dry himself. Then a man rolled up another truckload of fudge, only this time it was *vanilla* and all white and purty, and Slim jess stuck that old chocolate shovel in there and hauled it up, all streaky. When he spread the fudge with his hands he looked straight ahead and said, 'Phew!' because that was the only time he stoop up straight enough to talk to himself. That shore was some hard job and I knowed it.

Slim yelled to me, 'If I stop one second my arms are going to knot up round my kneck from Charley Horse!' and jumped back in the fudge. One time he said 'Ow!' and one time he said 'Whee!' and another time I heard him say, 'Oh Lord a mercy, I'll never eat a cookie again.'

Twelve o'clock, a big whistle blew and all the machines slowed down and ever'body walked off. But Slim, he only leaned there on the post and wiped his head and looked at his hands. Next thing you know, his right hand curled up and reached around for his wrist, and he said he was a *cramp*. Then half of his whole arm curled up like he was showin his muscles, but he wasn't, it was jess another cramp, and he pushed it back and forth and looked at it, and sighed, and cussed.

Well, he came out and we ate the lunch on the office steps in the hot sun. 'I hope my arms are better for this afternoon,' he said, and was glum and didn't say much more, even when I told him about the little boy I met. Come about one o'clock that big whistle blew again and Slim went back to work.

I watched again. Well, you know, that poor man couldn't grip the shovel when he reached for it, his fingers was so stiff. When he did close his fingers over it his arms began to shake and had no strength in them, and he couldn't hold the shovel at all. The man down the fudge-belt yelled, 'Start up that vanilla will you? We ain't got all day.' Slim called out to the boss and showed him his arms. Both of them stood shakin their heads and thinkin about this, because it *was* sad, and Slim tried again to grip the shovel and couldn't do it, and the boss rubbed his arm some, but Slim jess couldn't control his arms no more. They were red, and hot, and hurt him. Well, he wiped his hands with a rag, and they talked some, then by and by Slim came out the office door and joined me.

'What happened?' I axed him.

'I jess can't work any more today, my arms is tied in a knot.' And that's all he said, and went home with one mornin's pay in a envelope, $3.50.

Sheila came home at five o'clock, and hadn't found a job. Slim told her what happened and we ate supper most silent.

Well, it was the first time I seen Slim gloomy.

'Well, I'll tell you,' he said after supper, and jess soaked his hands in the hot water, 'I don't like them kind of jobs like I had today. I can't shovel fast enough to keep with no rollin belt like that and I used to be a prizefighter too. I don't like to sink my hands in no whole tub of fudge. Do you make your own cookies, gal, or buy it? Shoo, what's I goin to do with a thirty-five-dollar pay cheque anyhow when the groceries theirselves cost about twenty, and the rent's took up the rest. I can't be shovellin that dog-gone stuff up and down myself just so's ever'body can't pay extra bills and can't buy a hat, and my arms get so tired they hang like a broken branch in the tree. I don't want to complain all the time, but shucks almighty no matter how much I love the world and get my kicks every live-long day, and I think Pic here

137

loves the world and gets his innocent joys every day, and you love the world and feel fine in the mornin, it jess ain't the same when there's no dough and the house is black with money debts. It's like a closet you have to sit in, doggone it, 'stead of a house.'

'Well, you're just tired today,' said Sheila, and she kissed him on the ear and gave him a fine purty sidelook, and trotted off to make coffee on the stove. I reckon Sheila loved Slim like she was his slave. He didn't have to do anything but sit there, and Sheila loved him fine, and watched him, and never passed him in the house without she touched him and sometimes winked at him.

Well, it was mostwise a glum evenin, like you can see, but somethin else happened jest then.

A tall man all well dressed and smilin come in the door, and whooped – 'Slim you old tadpole,' and ever'body began laughin and forgot their troubles for then. 'You know why I'm here, man?' said the man, his name was Charley, and Slim lit up bright and said, 'You mean?'

'Yes, thass right, a job, and not only that, I got a *horn* for you.'

'A horn? A horn? My kingdom for a horn! Less go!' And we all went downstairs to the street. Some other man was in the car that had the horn in it, and Slim took the horn out the case and blooped in it a little bit, right on the sidewalk, and felt jess grand. 'Where we blow?' he said, and Charley said it was at the Pink Cat Club. 'Do I have to wear a suit?' Charley said he shore did have to because the boss man at the Pink Cat was jess complete persnickity about such things and wouldn't pay Slim no five dollars if he didn't like him.

'Well *hoe-down*! Here we go for five dollars Sheila baby,' Slim said, and ran upstairs as fast as he could run to put on his suit. Sheila hurried and put on a nice dress, and brushed *me* up some, and here we was all goin to the Pink Cat Club together not five minutes after Slim had sat so glum and sad. Grandpa, life ain't happy, and then it's happy, and goes on like that till you die, and you don't know why, and can't ask nobody but God, and He don't say nothin, do He? Grandpa, Slim and Sheila was so fine that night I *knowed* God was on their side jess then, and I thanked Him. Ain't I right, grandpa, to pray when I feel grateful and glad like I did then? Well, that's what I done.

The man zipped that car, and ever'body was glad, and it started rainin but nobody paid it mind, and we got to the club real early and set *parked* in front of it a minute whilst Slim and the men had theirselves a smoke and talked. We was still in *Harlem* about thirty streets up along the way, and it still looked like jess where we lived. The rain got on the street and made the purtiest manner of red and green lights, jess like a Arabian Nights and made rainbows. It was a fine rainy night for Slim to start workin inside that club in, and for me and Sheila to hear him. Well we shore had fun in that car. Slim took out the horn again and went *BAWP* with it to try out the lowliest note and then tried a run up and down the middles notes, and finished up with a little high *BEEP* and ever'body laughed. 'Ouch, my fingers,' Slim said. Those two fellows was fine fellows, Charley and th'other man, 'case they shore admired Slim and watched.

'Only thing, Slim,' Charley said, 'that suit of yours is a little beat.' Slim's suit was his onliest suit, and it was a old blue coat with the whitebelly insides showin out under the arms, and there was a rip in the pants he didn't have time to sew up. Charley said, 'I know it's the only suit but this Pink Cat joint is s'posed to be a *cocktail lounge*, you know, nobody's satisfied anymore with a regular old saloon.'

'Well,' Slim laughed, and didn't care, 'less go play some music.'

And we all went in the Pink Cat Club suit or no suit, on time or early or what-all, you know. Well, it was early. The boss wasn't there yet. The bandstand wasn't lit up. Folks was drinkin at the bar and playin the big *jukebox* machine and talkin low.

Slim ran up the bandstand, and clicked on the light. 'Come on Charley, let's have some piano.' Charley allowed it was too early and hung back shy, but Slim allowed no such thing and dragged him up there. Charley said the other boys in the band wasn't here yet but it made no difference to Slim. The other man that was with us, he was the drummer, and didn't say nothin, but just sat down behind Slim and knocked the drum and chewed his gum. Well, when Charley seen this he decided to sit down at the piano and play the music too.

Sheila bought me a Coca-Cola and made me sit down in the corner by myself to watch. She stood up right in front of Slim whilst he played his first number and didn't ever move from there till he was finished, and he played the whole first song to her. He blew in the horn, and moved his poor fingers, and I tell you grandpa he made the purtiest deepdown horn-sound like when you hear a big New York City boat way out in the river at night, or like a train, only he made it sing up and down melodious. He made the sound all trembly and sad, and blew so hard his neck shaked all over and the vein popped in his brow, as he carried along the song in front of the piano, and the other man swisht the drum with the broom brushes soft and breezy. And on they went. Slim never took his eye away from Sheila till the middle of the song, then he remembered me and looked across the room and pointed the horn at me and play extra purty to show me how good he could play even though his hands was hurt and he couldn't work in that old cookie factory. Then he turned the horn back to Sheila and finished the song with his head way down on the mouthpiece and the horn against his shoe, and stood like that bowed.

Well you know, ever'body at the bar clapped and was excited too, and one man said, 'You blowed that one, son,' and I could see they liked Slim better and shut down that *jukebox* by all means.

Sheila come over and sat with me, and there we was, right by the window and could see the purty lights out on the wet street, and see the whole bar and all the folks in front of us, and the bandstand perfect. Now Slim beat down his feet real fast and the drummer man walloped one, and off they went and jumped. Whoo! Slim jess grabbed that horn and hoisted it up and blew with all his might and moved his head from side to side with his jaws workin hard and fast like workin with his hands that day. When I seen that I realized how strong Slim was all over, and made of iron.

Ever'body at the bar jumped when they heard him.

'Yes, yes, yes, yes,' yelled the man at the bar and grabbed his hat and hung on to it and stepped up and down in front of ever'body jazzy. He shore could make his feets go, that gen'lman. Well, he was dancin to Slim.

Slim, he was walkin up and down where he was and jess carryin along that jump-song going as fast, well, like that *bus* I was tellin you about earlier. He was pushin the horn to go ever' old way zippin here and zoopin there, he then all drawed-out himself on one breath way high up, and threw it way down, *BAWP*, and back again in the middle, and the drummer-man looked up from his crashing sticks and yelled, 'Go Slim!' jess like that. Charley, he was poundin on the piano with all his fingers spread, *blam*, jess when Slim is catchin his breath, and *blam* again when Slim comes back. Grandpa, Slim had more breath than ten men and could go on all night like that. Wow, I never heard anything like it, and anybody makin some noise and music by himself. Sheila, she jess sat there grinnin at her old Slim and knocked her hands together under the table to the beat of the drum. Well, I done the same thing. I shore wished I could dance right then.

'Go, go, go!' yelled that man with the hat and flipped himself back and pawed at the air with his arms and said, 'Great-day-in-the-mornin!' jess as loud as a big old foghorn 'bove the noise. Whee, he was funny.

Well now Slim was startin to sweat because nobody wanted to stop, and he didn't wantsa stop neither and blew right on in that horn till the sweat begun pourin down his face jess like it did over the shovel in the mornin. Oh, he jess watered that bandstand from sweat. He didn't ever run out of anything to play ever'time he crossed from one end of the song to th'other, and had a hunnerd years in him of it. Oh, he was grand. That song lasted twenty minutes and the folks at that bar got out in front of the bandstand and clapped in time for Slim in one great big jumpin gang. I could jess see Slim over their heads with his face all black and wet and like he was cryin and laughin all at the same time, only his eyes was closed and he didn't see them but jess plain knew they was there. He was holdin, and pushin that horn in front of him like it was his *life* he was rasslin with, and jess as solemn about it, and unhappy. And ever' now and then he made it laugh too, and ever'body laughed along with it. Oh, he talked and talked with that thing and told his story all over again, to me, to Sheila and ever'body. He jess had it in his heart what ever'body wanted in *their* hearts and they listened to him for some of it. That crowd rocked under him, it was like the waves and he looked like a man makin a storm in that ocean with his horn. One time he let out a big horselaugh with his horn, and hung on to it when ever'body yelled to hear more, and made all kinds of designs with it till it didn't sound like a horselaugh no more but a mule's *heehaw*. Well, they axed him to hold that but he moved on to a high, long drawed-out whistle that sounded like a dog whistle and pierced into my ears, but after awhile it didn't pierce no more but jess was there like ever'thing was made dizzy like Slim felt from holdin that long note. It made you sympathize before he jumped on down back to reg'lar notes and made ever'body jump and laugh again.

A bunch of new folks come in and Slim seen them and decided to end the song there.

It wasn't time to play yet anyhow. He wiped himself with a towel from the kitchen and we all sat down together in the corner, with Charley and the drummerman. A man come over from the bar and axed Slim if he ever played with a big band. 'Ain't I seen you with Lionel Hampton or Cootie Williams or somebody?' Slim said no, and the man said, 'You ought to be with a big band and start makin yourself some money. You don't want to play for peanuts in a place like this all your life, with a taped-up horn. Go down see an agent.'

'Agent?' Slim said. 'Is that who you see to work with a band?' Slim was s'prised and didn't know any of these things.

Another man come by, and laughed, and shook Slim's hand and walked back to the bar, jess like that without talkin.

This was how they liked Slim, and what a real fine musician he was.

Well, here come the boss walkin in at nine o'clock, and the rest of the band is with him, includin the leader, who was Charley's older brother, and they all get ready to go on the bandstand. But that big sharped-up boss man seen Slim's tear under his coat and said, 'Haven't you got a better suit than that? No? Can't you borrow one from one of these boys?' Ever'body looked at ever'body else, and talked about it, and come to figure there wasn't but one suit they could loan him, only it was down in Baltimore. Well, Baltimore is a long ways off, and the boss had to admit it when he thought about it, but he jess didn't seem to like the idea of Slim in that poor awful suit. He hedged and hawed about it, and began shakin his head after awhile, and I began to see Slim's chance to make five dollars was all ready to go wrong. Slim seen that, and argued with the boss. He said, 'It don't make no difference, nobody'll see me, looky here I'll hold my arms down,' and showed him.

'Well,' said that boss, 'I know but I'm havin a big holiday crowd tonight and it'll be pretty *toney* as it gets in the later hours, and it just wouldn't look good, don't you see. It's just not, ah, hem, the *thing*.' And if you ask me, grandpa, I'd say he wanted to save that five dollars anyhow. One of the boys in the band was sick and Slim was only takin his place, and the boss figured he didn't need nothin or nobody, and didn't.

So out we went, Slim, Sheila and me, to go home, and walked it this time, in the rain. And you know the first thing Slim said? – 'I didn't really get goin on that horn tonight,' and that was what he was worried about. Sheila didn't say nothin, but jess held Slim's arm and marched along with him, and enjoyed the walk, and seemed gay.

Well, Slim asked her what she was so gay about, and she told him. You know how poor they was, and the money worries they had that very day, and the rent comin up in a day or two like Slim said. And you know how Slim was always talkin about Californy, and seemed to hint to Sheila about her comin there with him. I didn't tell you, but he come from Californy to marry her before he come to get me, and was out there most of the time since he left North Carolina in his boyhood. Well, Sheila took all that and wrapped it up in one package for Slim, like a Christmas present, and said, 'Let's use that hundred dollars in my girdle and go to California. I'll tell my mother we have to do it and can't help it. We'll stay at my sister's house in San Francisco to start with. Then we can get jobs, there as well as here I guess. What do you think?'

'Baby,' laughed Slim and hugged her, 'that's just what I want to do.'

And that's how we come to decide to go to Californy, on that day Slim lost two jobs.

CHAPTER 11

Packin for Californy

We spent two whole days packin. Sheila's mother lived right around the corner and come to visit us three, four times to argue with Sheila about goin to Californy *cold* like that. Seems Sheila's family lived in New York so long, with such long jobs, they didn't believe in traipsin around the country like that, and once tried to stop Sheila's sister from goin to Californy, that was Zelda, the one we was goin to live with out there. But Slim said, 'New York people are always afraid to move from where they are. Californy is the place to be, not New York. Didn't you ever hear that song Californy Here I Come, Open Up That Golden Gate? All that sun, and all that land, and all that fruit, and cheap wine, and crazy people, it don't scare you so much when you can't get a job because then you can always live some way if you even just eat the grapes that fall off the wine trucks on the road. You can't pick no grapes off the ground in New York, nor walnuts either.'

'Now who's talkin about eatin *grapes* and walnuts?' yelled Sheila's mother. 'I'm talkin about a roof over your head.' She was a woman of some level sense.

'You don't need one in Californy because it's never cold,' said Slim, and laughed in his head gleeful. 'Oh, you ain't never seen such nice sunny days when you don't need a *coat* most the year round, and don't have to buy coal to heat your house, or get overshoes or nothin. And you never die of the heat in the summer up north in Frisco and Oaklands and thereabouts. I tell you, that's the place to go. Ain't nowhere else to go in the United States and it's the last place on the map – after it, ain't nothin but water and Russia.'

'And what's wrong with *New York*?' Sheila's mother snapped up.

'Oh, nothin!' Slim pointed out the window. 'Atlantic Ocean is got the Devil for the wind in the wintertime, and the Devil's son

144

carries it down the streets so's a man can freeze to death in a doorway. God brought the sun over Manhattan Island, but the Devil's cousin won't let it in your window unless you get yourself a penthouse a mile high and you don't dass step out of it for a breath of air for fear you'll fall that mile, if you could afford a penthouse. You can go to work, but probably wind up havin two hours left to yourself after a eight-hour day made into twelve hours by subway, bus, elevated, tube, ferry, escalator, and elevator and waitin in between, it's so *big* and hopeless town. Ain't nothin wrong with New York, nope. Go around the corner to see your friend after supper, see if he's there or ten miles downtown wishin he could see you. Try to have a ensemble evenin when your pockets are empty, like any country boy, and the man'll look for a blackjack in your pants.'

That's how *he* talked about things.

'Future of the United States was always goin to Californy, and always bouncin back from it, and always will be.'

'Well don't come bouncin back on *me* if you go broke out there,' said Sheila's mother and said it to Sheila.

'We're broke as it is,' Sheila said, and that woman her mother shore didn't like any of it.

Well, I didn't tell you about the money, but there wasn't enough for all three of us to go by bus. Sheila was goin to have her first baby before six months so she had to take sixty dollars of the hunnerd and go by bus and *eat good*. Me and Slim, we had the forty dollars and some more him and Sheila still had, and because rent was due in two days we was movin out, and sendin clothes and dishes in two big old suitcases and a smaller one, by railroad, and then me and Slim, with that $48, was *hitchhikin* to the Coast right away, and eat good too but be *on the bum with our thumbs* and sleep in beds only part of the time, mostly in cars and trucks and parks in the afternoon.

It shore sounded good and fine to me. But I didn't know *then* how far that Californy Coast was.

The last night ever'thing was packed and ready to go in the mornin and we had coffee in the kitchen and house looked so bare Slim seemed most gloomy about it. 'Look at this place we've been livin in. We leave it, someone else comes in, and life is jess a dream. Don't it remind you of old cold cruel world to look at it? Those floors and bare walls. Seemed we never lived here, and I never loved you inside of it.'

'We'll make ourselves a new home in Californy,' said Sheila, gladly.

'What I want is a *permanent* home and spend our lives in one neighbourhood, up on a hill till I get old and grandpa.'

'We'll see,' said Sheila, 'and pretty soon Pic'll have a little brother in Californy.'

'First we've got to go three thousand and two hundred miles,' sighed Slim, and I remembered that later. 'Three thousand and two hundred miles,' he said, 'over a plain, a desert and three mountain chains and any and all the rain that feels like falling down. Praise the Lord.' Well, we went to bed and slept the last night in that house, and sold the beds in the mornin. 'Now we're out in the cold,' Slim said, and he was right. In the afternoon we left the house dead empty except for a old bottle of milk, and my North Carolina socks too.

Sheila had her suitcase, and me and Slim had one suitcase with all our things in it. Off we went, to the bus station, and bought Sheila's ticket and waited around for her time to go.

By the time her bus was ready we all felt terrible sad and scared. 'There I go into the night,' Sheila said when she saw that bus that said CHICAGO on it. 'I'm goin and I'll never probably come back again. It's jess like dyin to go to Californy – but here I come.' Grandpa, I ain't forgot that minute.

'It'll be more like livin when you get there,' Slim laughed, and Sheila said she hoped so. 'Don't let no boys mess with you on that bus,' Slim said, 'because you're plumb alone till Pic and me get there, which I don't know when.'

'I'll be waitin for you, Slim,' and Sheila begun cryin. Well, Slim didn't cry but he looked it when he hugged her. Poor girl – she shore seemed pitiful that night, and I shore loved her plenty, jess like Slim said I would on that first night in the woods. Jess a young mother, and don't know what'll happen to her on the other side of the country, and all that nighttime alone in front of her till Slim and I got there. Jess like the Bible said, A fugitive and a vagabond shalt thou be in the earth, only she was a girl. I reached out and touched her cheek, and told her wait for us in Californy.

'You be extra careful with yourselves hitchhikin,' she said. 'Still seems to me Pic is too little for such hard travelin, well, and I don't feel right about it.'

146

But Slim said I'd be safe and sound with him, as much as *he* could be by himself, and if he couldn't make it nobody could. This's how Slim felt, and was sure, and watched over us. So him and Sheila kissed, and then she kissed me so soft and sweet, and in the bus she goes.

'Goodbye Sheila,' I said, and waved, and felt more so terrible lonesome and scairt than when she cried, and goodbye, goodbye ever'body else was sayin to ever'body else round the bus, and grandpa that's how sad it is to travel and roam, and try to live and go about things, I reckon till the day you die.

So Sheila went, and was gone, and now me and Slim had to catch up with her hitchhikin over that land.

We walked from the bus station to a big lit-up street called Times Square, and Slim said we was goin out the way we come in, at the Lincoln Tunnel, and hoped that old hole would point us to the West and nowhere else when we shot out of it. 'First we'll have our Hot Dog Number One on Times Square,' he said.

That's what we done, and grandpa I'll never forget that night of Hot Dog Number One in Times Square, jess about an hour it took us to eat it, before we hit that road.

CHAPTER 12

Times Square and the Mystery of Television

There was a whole lot of men standin on the corner of Eighth Avenue and Forty Second in front of a big grey bank that was closed for the night. In the middle of the road it was all tore up from constructin work, and cars bumped by over the rocky sand along the sidewalk. It was a cold night for spring, felt more like autumn weather, and a whole lot of papers blowed by in the wind and the lights shined ever'whichside and flashed in that wind like so many eyes twinklin. It was jolly, and people had to be a wee bit frisky to keep warm, so they jumped about. Me and Slim bought the hot dogs and spread some mustard on em, and strolled over to the corner to see what was goin on while they cooled a minute.

Lord, there was a couple two, three hunnerd men on one side of the street. Most of them was listenin to the speeches of the Salvation Army. Four Salvations took turns makin speeches, and while one was speakin the other three jess stood there like ever'body else lookin up and down the street to see what else was goin on. Here come a tall white-haired man of ninety years old clompin thu the crowd with a pack on his back, and when he seen ever'body listenin to the speeches he raised his right hand and said, '*Go moan for man*' as clear and loud as a foghorn in the wind, and clomped right on by like he hadn't a minute to stop awhile. 'Where you goin' Pop?' a man said in the crowd, and the old man yelled it back over his head – '*California* my boy' – and he was gone around the corner with that white hair flowin.

'Well,' said Slim, 'he's not lyin and that's the tunnel he's headed for.'

Then here come a loud siren motorcycle, and then another, and a third, all screechin together and escortin the way thu the traffic fo a big black limousine with a spotlight on it. All the men on the corner stooped down to see who was in that car. Me and Slim coulda reached out and touched it and made it a sign, it was so close. The limousine slowed in the sand, and started again, and a man in the crowd yelled, 'Look out for that Arkansas clay,' and some of the men laughed because here it was New York clay and not much of it. Well, wasn't nobody inside the limousine except two, three men with hats on, you know.

Then, grandpa, the word come floatin by in the heaven and I was so scairt, I'd never seen no such thing in all my born days like a word floatin by in the heaven, but Slim said it was jess a old balloon with a electric sign on it nudgin down close to Times Square for ever'body to see. Well, a couple folks looked up and din't look s'prised, and I *knowed* these New Yorkers was ready and used to ever'thing. It was purty balloon, and hovered around the longest time, and had to fight with the wind, but tacked and rassled right up there for Times Square. Not so many folks was lookin at it, a shame, bein such a purty balloon like that. Well, my cousins back in Carolina would appreciate it shore a lot. I know I did. It turned its nose into the wind, and wobbled, and jess floated back like a breeze and turned its nose around again and had to buck on back. It was best when it missed and ballooned. I couldn't hear what the poor thing sounded like, there was so much fuss below.

A number of things like this was goin on, and those Salvation Army speechers howled right along in the noise and roar. The Lord *this* and the Lord *that* is all they kept sayin, and I don't remember exactly, except about *burning in the fires of repentance* and them talkin to ever'body like they was sinners. Well, maybe ever'body do be sinners but it ain't innerestin on the street corner to hear it challenged, 'case there ain't nobody likely to step up and confess all his sins in front of the police-man that's always teeterin on his heels right there. What's I goin to explain to the police-man about the fire I started in Mr Otis' cornfield that cost him twenty dollars of feed and nobody ever knowed it was me? Well, no New York man that lives right there is goin to step up and tell how he threw his cigarette away and burned down the hospital in his block, and any such thing. Besides of which, why don't the speechers go into detail about *their* own sins they keep repentin and folks could work from there and judge. But it grew innerestin when a new man stepped up on the other side of the corner and started a speech of his own. He had a much louder voice and drew a bigger crowd. And it was the shabbiest crowd drew about *him*. He was jess a ordinary lookin man in a black hat, with shiny eyes.

'Ladies and gentlemen of the world, I have come to tell you about the mystery of television. Television is a great big long arm of light that reaches clear into your front parlor, and even in the middle of the night when there ain't no shows going on that light is on, though the studio is dark. Study this light. It will hurt you at first, and bombard your eyes with a hundred trillion electronic particles of itself, but after awhile you won't mind it no more. Why?' he yelled way up loud and Slim said, 'Yes!' The man said, 'Because while electricity was light to see by, *this* is the light comes not to see by, but to *see* – not to read by, but to *read*. This is the light that you *feel*. It is the first time in the world that light has been gathered up from the sources of light and shot through a tube in a way that it can be watched and studied instead of blinked at. And it has taken the shape of men and women who are real flesh and blood at the studio but come streaming into your parlor in *light* with all their sounds shot in sidetrack. What does this mean, ladies and gentlemen?'

Well, nobody knowed that, and waited, and Slim said, 'Go man!' and to hear it.

'It means that man has discovered light and is fiddling with it for the first time, and has released concentrated shots of it into everyone's house, and nobody yet knows what the effect will be on the mind and soul of people, except that now there is a general feeling of nervousness among some, and sore eyes, and twitching of nerves, and a suspicion that because it has come at the same time as the ATOM there may be an unholy alliance betwixt one and the other, and both are bad and injurious and leading to the end of the world, though some optimists claim it is the opposite of the atom and may relax the nerves the atoms undid. Nobody knows!' he moaned way out loud, and looked at ever'body frank. Well, ever'body was innerested and paid no attention to the speeches about *repentance*, and Slim agreed, most amazed.

'And, ladies and gentlemen,' he said, 'it is the old-time Depression travelling salesman that used to put his foot in your door and now has got a leg in your parlor, except he looks so doggone strange in light you just can't believe his transformation. And don't think *he* ain't more nervous than the Depression days jiggling behind all that light and looking out into the unknown

150

America. Yes, ladies and gentlemen, and I seen a salesman on television last night who put on a mask for fun and yet his eyes looked awfully scared peeking from behind that mask at a million other better-hidden eyes. What does this mean?' he demanded, and ever'body was ready to kneel to find out, so to speak, and Slim yelled, 'Go!' and socked his hands together.

'The day shall come when one giant brain shall televise the Second Coming in light and everyone in the world shall see it in their brains by means of a brain-television that Christ Himself shall cause to be switched on in a miracle, and no one shall be spared from knowing the Truth, and everyone shall be saved forever, and men and women of the world I warn you, live as best as you can and be hereinafter kind to one another and that is all there is to do now. We all know this.' And off he trots jess as calm as you please, and Slim looked after him with the most satisfied and glad look and clapped his hands, so that a whole bunch of others clapped their hands too, and the speecher vanished in glory. Grandpa, it was as strange as that.

Then the Salvation Army man howled out at us, 'Don't you realize the Lord is coming?' and jess then a loud screechin and crashin come down the street flamin red lights ever'whichway and I ducked, it was the fire engines barrelin to a fire with a whole bunch of firemen hangin on to their hats most solemn and displeased, and goin a hunnerd miles a hour. Whoo! that roused us, and Slim said, 'Whee!' and ever'body shore looked amazed and innerested. Then ever'thing got back to normal and people slouched around bored like always.

Well, it was time to go, and Slim said, 'We'll come back to Times Square sometime, but now we gotsa go across that night, like the old man with the white hair, and keep goin till we get on the other side of this big, bulgin United States of America and all the raw land on it, before we be safe and sound by the Pacific Sea to set down and thank the Lord. Are you ready, Pic?' he said, and I said, 'Yes,' and off we go.

CHAPTER 13

The Ghost of the Susquehanna

It was eight o'clock when we went and stood in front of the Lincoln Tunnel in all that yaller light, and it started mistin jess a little, enough to worry me and Slim even before we was begun on the road. But for the first time since that time, we got a ride inside a minute; seemed like the man at the wheel come around the corner sayin, 'pleased to meet you' before we could even show our thumbs. He lit up with a smile and throwed open the door. It was a big gigantic yaller truck that said PENSCO on it, with a tractor-cab in front a good twelve feet high, and the biggest tyres in the world, and hauled a trailer you couldn't see over of without backin up across the street. A mighty gigantic thing, that Slim had to throw me up to get in, and the man cotch me like a football. When I sat up there it felt like bein in a tree, it was so grand and high. Slim jumped after, and hauled in that suitcase that had all our clothes, and here we go.

'Going someplace with your kid brother?' the driver said. 'It don't do for him to get caught in the rain,' and with that he kicked down, and grabbed two clutches, and socked ever'thing around and pumped his feet like an organ-player, and boom! that big truck started to roll and growl, and bowled down into the tunnel like a mountain. It was a white man driving it. His name was Noridews. And he made that tunnel shake and reverberate from there to New Jersey.

Not only that, he didn't say another word till we got to Pennsylvania hours later, and all Slim and me had to do was sit and enjoy the way he throwed that gigantic machine down the highway. He was ever so much stronger than a poor *bus*, and that is a heap of strength. People in the other cars seemed to quake and wobble when we come by spitboom eatin up everything in sight. Only time he stopped was on a hill, and only stopped *passin* people then, didn't stop rollin at all. He had the mightiest brakes in the world to stop that trailer bumpin us down the back at ever' red light, and had to kick for his life on the brakes they handled such powerful stops and was so supple. Then the trailer bucked to a stop, like a mule, and edged along like it couldn't wait too long at no red light, and the driver told it to hold fast but it edged along no lesser. 'She's got to go,' he said.

Well, the mist was rainin in New Jersey, and grandpa, the first thing Slim and I seen was that old white man with the silver hair flowin around his head, walkin along in the highway in all that yaller light with the rain blowin over him like the smoke. Oh, he looked pitiful and grand all at the same time for an old man. Slim said, 'He got a poor short ride from New York.' We looked at him when we boomed by, and seen his face stuck out in the rain and him deep in thought of somethin like it never rained and like he wasn't anywhere but in his room, you know. 'What's he goin to do?' Slim said, and 'Oh that wonderful gentleman, he puts me in the mind of Jesus, trackin along like that in this dismal world. I bet he don't pay no taxes, neither, and his toothbrush was lost in Hoover's Army. Ah,' he said, 'ever'body's bound to make it at the same time if *he* ever makes it.' The old man had the bluest eyes, I seen that when we rolled by. Seen him later, tell you when some day.

We rolled through all the crowded streets of New Jersey, and got on the road, and come to a sign that said 'South' with an arrow pointin flat to the left, and 'West' with an arrow pointin straight down, and stayed right on the straight arrow down into the West. It got dark, and countrylike, and pretty soon there was hills.

It took some hours to get to Pennsylvania where the man was drivin to, and about five to get to Harrisburg, Pennsylvania, where he lived. I slept some of the way. It kept right on rainin. Inside the cab was warm and comfortable, and a good start it was for me and Slim. He said he wasn't far behind Sheila after all.

At Harrisburg at midnight the man said he could save time by droppin us off outside town at a junction, and pointed to it when we passed, and it was a lonely rainy junction that made me gulp it was so dark, but he said he would take us in anyhow to make sure we connected right for Pittsburg and points west, and added he knowed another short cut downtown.

That was good for us, that short cut. Harrisburg was all lit up in halos in the rain and looked quiet and gloomy. There was big grey bridges, and the Susquehanna river below them, and the main street in town where ever'body was waitin for buses at midnight.

Me and Slim jumped out of the tractor-cab at the red light, and the man repeated his instructions over whilst Slim thanked him gladly, and then back we was on foot, goin slant across town for the other highway with hopes on high. 'That was a good ride,' Slim said, 'and I wouldn't of got one like it alone. Ever'body'll sympathize with you bein so little and we'll make time to the Coast. Pic, you're my goodluck chile. Come along with me, you old daddyo.'

The houses in Harrisburg is extremely old, and come from the time of George Washington, Slim said. They's all old brick in one part of town, and have crooked chimbleys and ancient shapes but look all neat. Slim said the town was so old because it was on a great old river. 'Ain't you ever heard of the Susquehanna, and Daniel Boone and Benjamin Franklin and the French and Italian wars? In those times ever'body was here, and come from New York where we was, with pushcarts and oxes over the hills that truck groaned on, in rain and high weather, and suffered and died jess to reach it here. It was the beginnin of the big long push to California and now you remember how long it took us to get here by truck then figure it by ox, and *then* tell me about it when we get to San Francisco – about the ox. I'll ask you about it when we go over the sink in Nevady. In Nevady they's a sink that took down a *whole ocean* and's been dry ever since, and takes a month to measure the edges of it. Ain't nobody wash their teeth over that sink. You ain't seen nothin yet, boy.'

Well, we was still in Susquehanna and hungry enough to be in Nevady, so Slim said we'd have Hot Dog Number Two and Hot Dog Number Three and maybe Four. We went to a diner and ate them, and had a side dish of beans with katchup, and coffee both of us. Slim said I had to learn to drink coffee to keep warm on the road. He counted his money, said we had $46.80 left, and dug down in the suitcase to put on more clothes in case it rained bigger. He said he hoped we got a ride soon so's I could sleep, and wished I could wake up in Pittsburgh and then we'd move right on 'stead of sleepin. 'Up ahead the sun is shinin in Illinois and Missouri, I *know* it,' he said.

By and by we hit the night again, and Slim brought along two packs of cigarettes that left us $46.40, and we walked to the outskirts of town. Folks looked at us curious and wondered what we was doin. Well, that's life. *A man's got to live and get there*, Slim always said about that. 'Life is a sneeze, life is a breeze,' he said. Along come a car with a man goin home from work and Slim didn't care, he threw out his thumb and whistled 'most shrill through his teeth, and when he seen the man wouldn't stop, why he stuck his leg and pulled up the pants and said, 'Have pity on a poor young girl of the road.' Tickled me the way he fooled around ever'where he went.

It was cold, and it *was* raw, but we felt real fine jess like we was home. Ever' now and then I got to worryin about findin a bed and home in Californy, and worried about Sheila, and worried about gettin tireder than I was, and damper, in a darker place than this, but Slim made me forget it the way he went along. 'It's the only way to live,' Slim said, 'jess don't die. Whoopee, sometimes I feel like dyin but now I wantsa wait the *longest* time. Bein that you bring it in some more, Lord, I ain't afraid of a few cold toes so long's my whole foot don't crack. Lord, you didn't give me any money but you gave me the right to *complain*. Whoo! Complain so long on the left hand, the other hand'll fall off. Well, I've got my baby. I'll hold on jess a while longer, and see what Californy looks like now, and look around inside myself, and bet. I can't do no more than *kick*, Lord, kick this way, kick that way, and then I kick it proper. Look out for you boy, Lord.' Slim was always talkin to God like that. We got to know each other fine and could talk to ourselves anytime, the other one only listened. I'd say 'Tick, tack, toe!' countin my footsteps and Slim would say 'There you go' jess as absent-minded and thinkin about somethin else. It was the grandest fun, and good.

Someday, grandpa, I'll make a whole lot of money for you and me, but I'll enjoy it like Slim enjoyed it *without* no money, and make sure to be a happy man.

We crossed over the town, and pretty soon there we was

on the highway and there was the Susquehanna River runnin right with us, most solemn and black and not makin a sound for miles.

And here come a man with a little tiny suitcase hurryin along most jaunty from the shore, and seen us, and waved, and said, 'Walk a little faster if you want to keep up with me, for I'm goin to CANADY and I don't aim to waste time.' Well, he wasn't even caught up with us and talked like that, but soon enough he passed us. 'Can't lag, son, can't lag,' he said, and was lookin back. Me and Slim hurried on after him quick.

'Where you headed?' Slim said, and the man – he was jess a little old man, white, and poor – said, 'Why, I'm gonna get me a *hiball* up the river here soon's I cross the bridge. Member of the Veterans of Foreign Wars and the American Legion. Red Cross in this town wouldn't give me a dime. Tried to sleep in the railyards last night and they put a spot-light on me. Told them, "You'll never see me in *this* town again," walked away. Had a good breakfast last week, Martinsburg, West Virginia, pancakes, syrup, ham, toast, two glasses milk and a half, and a Mars candy bar. Always like to load up for the winter like a squirrel. Had grits and brains in Hippensburg two weeks now, and wasn't hungry for three days.'

'You mean Harrisburg?'

'Hippensburg, son, Hippensburg, Pennsylvania. I've got to meet my pardner in Canady by month's end so I can go into a uranium deal. Know upstate New York!' he said wavin his fist most determined. He was a funny old man, was short and thin, all weazled up his face that had such a long horny nose, and looked so shrunk and wan under his hat I wouldn't recognize if I seen him again. 'Walk fast,' he yelled to usn's behind, 'knew a boy three years ago on this road jess the same as you. Lazy! Slow! Don't lag!' We followed him and had to hustle some.

We walked about two mile.

'Where we goin?' Slim said.

'Know what I had me in Harrisburg last night? One fine meal I tell you, in any diner in the world. Had candied pig's feet, yams, with peas, peanut butter sandwich and two cups tea and Jello with fruits in it. Old Veteran of Foreign Wars cook behind

156

the counter. On the twelfth of this month had me a cold shower followed by hot, in the Cameo Hotel, won't tell you where, desk clerk was Jim, Veteran of Foreign Wars, I caught a cold and sneezed myself all over.'

'You sure keep movin along, Pop,' said Slim.

'Old silver-haired man with a pack an hour ago couldn't even keep up with me. All set for Canady, I am. Got things in this bag. Got a nice new necktie, too.' His bag was a poor little tore-up piece of cardboard and was held together by a big belt tied around it. He kept fiddlin at the belt. 'Wait a secont while I take out that tie,' he said, and we all stopped in front of a empty gas station and he kneeled down to undo the belt.

I sat down and caught back the rest in my legs, and watched. That man was so funny, that was why Slim was followin him and talkin to him so. Slim jess went along trailin what innerested him, you know, and couldn't say no to any old man like that.

'Now where can that tie be?' said the old man, and fiddle-faddled around in his busted satchel the longest time, and scratched his haid. 'Now don't tell me I left it in Martinsburg. I packed two dozen cough drops that morning and remember the tie was stuck up alongside. No it wasn't Martinsburg at all, at all, at all, now where was it? Harrisburg? Ah shoot, this old tie will do till I get to Ogdensburg, New York State,' and off we went again walkin. He didn't have no such a tie.

Grandpa, don't believe it if you will, but we walked SIX more miles along that river with that old man, and somethin was supposed to be around the bend ever' time, but there never was anything. I never walked so much and minded it so little, he talked so crazy. 'I have all my papers,' he kept sayin, and told us what he done in ever' town for the past month to eat, how he showed his cridentials at places, and what the meal was, and how much sugar he put in his coffee and crackers in his soup. It made me and Slim hungry to hear him. He's so small, and loved food so large. And walked and walked.

Well, that somethin never showed up and we had walked clear into the wilderness where the road was lit in only the longest spaces.

Slim stopped cold, and said, 'Say, you must be . . .' but didn't want say 'crazy' and just said, 'You must be . . . Pop, me and my brother better turn back.'

'Back? No back about this part of the country. Heh, heh. I just misjudged you boys like I misjudged that young man three years ago, that's all I done. I'm ready to go on if you aint.'

'Well, we can't walk all night,' Slim said.

'Go ahead, give up, I'm all set to walk to Canady and straight on through New York City if that's how the chips fall.'

'New York City?' Slim yelled. 'Did I hear you say? Ain't this the road west to Pittsburgh?'

Slim stopped, but the man hurried right along. 'Say did you hear me?' Slim yelled. That old man heard him all right but didn't care.'Keep walking,' he say, 'maybe I'll be in Canady, maybe I won't. Can't wait around all night.' And he kept talkin, and walkin, till all we could see was his shadow fadin in the dark and gone like a ghost.

'Well,' Slim said, 'it *was* a ghost.' And he worried himself to death standin there with me in those fearful river woods, at midnight, tryin to figure where we was and how we got lost. All I could hear now was the pat of rain on a million leaves, and the chug-chug across the river, and my own heart beatin in all that open air. Lord, it's somethin.

'Why'd I go follow that crazy man?' Slim said, and seemed lonesome, and looked for me, and reached some. 'Pic, you there?'

'Slim, I'm scairt,' I said.

'Well don't be scairt, we'll walk back to town and get back to those lights and folks can see us. Whoo!'

'Slim, who was that man?' I asked him, and he said, 'Shoo, that was some kinda ghost of the river, he's been lookin for Canady in Virginia, West Virginia, West Pennsylvania, North New York, New York City, East Arthuritis and South Pottzawattomy for the last eighty years as far as I can figure, and on foot, too. He'll never find the Canady and he'll never get to Canady because he's goin the wrong way all the time.'

So grandpa the next three cars swished by, and the fourth one stopped for us, and we ran for it. Was a big solemn white man in a beach-wagon truck. 'Yes,' he said, 'this is the road west to Pittsburgh but you better go back to town for a ride.'

'That old man is goin to walk west all night, and he wants to get to the North to Canady,' said Slim, and it was the God-awfullest truth, and we was talkin about that Ghost of the Susquehanna for the next three months, I tell you, when we got to Sheila in San Francisco.

CHAPTER 14

How We Finally Got to Californy

I'm goin tell you it was a long trip, grandpa. That man rode us back to Harrisburg in the rain. He told us how to take a left and then a right and then left and then right and go down to a lunch wagon where he say they made very good sweet yams and pigs' feet and also seven-inch-long hot dogs with Piccadilly Circus on it. Me and Slim went in there and sat down in the eatin part of the restrant, th'other side was a spittoon place with a big bunch of men argufyin about how they was Jindians.

'Don't tell me that, you're no Indian!'

'Oh I ain't, ain't I? – I'm a Pottzawattomy from Canady and my mother was pure-bred Cherokee.'

'If you're a Pottzawattomy from Canady and your mother was pure-bredded Cheroke I'm James Roosevelt Turner.'

'Well turn around, son, and I'll give you the biggest whompin you ever got.' And then there was the sound of glasses breakin, and fights, and hollerin, and women yowlin, and this woman came over to the table where me and Slim was eatin and sat down with us with a nice smile, and said, 'May I join you?' just as a big flock of police-men came in out of a squad car. The woman, girl actelly, said to Slim, 'May I sit?'

And she smiled but Slim he was feared of the police-men and never smiled back at her smile, besides Slim is married to Sheila, but the woman sat there actin as though she was at the same table with us and no one of the police-men offered up to bother her. Slim didn't say no, and he didn't say yes. The police-men took away the skeedaddlin Jindians and ever'thing was peaceful again.

Me and Slim ate up all our money on candy yams and pigs' knucklets feets and seven-inch-long hot dogs and Slim didn't pay no intention which-however to the woman. It was a barnyard. But you know, grandpa, a whole lot of black men have Jindian blood, as I discovered up when I saw all those Jindians in Nebraskar,

Ioway and Nevady, not to mention Oakland.

But now we were pretty well filled up with food-supper and ready to roam on in the rainin, only now it was slower now, pizzlin, and Slim said, 'Now next step is to get to Pittsburgh down this Route 22.'

It was early mornin sunrisin and an au-to went by and squished a blue-color bird under the rollin wheel.

It made me sickish to hear the squeak of it. I wished there was a better place. I felt missilated. A plumber gave us a ride to Huntingdon, then a light-bulb man gave us a ride to Holidaysburg, then a man called Biddy Blair gave us a ride to Blairsville, then we wound up in Corapolis with a country folk truck driver whose son had jess had a hernia belly. It was awful all them stories you heard. But I had a feelin in my chest that ever'body was doin their best, I guess.

Now it was about seben o'clock in the mornin and Slim bought some Sin-Sins to put sugar in our mouth. He was rare worried he'd never get to Sheila. He didn't not ever tell me how long it was to Oakland for fear I'd get scairt. I told him I didn't know there was so many white people in the world, comin as I done from North Carolina countryfolks.

He said, 'Yep.'

Then he said, 'I wonder if Mr Otis sent out the cops after me for kidnapin you. Well, he won't find us now. Here's stoppin a car with two men in it.'

They were goin eighty miles an hour or somethin like that but they stopped, squeak. We got in the back. They said, 'Where you goin? – Shoot, we Montana-bound, you got money?'

Slim said, 'Not much so.'

So they said, 'We'll drop you off at Pittsburgh.' It was rainin, grandpa, when we got to Pittsburgh. Me and Slim went inta the railroad station, to get out of the rainin. Two men in blue choo-choo master suits told us to get out. So we pulled up our collars and draddled on down the street, we saw a church, with a cross on top of it. Slim said, 'Let's go in there and dry up some. Don't reckon they'll throw us out of there.'

It was chilly-like but there was a runnin heat comin from the furnace in the bottom down-belows, and a man upstairs was playing the big organ piano. Slim said it was the Have-a-Maria, and then a fellow come by with a lighted stick and went rush-up lightin candles at the front part, 'The Halter,' said Slim (said it laughin), and outside it was rainin cats and dogs.

Grandpa, when I heard that music I shushed Slim, and I said, 'Can I sing?'

'Slim wants to know if you know the tune?' said Slim.

'Well I'll jess hum.'

Slim said, 'Here comes the big man in the black coat.'

By this time I was already hummin.

The big man in the black coat said, 'You have a beautiful voice, what's your name?'

'Pictorial Review Jackson of North Carolina.'

'And who's he?'

'My brother John Jackson.'

The priest axed, 'Do you know how to dust pews?'

Slim says, 'I just worked in a cookie factory and I'd rather dust pews.'

'Do you know how to mop floors in the basement? Two Army cots beside the furnace, hundred dollars a month, fifty each, free food, no rent.'

Slim says, 'Tsa deal, we are goin all the way to Californy to join up with my wife.'

'What's your wife's name?'

'Sheila Jackson, born Joyner, North Carolina.'

'I am Father John McGillicuddy.'

Slim sez, 'Ain't you the guy that managed the Philadelphia Phillies?'

'No, that was Cornelius McGillicuddy, some distant cousin ... Philadelphia Athletics ... I am Father John McGillicuddy, Society of Jesus, Jesuit Order. Now little Jackson Picture, you want to go up sing in the choir? What's your favourite tune?'

Grandpa, I told him *Our Father Which Art in Heaven*, coulda made Lulu cry to hear me sing like that in her porch.

So Father McGillicuddy took me up to the attic LOFT, and sat me by the man with his hands on the keys of the ORGAN. Grandpa, I even whistled and I wisht I had my harmonica, and the priest man sing up and said I sung up like an angel.

By and by, Slim was present down at the cellar moppin up the floor, he said he sure wisht he had his horn, but said he found a horn in his little brother's voice.

So we told Father McGillicuddy soon's we pick up one hunnerd dollars pay we would fetch for Oakland on the Greyhound Bus, but Father McGillicuddy said it was comin up close to Sunday mornin, as it was Adventist or adventurous night now, and Saturday too, and wanted me to sing before the intire congregation the Lord's Prayer, which I done, up in the LOFT, like best I could. Father McGillicuddy was s'tickled he was sunrise all over. Them Irish mans is so tickled they's pink as a shoat all over, but I feasable say they got troubles of their own, so we had our hunnerd dollars and took the road bus with the picture of the blue hound dog on the side of it, Greyhound it's called, and we peewetted across Ohia and clear inta Nebraskar, Slim was asleep in the back seat all alone stretched out legs all over, and I was sittin in a reg'lar seat near-up with a ninety-year-old white man, and when we come to a stop just before Kearney, Nebraskar, the old man said to me, 'I gotta go to the toilet.'

So I led him out of the bus holdin his hand, 'case he was about to fall in the snow, and ask the gas man where was the men's room. Finished, I took the old man back in the bus, and the bus driver yelled out, 'Somebody's drinkin around here!'

And the bus driver was wearin black gloves. Two men was in the front seat next to him holdin hands together.

Slim was still snorin on the back-seat bed. Then he got up said to me, 'Hi, Baby.'

First thing you know, no more snow. Heard another old man behind me say, 'I'm goin back to Oroville and bank my dust.'

We then was now in the Sacramenty Valley, grandpa, and quick we saw Sheila's ropelines with wash on hooks of wood hung dryin, flappety-flap.

Slim, he put his two hands on his back, limpied around the yard, and said, 'I got Arthur-itis, Bus-itis, Road-itis, Pic-itis and ever' other-Itis, in the world.'

And Sheila run up, kissed him hungarianly, and we went in eat the steak she saved up for us, with mashy potatoes, pole beans, and cherry banana spoon ice cream split.

PENGUIN MODERN CLASSICS

LONESOME TRAVELLER
JACK KEROUAC

'Full of startling and beautiful things … one sees, hears and feels' *Sunday Times*

As he roams the US, Mexico, Morocco, Paris and London, Jack Kerouac
breathlessly records, in prose of pure poetry, the life of the road. Standing on the
engine of a train, as it rushes past fields of prickly cactus; witnessing his first
bullfight in Mexico while high on opium; catching up with the beat night-life in
New York; burying himself in the snow-capped mountains of north-west America;
meditating on a sunlit roof in Tangiers; or falling in love with Montmartre and the
huge white basilica of Sacré-Coeur – Kerouac reveals the endless diversity of
human life and his own high-spirited philosophy of self-fulfilment.

'Piquant writing, the best part of its flavour being … the hunt for the big
experience, a touch of Hemingway and Whitman' *Guardian*

read more

PENGUIN MODERN CLASSICS

ON THE ROAD
JACK KEROUAC

'A paean to what Kerouac described as "the ragged and ecstatic joy of pure being"' *Sunday Times*

On The Road swings to the rhythms of 1950s underground America, jazz, sex, generosity, chill dawns and drugs, with Sal Paradise and his hero Dean Moriarty, traveller and mystic, the living epitome of Beat. Now recognized as a modern classic, its American Dream is nearer that of Walt Whitman than F. Scott Fitzgerald's, and the narrative goes racing towards the sunset with unforgettable exuberance, poignancy and autobiographical passion.

With an Introduction by Ann Charters

Penguin Modern Classics

THE DHARMA BUMS
JACK KEROUAC

'A descriptive excitement unmatched since the days of Thomas Wolf' *The New York Times Book Review*

Following the explosive energy of *On the Road* comes *The Dharma Bums*, in which Kerouac charts the spiritual quest of a group of friends in search of Dharma, or Truth. Ray Smith and his friend Japhy, along with Morley the yodeller, head off into the high Sierras to seek the lesson of solitude and experience the Zen way of life. But in wildly bohemian San Francisco, with its poetry jam sessions, marathon drinking bouts and experiments in 'yabyum', they find the ascetic route distinctly hard to follow.

'A vivid evocation of a part of our time' *New York Post*

Contemporary ... Provocative ... Outrageous ...
Prophetic ... Groundbreaking ... Funny ... Disturbing ...
Different ... Moving ... Revolutionary ... Inspiring ...
Subversive ... Life-changing ...

What makes a modern classic?

At Penguin Classics our mission has always been to make the best books ever written available to everyone. And that also means constantly redefining and refreshing exactly what makes a 'classic'. That's where Modern Classics come in. Since 1961 they have been an organic, ever-growing and ever-evolving list of books from the last hundred (or so) years that we believe will continue to be read over and over again.

They could be books that have inspired political dissent, such as *Animal Farm*. Some, like *Lolita* or *A Clockwork Orange*, may have caused shock and outrage. Many have led to great films, from *In Cold Blood* to *One Flew Over the Cuckoo's Nest*. They have broken down barriers – whether social, sexual, or, in the case of *Ulysses*, the boundaries of language itself. And they might – like *Goldfinger* or *Scoop* – just be pure classic escapism. Whatever the reason, Penguin Modern Classics continue to inspire, entertain and enlighten millions of readers everywhere.

'No publisher has had more influence on reading habits than Penguin'
Independent

'Penguins provided a crash course in world literature'
Guardian

The best books ever written

PENGUIN 🐧 CLASSICS

SINCE 1946

Find out more at www.penguinclassics.com